The Girl with the Red Nails

G. SPENCER MYERS

Creator of the Dr. Derk Bryan Eco-Thriller Series

Other Books by G. Spencer Myers

Pest:

A man experiences a deadly premonition while fishing in the Florida Keys. A murder in Michigan causes a toxic spill. Dr. Derk Bryan, the Indiana Jones of the EPA, soon discovers that these two disparate events threaten every drop of water on the planet and every important relationship in his life. His laisse faire life on the beach is on a collision course with the maniacal chemical company magnate, Jack Von Lleuwan, and his bodyguard, Jimmy "Gloves Swingle, an ex-wrestler with anger management issues.

Von Lleuwan's newest product, *PESTfree©*, designed to replace the chemicals that are contaminating food and water worldwide, contains a deadly flaw. As a result, Kate McCardigan, Derk's college sweetheart, becomes a target when she blames Von Lleuwan for crippling her son and others. As the body count grows, Derk Bryan races against the clock to thwart disaster and save McCardigan from becoming another victim.

Praise for Pest:

"Murder leads Derk Bryan, the EPA's most creative investigator, from a chemical spill in West Michigan to Tampa Bay and back to Ohio. Pest will make you laugh and make you cry. Ultimately, you will ask, Will I be the next victim? A must-read book."

- **Ervin Harmon, Book Reviewer, and Critic**

"The engaging narrative of Pest contains much to think about regarding toxicology, environmental awareness, and the balance of nature. . . Pest leaves one wondering how closely the story resembles a true one."

- **Rachel Elaine, Author of Thoughts for Thought.**

Dead Wrong:

A truckload of toxic chemicals crashes into Tampa Bay, a bank president's son and a senator's daughter die after smoking weed at a fraternity party, and the publisher of a weekly entertainment rag accuses the cops of murder. As one of the EPA's top investigators, Derk Bryan refuses to accept the ME's conclusion that the spill was an accident and that these events are not related. With three monster hurricanes on a collision course with Florida, Bryan races against the clock and the bureaucracy to uncover the clues in this ecological crossword puzzle.

Praise for Dead Wrong:

"Using an EPA investigator is unique for a crime novel. I really like Derk Bryan and I really liked this book."

- **Ann Bocock WXEL-TV, "Between the Sheets" Summer Reading Series.**

"Dr. Derk Bryan is a hero without a Messiah complex."

- **Buch 1-DM, Online Book Club**

"Impressive characters headline this suspenseful tale with an ecological bent."

- **Kirkus review**

". . . interesting, thought-provoking, and thrilling . . . There is no doubt that audiences will be anticipating the next adventure."

- **Gretchen Hansen, The US Review of Books**

We Are Playing Roulette With Your Future:

G. Spencer Myers issues a profound warning to Ian, his grandson, and Ian's generation that involves a threat to humanity so great that scientists have given it a name: The Anthropocene—a human caused extinction.

Using a series of short stories Myers challenges grandsons from eight to eighty to think big and be bold in your ideas in the face of the crisis of your lifetime: Global Warming. In 1980, he became the first person in the U.S. to put 400 sq. ft. of solar panels on a multi-family residence listed on the National Register of Historic Places. Today, he drives an EV and fuels it with sunshine. Having devoted his life to reducing his own carbon footprint, he says, "There's hope. We know what to do." Read it and become inspired.

All books are available at: www.GSpencerMyers.com or your favorite online book provider.

Foreword

With hurricanes, floods, drought and fires filling our evening news broadcasts the release of The Girl with the Red Nails is as timely as ever. Between its covers you will meet Estee Sparks, a woman so committed to seeking for revenge for the death of her son, the breakup of her marriage and the loss of her family's business, she has covered her body with tattoos of extinct animals and gone into attack mode. She enlists the help of a group of law students taking on the plastic manufacturers and a dogged reporter living out of his car while recovering from opioid addiction. Their efforts will lead Dr. Derk Bryan, the Indiana Jones of the EPA, to the doorstep of Pendleton Danswirth III, a leading manufacturer of the plastics that are contaminating the water supply throughout the world. Enjoy the quirky characters and Dr. Derk Bryan's obsession with corralling the bad guys and reducing his own carbon footprint.

As you read, I would like you keep this mind. The increased frequency and severity of these natural disasters are the result of our rapidly warming planet due to the release of greenhouse gases. In 1979, at the first World Climate Conference in Geneva, an alarm was sounded, "We have an excellent chance of slowing carbon emissions to avert catastrophic climate change."

The fossil fuel industry had yet to mobile to challenge climate science, and Republicans and Democrats saw climate policy as a nonpartisan issue.

When the IPCC (International Panel on Climate Change) met in 1989 to set enforceable standards the United States, Britain, Japan and Russia refused to commit to freezing emissions. Since then, more carbon has been released into the atmosphere than in the entire history of civilization.

If we continue on this path, by 2070, one third of the Earth's inhabitants will be living on land that is unsustainable. This is already leading to massive migrations, cultural clashes, political discord and armed conflict. We owe it to our grandchildren not to let this happen.

This is why I have included a Climate Fact and What You Can Do About It before each chapter. If each of us reduces our own carbon footprints we can make a more just, peaceful and livable world for our children and grandchildren.

Contents

1

Instinct. It was pure instinct that caused him to leap from the airplane. He was part of a team of scientists that wanted a close look at the exposed rocks in the Grand Canyon. As a result of a man nourished drought, global warming had depleted the river to the lowest level any human had ever seen.

Dr. Derk Bryan was five thousand feet above Lake Havasu City and falling at thirty-two feet per second per second or roughly 120 MPH. At that speed he would hit the ground in less than thirty seconds. He wasn't a sky diving expert, but he knew the physics.

He also knew he had to grab onto Doctor Susan Carlton, who had fallen from the airplane, secure her to his body and engage his parachute in less than ten seconds. Chances were slim he could do it, and he would later wonder if he would have jumped if he had calculated the odds.

During the short bus ride to the airport Derk couldn't take his eyes off her. She was fit, had a mind like an encyclopedia, the wit of a comedian and something else. When he asked if this were her first jump, she said, "First solo. I'm used to being tethered to someone. Would you like to accompany me," with the most seductive brown eyes he had ever seen. As she approached the jump hatch, she stumbled while trying to put her second arm through the parachute. That seemed unusual for someone training for the Mission to Mars, Derk would later recall. Now she was tumbling through space still trying to get the strap around her arm.

Derk streamlined his taut body and dived toward her like that guy in the Ironman movies. He hoped she wouldn't bounce off him. In that event each of them would likely crash down near the old London Bridge that traversed the Colorado River. If they landed in the river, which would be much softer than on land, they might survive, but the current in the Colorado was so strong they would probably be dragged under before they could free themselves of their gear. He considered none of this before leaping. His only thought was of saving her.

She saw him coming. He expected terror in her eyes, but she smiled and spread her wings like a butterfly. A roaring wind distorted his tanned face as they connected with a hard thud. Strong arms wrapped around him like tentacles. He pulled the ripcord and awaited the reaction that met the chute had opened.

At two thousand feet above Lake Havasu, Derk got only a glimpse of the people watching from the bridge. The silliness that someone had dismantled a bridge in London and shipped it here at the behest of Robert McCulloch, of chain saw fame, flashed through his head.

He was hesitant to let go of her, but he needed both hands on the steering lines. "Hang on!" he shouted. He didn't know if she heard him over the howl of the wind, but her fingers almost penetrated his jumpsuit. Within seconds, they splashed into the river.

He struggled to release the chute from his shoulders. The Colorado is deep, cold and fast. His athletic physique, normally an asset, reduced his buoyancy, allowing the current to drag him under. Each time he surfaced he gasped for air. The jump suit was already waterlogged. He went under again and again, each time swallowing more water than air. When he tried to stand the current took him. With the coldness sapping his will he took one last, deep breath, went under and released the parachute.

Thud. He bumped into Doctor Carlton as he surfaced. Without a worry line on her face, she grabbed him under his arms and started paddling toward shore. They were swept another fifty yards before reaching an outcrop near a craggy shoreline. She sat up while he collapsed on a large rock next to her. When his shivering subsided, he wrapped her into his arms.

It seemed longer but it was probably only minutes when a rescue squad showed up, followed by a man and a woman in military fatigues with NASA patches on their sleeves. Each of them was armed. Doctor Carlton and he were rushed to the local hospital and rolled into separate rooms.

***

"Doctor Carlton, Doctor Carlton, how is she?" He kept asking.

"Fine, Doctor Bryan. Does that hurt?" People in white coats were poking him.

"Ouch!" he said as the doctor ran his fingers over his ribs.

"She's fine," Someone responded.

"Fine! How can that be? It hurts me to breathe," Derk said.

After the examining physician placed one arm in a sling, Derk convinced him they could remove the IV. His core temperature had returned to normal, and the threat of shock had been eliminated. He hobbled to the nurse's station and was told that Doctor Carlton had been released.

"Already!" Derk said.

He found her waiting in the lobby. She smiled and took his hand.

He urged to her turn in a complete circle. "You're okay," he said, seeing no visible sign of damage.

She nodded and winked at him. He whispered into her ear while the woman with the gun and the NASA insignia stood by. Another nod and wink told him she understood. As he walked down the corridor he turned and watched her make a gesture of dismissal to her armed escort.

A few minutes later she joined Derk at the freight entrance. The Uber he had summoned was already only minutes away. By nightfall Doctors Derk Bryan and Susan Carlton, strangers only six hours earlier, were in a local hotel clinging to each other like desperate lovers.

That's when the call came.

"Dr. Bryan, I have a call for you from Sahith" Joyce said. She was the Administrative Assistant for the director of EPED, the investigative arm of the EPA.

Derk interrupted her, "I thought you retired when Ben left."

"Next month. He came in a month before me. I'd like to talk but he's on the line."

"Who?"

"Sahith Cromwell, the new director."

"Doesn't he know I'm on a sabbatical?"

"You've been talking retirement for years. You'll never do it. You love this job, and now you're a hero. Are you alright?" Joyce said.

"What are you talking about?" Derk said.

"Yes, he's on the line," she said but it wasn't to Derk. "Take care of yourself, hero."

"This is Dr. Cromwell. As you know I took over for Ben Waitley. We've got a situation and I'd like you to handle it."

Derk started to say, "I'm sort of retired and it's not a good time," but Cromwell interjected, "We saw what happened. Are you okay?"

Good grief, he was already on the news and they're calling him a hero. The truth was if Doctor Carlton hadn't latched onto him, he would have been no better than driftwood on the way to the lemon groves of southern California. He may have saved her, but he was alive because of her. What each of them had done had created an instantaneous bond between them, and he was in no mood to share any of it with the media.

"Not really and this isn't a good time," Derk said.

He got out of bed, put on the white boxer shorts and tee-shirt he had donned before his trip to the canyon, and paced in front of a mirror while he assessed the damage. It hurt a little when he sucked in his tummy. It also hurt each time he exhaled. In the reflection of the mirror, the desire in Susan Carlton's eyes summoned him back to bed.

She whispered, "Do you have to go?"

He shook his head and whispered, "I don't know."

"Can I call you back?" he said to Cromwell.

"Sure, the body's not going anywhere."

"Body?" Derk was surprised but he shouldn't have been. He was only called when someone was found in a waste dump, a toxic spill or during some environmental mishap under circumstances that always involved foul play. It was grim work, and he took pride in locking up the maniacal bastards who had no qualms about raining hell upon the environment, particularly when it involved his own slice of paradise. He lived on the beach.

"I wasn't going to bother you, but—"

"You've got a situation. There's always a situation. We're the damned EPA," Derk said and winced. He had removed the sling from his arm when he got into bed with the astronaut.

As Susan Carlton summoned him with an outstretched hand, her dark brown hair cascaded over her sturdy shoulders, and there were two hard raps on the door followed by a stern female voice.

"Doctor Carlton, we have to get you back. Please open the door."

"Okay Cromwell," Derk said with a sigh, "Call me back in ten minutes."

Climate Fact:

Each week we ingest enough micro-plastic particles to make a credit card. Only 9% of plastic is recycled.

What can you do about it? If you must use plastic for any purpose, recycle the container.

2

Reverend Huck's guest on today's show, *Don't Back Talk God—* radio's Pulpit Fiction—is Fonnie Faith. Her claim to fame: she can call upon the universal force, she referred to it as Ja, that would allow her to materialize things.

"What kind of things?" Reverend Huck smirked as he leaned back in his chair. He had interviewed so many quacks it was difficult to take anyone seriously anymore.

"I once made a ring appear that had been lost for five years," Fonnie said.

"Uri Gellar stuff," said Huck. Uri Gellar claimed he could make things appear out of thin air. Some claimed to have seen him do it. True or not, it was an ingenious con. Huck had tried almost everything from grifting to insurance fraud. The latter netted him five years in Texas State Prison. He preferred a con that required skill and showmanship so Fonnie Faith's idea humored him.

When Fonnie whispered, "Uri who," Reverend Huck moved on.

"You do this all by yourself?" Huck preferred to work alone.

"No, Mon, usually in groups. The Ja is stronger, more amplified, the more believers there are." Her accent was from the islands, but Fonnie Faith was as white as Wonder Bread.

"Believers? You talking about God?" Huck said. He had found Jesus, at least, he had been able to convince the prison chaplain of that, which became his ticket to freedom. As far as he was concerned religion was the biggest con of all. He got this radio gig when Pendleton Danswirth III, a wealthy plastics manufacturer, hired him to host the show.

"Faith, Mon." She looked like Lady Gaga, but talked like Bob Marley with an English accent.

"What's the largest thing you've—" he hesitated while searching for the correct description, "materialized, Mon?"

"A bus," she said with a frown.

"A bus! Get outta here."

"Actually, a VW van."

Reverend Huck shook his head while he scratched the back of his neck. "Well, listeners, it's said that faith can move mountains. What do you think? 555-Believe. I want to hear from you now," Reverend Huck said.

Huck couldn't hide his smirk. They paid this charlatan five grand for an hour appearance, expecting to get ten to twenty times that in donations. Last week he hosted three cancer survivors who claimed they overcame the disease through prayer. That show grossed eighty grand.

The first call came from a woman who said she saved her husband by warning him not to get on an airplane after the image of a crash came to her when she passed a flight attendant on the first floor of Macy's.

The next call came from a guy with gout. A friend had brought him fibers he claimed he scraped from the Shroud of Turin, the one that belonged to Jesus. Since Jesus had immense healing powers, he wanted to mix the DNA of Jesus with his own to heal himself. The doctor refused to perform a DNA analysis on it.

"Can you help me, Fonnie?" he asked.

Reverend Huck responded with as much respect as he could muster, "While your theory is intriguing, that particular Shroud has been analyzed by scientists and determined not to be old enough to belong to Jesus. So, I doubt its DNA will help you. But I am sorry to hear about your health issues. You might want to stop smoking, give up red meat and exercise your fat ass, but who am I to judge."

The caller was disconnected after a torrent of four-letter words.

The most profound response came in person as a well-dressed, middle-aged man barged into Huck's doublewide slash pulpit slash studio with venom on his tongue.

"You moron. You fucking dim wit. I asked you to do one simple fucking thing and—"

Pendleton Danswirth's hands and arms were flailing.

Reverend Huck waved at Danswirth to stop while he smothered the microphone with his other hand.

Danswirth ran one finger, like a knife, across his throat. "Now!"

Danswirth's tirade slammed into Fonnie Faith like a tsunami. She repelled until her chair hit the wall and came to a stop under the plastic Jesus. The lighted halo flickered before fading and dropping onto her head. With fear in her eyes, she scrambled for the exit. Her headset, still tethered to the equipment under on the table, jerked her back and she fell to the floor. The microphone emitted an ear popping screech.

"He Satan!" Her Jamaican accent lingered in the room after she ran out.

With thirty minutes left still remaining on the interview with Fonnie, Reverend Huck calmly said, "Our guest has parted so that's all for today, Believers. In God you know you've won."

He hit a switch on the keyboard that turned off his mic and turned on the show's theme music. The voice of Eric Burden filled the studio with *House of the Rising Sun.*

"You should have told me what was in that box," said Reverend Huck.

"What difference would that have made? You'd still be an imbecile. And turn off that music!" Danswirth shouted.

"How would I know it would drift? I don't know anything about the tides. I'm not a mariner. I'm a man of the cloth," Huck said as he flipped a couple of switches. The room became silent.

"My tailor is a man of the cloth," said Danswirth. "You're just an ex-con with a microphone and a pulpit on wheels."

That was essentially true, but it didn't deter Huck. His pulpit was propped upon a table from which two microphones extended into the air. Huck sat behind the desk in the same seat he occupied when he gave the morning sermon and interviewed guests. His broadcast targeted Believers. The plastic Jesus, with a lighted halo, was given to him by Danswirth along with a certificate granting legal status to this side of the trailer as a formal ministry. Both had been displayed on a wall of knotty pine that was draped with red velvet and featured a life-sized Jesus which was embroidered upon it.

The whole set-up had been financed by Danswirth whom had been introduced to him by the prison chaplain. Originally Huck had assumed that Danswirth, one of the richest guys on the planet, was also a man of faith and charity. Why else would he have founded a radio network and employed him to host the show?

It didn't take long for Huck to realize that Danswirth was as steely cold as anyone he had ever met, including some heartless bastards in the State pen, but he couldn't be too angry with him. Danswirth had allowed him to take his forty-foot Baja speed boat out for the weekend and asked only one thing of him, "Please bury Farns at sea."

Reverend Huck was elated. He wanted to take Germaine and her bi-sexual girlfriend along in anticipation of a threesome, while he took the boat out for a test run. A former cell mate had turned him onto a guy on the outside who was looking for runners, people to transport stuff throughout the Gulf --- guns, people, drugs--- all illegal, but nobody got hurt and he could score some quick cash. He was building a nest egg to open a jazz bar in Key West. All he needed was a fast boat.

Before he mentioned Germaine, Danswirth said, "Absolutely no one goes with you. You've got to do this alone."

He should have been suspicious, and more so, when he found the package, wrapped in burlap and tied with rope, left at the stern of the boat without a word in memoriam. He assumed it was Danswirth's old black lab, Reginald Farnswirth. Raised from a puppy, the dog had been with Danswirth for fifteen years. Danswirth had come by the studio one day after taking Farnswirth to the vet. That's when Huck was told about the bladder cancer and that the dog had to be put down.

"I can't do it myself," Danswirth said. The unconditional affection Danswirth felt for that dog was something Huck was sure Danswirth never felt for any person. For the most part he was a manipulative narcissist --- a trait with which Huck was familiar.

Thurgood Marshall Hucklebee, during his three-year stretch for fraud, had come in contact with many of them. Gangs roamed the prison. When asked by those wanting him to pick a side, he would always repeat what his mother had told him, "One of those boys must have gotten that other boy really vexed." Then he would step away. For the most part, he was seldom bothered.

Father Trout, the prison chaplain, told him, "Somehow or another you have a calming effect upon people. It's your voice, I think."

Reverend Huck learned later, when introduced to Danswirth by Father Trout, "You've got what one in ten million have, the radio voice."

It didn't hurt that he was Hollywood good looking --- before prison women passed under him like he could fly --- and that his parole required stable and verifiable employment.

He had tried pool hustling, poker and illusion without success. He thought about a career in theater, probably due to a bit part in the high school version of West Side Story, but he would eventually slip back into what worked best for him: verbal trickery.

What stressed him was at fifty-five he was broke and aware that he only had a few more good years to reach his goal. After a weekend in Key West, twenty years ago, he got hooked on the lifestyle --- the music drifting from the bars on Duval, the glowing evenings nourished with mojitos and summer breezes that wafted in from the Caribbean. In spite of her failings his mother had done one very good thing in his life. She forced him to play an instrument. Fortunately, although it didn't appear that at the time, it was the organ at the local church. He wanted to play jazz guitar, George Benson style, but they couldn't afford one.

Father Trout, the prison chaplain and a wannabe organist, asked Hucklebee to play at church services in prison. It was a cushy job and exempted Huck from other more dangerous activities. Huck modified some religious cantatas to organ music. Father Trout was so impressed he took Huck on as a rehab project. Over time he convinced Hucklebee to give himself over to God which is exactly what Huck did when he found the chaplain could recommend him for early release.

Although the three years in the State pen were more than an inconvenience it was Father Trout that introduced him to Pendleton Danswirth III. The guy was pert and self-absorbed, but his suits were Italian, his watch was Rolex and he was always well manicured. That meant he either had money or good taste, and Hucklebee aspired to each of those things. Danswirth appeared to be a man of faith and spoke of his aunt's influence upon him as a youth. He wanted Huck to host a religious radio program on a network he had founded. The idea was intriguing but Huck wasn't a preacher, and he certainly didn't measure up to those Commandments he had read about.

"You don't have to be a preacher to host a radio program," Danswirth said. Father Trout confirmed with an anxious nod.

"You would be collecting donations from listeners and sending the money to deserving charities," the chaplain said, encouraging Huck to take the job.

"Of course, after we pay the overhead and ourselves," Danswirth added.

Nothing was as easy as it looked, but Thurgood Marshall Hucklebee, soon to be ex-con, had to consider that this may be his last, best chance. He recalled his own Momma watching the television pastor every Sunday. Once she sent fifty dollars, which was a lot for them, to a post office box after watching a man in a wheelchair get up and walk again. For Huck, it was an absolute miracle, not that the man walked after the television reverend laid his hand on cripple's head, but that thousands of poor souls like his mother sent in their last dollar in hope that some kind of miracle would visit them.

His reservations were quelled by Danswirth's closing sales pitch, "You'll be famous—the next Falwell—and rich."

There was one more thing that Huck needed before accepting the job. Behind bars he learned if you had nothing to trade you got fucked, every which way. He anticipated that Danswirth wanted something from him.

"Praise the Lord," exclaimed Hucklebee when Danswirth's said, "You'll have to upgrade your wardrobe."

"That's all!"

"Preachers don't wear orange coveralls," said Danswirth with a chuckle. It was the last time Huck saw him smile.

"I'm a little short on cash." Huck pressed for more.

"Don't get ahead of yourself." Danswirth's eyes narrowed into frown. "You'll be paid."

"Oh, one more thing," Hucklebee said, reluctantly. "I'll need an instrument."

On the day Thurgood Marshall Hucklebee left prison Danswirth drove him to a pawn shop to pick out a used organ. The next day Hucklebee petitioned the court to change his first name from Thurgood to Reverend.

Since then, his relationship with Danswirth had been more profitable than he could have imagined. For that he was grateful. But the Pendleton Danswirth standing in his home today was the one he had always feared—the one whose eyes defied his smile. This was the side of Danswirth that Huck knew would eventually surface.

"I know you paid for this trailer and got me this job, and I know what you're having me do is legal, but this doesn't seem right," Huck said as he motioned for Danswirth to calm down and take a seat.

"Right or wrong, you've got a serious problem on your hands," said Danswirth, still standing.

Huck couldn't deny that. He had taken out Danswirth's boat because it was an opportunity to score some quick cash. The Salty Glider, as Danswirth had named it, could transport six, perform in deep seas and, with its three Mercruiser four hundred and twenty-five horse power motors, was as fast as wind through a duck's ass. Huck's plan was to dump the dog while transporting some illegal immigrants through the Gulf of Mexico. Danswirth would have been none the wiser if the discovery of the woman in the block of plastic hadn't made the evening news. Danswirth's tirade made it clear that it was the same package Huck had buried at sea. Fifty miles off the east coast of Texas, in calm seas with a million stars illuminating the night, he slid the burlap wrapped block of plastic into the Gulf.

He had no idea, nor did he care, that it would drift into the Hypoxic Zone, a swath of toxic blooms that emanated from the pesticides and fertilizers of the Midwestern industrial farms and cities that fed the Gulf from the Mississippi River. In this morass the lines surrounding the burlap dissolved and frayed. Sharks, that can smell blood through sheets of plastic, gnawed at the ropes until the burlap loosened. The body in its plastic tomb drifted six hundred miles east before getting tangled in some discarded fishing nets south of Apalachicola.

"Me? I dumped a dead dog into the sea. Give me one good reason I should be worried."

"I'll give you a million reasons," said Danswirth. That was the amount of tax-free revenue that Reverend Hucklebee's broadcasts had taken in each year since Danswirth's accountant had obtained an IRS designation for Hucklebee's scam as a church. Hucklebee's 401K was already half way to his goal.

Huck knew his balls were in a vice and Danswirth's hands were on the crank. Danswirth controlled the foundation that owned the land on which Hucklebee's trailer home was parked. He also owned all of the chattel property thereon. This meant that Danswirth could haul away Huck's home and pulpit whenever he got a bug up his ass and, along with it, his Key West dream. He might be operating a street legal ministry, but it was not a house of worship and he was not an ordained minister. If he got caught up in anything illegal, which surely included dumping a human body into the Gulf, it would result in an express bus back to the Texas State penitentiary.

"And who was that quack? I told you to call Senator Esau Lionshaim."

"Lionshaim's been on three times in the past month. People are more interested in characters like Fonnie Faith," said Reverend Huck, questioning why Danswirth preferred elected officials and right-wing religious freaks as his guests on the show. Huck sat on the edge of his chair, ringing his hands. "The likes of Fonnie Faith bring in three times the donations of oil barons and CEOs in their eight-hundred-dollar suits. And about that problem, we need to get rid of the boat. That's all. I'll handle it."

Danswirth, with pursed lips and squinted eyes, looked as if he had swallowed a dill pickle.

"Yeah, you better."

3

Derk felt a twinge as he took a deep breath, testing his bruised ribs. He had removed the sling, but there was a slight twinge in his right shoulder when he lifted his arm. The image of Susan reaching out to him from the bed in the hotel relieved the pain.

He was standing in front of a beach bar in the Panama City because Estee Sparks, the woman who discovered the body, told the EPA she would speak with their agent, but it had to be at the Salty Dog Saloon. His short-lived sabbatical had come to an abrupt end, and he was back on the job.

Before arriving in Panama City, he stopped to view the body at the coroner's office in Apalachicola. A dead body wasn't unusual in his line of work. EPED, the EPA's enforcement division, didn't call him unless someone turned up in a polluted lake, a toxin laden stream or a cesspool of poison, but the director described something so bizarre Derk had to see it.

He had taken a flight from Phoenix to Tallahassee, rented a car and headed to the coroner's office in the Florida Panhandle. Unlike most corpses that are kept in cold storage to prevent deterioration prior to autopsies or burials, this one was left on a stainless-steel table in the middle of the room. A tag on a leg of the table, labeled Jane Doe, was the only identification for the body imbedded within what appeared to be a clear solid block of polycarbonate.

"What the f—!" was his reaction.

Visible through the plastic was a female in her mid-twenties and possibly Hispanic. Once an attractive gal, the only thing she had on was red nail polish.

He guessed she had been put in this plastic tomb while a transparent kind of lava was poured into the structure. She was buried alive as the plastic hardened around her from her feet up. He had seen some gruesome stuff, but this gave him goose bumps.

"That was my first reaction," said the coroner who was scanning the surface of the coffin with a magnifying glass.

"What are you looking for?" Derk said.

"A seam, a break or any imperfection," said Dr. Armand Corji, a bespectacled and fidgety man of fifty with a receding line of burnt orange hair. "How am I going to do an autopsy?"

"Drill it, saw it. It's just plastic."

"I tried. I've never seen anything like this."

"What do you mean?"

"It's as hard as steel, and it won't melt." The doctor shook his head as he waved his hands over the solid, glass-like casket. "It looks like plastic but acts like rock."

Derk slid his hand across the top of the block. "Feels like plastic." He held out his hand for the magnifying glass, took it and held it against the surface.

"Clear as daylight," said Dr. Corji with a lurch of one shoulder, one of many nervous tics he displayed.

"How can that be?" said Derk.

"I can't determine the cause of death, because I can't get at the body."

Derk had seen bodies melted by corrosive chemicals, the remains of human offal discarded like trash and the stench of dead marine life as thick as gravy, but this was just plain bizarre. Terror was frozen in her eyes.

"I see. You've got no name, no address and no DNA," Derk said.

Doctor Corji nodded. "Got any ideas?"

"None that don't involve disfiguring the body or contaminating the evidence," Derk said.

No one knew more than where and by whom the body had been discovered. It was a challenging case to be sure, but Derk didn't see how this was an EPA matter. He assumed the only reason he had been called was that the woman who found the body had requested it. In fact, she had insisted. She told the director she had relevant information about the case and would reveal it only to an EPA agent in person. He got the call because Cromwell didn't want to commit full-time personnel to a Q&A with a side show freak.

He had been warned that the Sparks woman might be a little different, but that wouldn't be new to him. He had dealt with an ex-wrestler with a false ear and a redneck who got his Emus stoned to fatten them up. Unless she was from another planet, he didn't think anyone could surprise him.

On his way to Panama City, he left a message on a number Doctor Carlton had written onto a piece of paper as she was leaving the motel. He had known her for less than twenty-four hours, but the bond created, driven by survival instincts, was unrelenting.

"I'm afraid to let go," he told her as they spooned like clams in the motel room. "I'm afraid if I let you go, you'll disappear."

They had embraced with a need that was all encompassing. As their breathing coincided, they made love. Their frenzy was only ameliorated by the mechanics of the act. She was like no other lover he had ever known; eager without foreplay, but not sure of herself. He had never felt anything like her, emotionally and physically. She seemed to follow his lead. Steadily they gained momentum until a crescendo, like the finale of Swan Lake, consumed him. As it had risen her breathing subsided with his, and she maintained her grip around him. He had to pry himself from her grasp to use the bathroom. After relieving himself the trembling returned. He stopped shaking only after he was back in her arms.

On the way to meet Ms. Sparks separation anxiety returned. He was an unafraid and adventurous guy, used to living within a set of emotional guardrails, but Susan Carlton has gotten a grip on him like a narcotic. He should probably wait for her to return his call, but she was preparing to leave the planet on a trip that might separate them for years. This time, after a series of beeps, he left the same message, "Please call. I want to know if you're okay."

He tried deep breathing, a technique he learned at a yoga class years ago. In and out, in and out. It was working until he became distracted by larger and larger piles of debris that lined the coastal highway. Two weeks ago, the stacks of lumber and appliances that appeared like cookie batter on a baking sheet, had been homes and businesses. The Cat 4 that ravaged the Panhandle aroused another emotion. He was one of the forty percent who lived within sixty miles of a coastline. Like these people his Pass-a-grille home was a target for violent storms. He lived with the realization that every aspect of his life could be so easily disrupted. He was still reeling from the loss of his mother and his wife within a few months of each other. The debris along the road aroused a trepidation that came with an omen. Mother Nature was self-correcting the faults of mankind. She was unlikely to stop soon. He loved living on the beach but his home and the prospect of romance were each threatened. He focused upon the breathing. In an out, in and out.

It was late afternoon when he arrived at the Salty Dog. When he asked the bartender to point out S. T. Sparks, he was directed to the back patio over-looking the Gulf of Mexico. Beyond the patio and the fine white sands was a calm blue expanse of water that defied the anger it thrust upon the shore two weeks ago. Only a single couple with a young child walked the beach, occasionally scurrying back and forth to avoid a tide that barely crept onto the shore.

A glance at his watch indicated it was Happy Hour, but the dearth of people in the bar suggested the tourists were shy and the locals had no reason to celebrate. On the patio three men in their late thirties sucked on longnecks, while engaging in a somber conversation. One of them stopped, took a long drag on his cigarette, and blew a smoke ring into the air. Two of them wore tee-shirts with fishing themes on them. Each of them sported tattoos. A tall man, the youngest of the group, sported a full beard and white rubber boots, the kind that people wore in fish processing operations. The only woman in the group rose from their table to greet him.

"Simeon Sparks," she said as she offered Derk her hand. She wore a tee-shirt with a red "X" drawn through a plastic bottle that floated atop cobalt blue waves that were brushing a tropical shoreline. A child frolicked in the surf while porpoises played Dolphin games nearby. Palm trees gently swayed in the wind. *Imagine* was embossed above the scene and below it were the words *a world without plastic*.

With reservation he said, "S. T. Sparks?"

Standing in front of him was the most unusual woman he had ever met dressed in shorts and a tank tee. Stunning? No. Breathtaking? No. Still, he couldn't take his eyes off her. Waves of burnt red hair flowed freely to the middle of her sinewy back, which was adorned with wildlife. Fit as a gymnast, her lithe limbs sported creatures so artfully engraved upon her skin they looked 3D.

"I surprise people," she said.

"I'll bet you do," he said.

"It's actually Simeon Teresa Sparks."

"Estee, of course" he said. When he stopped alternating glances between the Mastodon and the Auroch imprinted upon her thighs, he offered his business card. "Derk Bryan, EPA."

"We know who you are," said one of the men sitting with her as he blew another smoke ring into the late summer sky.

Accounts of his travails must have traveled fast. He tried to conjure a comical retort that would politely dismiss any of their inquiries, but he settled for, "You said you have information about a body you found."

Her friends seemed surprised by his announcement.

"Have a seat," Estee said as she motioned to one of the guys to give up his chair.

When her colleague resisted, she kicked the leg of his chair. "Hey, Bubba, be a gentleman and let Dr. Bryan sit down."

Bubba, if that was his real name, rose slowly while the others grumbled in low tones. Estee Sparks was clearly the Alpha dog in this group.

"Sorry for the cold welcome, but Sandy here," she said as she opened her hand in his direction, "doesn't think there should be an EPA. And Chris, well, he doesn't like the EPA. Doesn't think you're doing your job. Bubba, he prefers dogs to most people so don't take it personally."

Bubba started to object, but Estee held up her hand.

"And you?" Derk said.

Before Estee could answer Chris spoke, "They keep polluting our water and we still haven't gotten compensated us for the BP thing."

Estee held up her other hand. "Chris, we'll get to that. We're all hurting here, Dr. Bryan, and we want to know what our government is going to do about it."

The agenda was clearer. These boys were in the fishing business, and the Panhandle had been hit hard by the BP oil spill, multiple hurricanes and a lot more. They blamed the EPA.

"BP had paid out millions for the oil spill," Derk said. "I gather you didn't get your share."

"Yea, we got paid," said Bubba, "but our oyster catches are down two thirds. We're holding on by threads."

Chris added, "Then they released fresh water into Lake Ponchartrain. That was a fucking disaster."

"We were told it was to prevent a repeat of the flooding that crippled New Orleans during the hurricane," Sandy said. "What it did was wipe us out. Why is there an EPA if you're not going to stop these things?"

"I am aware that to counter the problem fresh water from the Bonnet Carre Spillway was released into Lake Ponchartrain which flows into the Gulf. That much fresh water upset the natural balance, but ---" Derk said.

Bubba interrupted him, "But nothing. It killed the oysters, the blue crabs and the shrimp. Her family's the only one left in the business and we're making minimum wage."

"Please, Bubba," Estee said.

"No, Estee," Bubba continued, "Chris lost his boat and his wife."

Chris covered his face as if he were embarrassed by such a public pronouncement.

"Dr. Bryan, our entire way of life has been destroyed by runoffs, oil spills and hurricanes, and all the stuff that's been dumped into our water. We want to file a suit against the EPA," said Chris.

"You're an attorney?" Derk said to Estee.

"She's sitting for the bar exam next year," Bubba said and pointed at Estee.

"Paralegal," Estee said.

Derk nodded. "I'm sorry to hear that."

"You don't like lawyers?" she said.

"No, about your losses," he said. He wanted to address Estee but Chris was determined.

"So, when is the EPA going to do something?" said Chris.

"We're trying," Derk said, then faced Estee. "Tell me about the lawsuit. What's your claim and why the EPA?" Her tout limbs and short shorts belonged on someone in her twenties, but the little cobwebs that spread out from her eyes suggested she was older than that.

"Because you failed to do your job. You didn't protect us," Chris said.

Estee held up her hand again. She had closely filed nails with clear polish and no frills other than coral earrings.

Sitting across from him was a lioness and three cubs. He wondered what was so alluring about Estee Sparks that they followed her lead. He soon found out.

When she spoke she was polite and deliberate. "We think that all the chemicals that have been dumped into the bay, the runoffs from the industrial farms, the oil spills, and all those other things are the responsibility of the EPA."

"And we want the courts to force you to do your job," said Chris.

Derk spoke directly to Estee, "As someone in the legal profession—"

"She's taking the bar exam next year," Bubba interrupted.

"Good for you. What school?" Derk asked.

"Hard-knocks," said Sandy and everybody laughed.

"FSU," Estee said.

"Then you should know about jurisdiction," Derk said. The EPA was too often subject to the whims of politics and found itself regularly defending itself against lawsuits claiming overreach. He didn't want to encourage another one.

"Of course."

Derk continued, "If your claim occurred within nine miles of the coast, it's a State matter. If it occurred from there up to twenty-four miles out, it's a federal matter. Beyond that it's in international water and that's gray matter."

"Not really. Two hundred miles from the shore of any country is considered an exclusive economic zone of the country involved, thus granting that country jurisdiction over its territory." She spoke like seasoned counselor.

"If only it were that easy. Even though one hundred and ninety-six countries hammered out the terms of the Paris Climate

Agreement, few have actually done anything about it," Derk said. "It's damn discouraging."

"That's why we want to sue the EPA. We're all within that two hundred miles and we want you to do your job." Chris said. He sat back in his chair and blew another puff into the air.

Sandy said, "The stuff they used to break up the oil spill contaminated most of the seafood around here. Then you guys shut down access to our beds. What else can we do?"

"We've been fucked and no one seems to care," Chris said.

Estee winced. She began to say something when Derk cut her off.

"When I'm done here, I'll give you the names of people who may be able to help you. Right now, I'm here to talk with Ms. Sparks about a body that ended up in her net, and unless you know something about that, would you please excuse us."

Derk rose from his seat and motioned for Estee to join him at another table.

"Not so quick," Chris said. "We were promised."

"Promised what?" said Derk.

"Relief and change."

"By whom?"

"FEMA," Estee said.

Derk took a piece of legal paper from his note book, and held up one hand while he wrote down several names.

"This is the name of the Director of FEMA. If you are due anything he should be able to help," Derk said.

"Been there, done that," the choir sang.

Derk wrote down more names and numbers. "This is your congressman and these are your two senators. I would be calling them and asking why they have not supported legislation to stop the runoffs coming down the Mississippi River. While you're at it, ask them why they haven't recognized that our thirst for fossil fuels is not only ruining our planet, it was the reason for the spill that disrupted your lives. And, if you're going to rely upon the courts to resolve your problems, keep in mind the Supreme Court recently denied the EPA the right to regulate carbon emissions. This may not be what you want to hear, but it's the current reality."

"No, no, no, no," Sandy said along with more grumbling.

"I would like to be able to help you, but someone killed a young woman, shaved her like a naked rabbit and stuck her in block of plastic so hard she can't be identified. If any of you has any information that can help me, I'm all ears."

This news silenced them. It appeared as if Estee had not shared the details of her discovery with them. They may have grievances, but he had a job to do. It probably wasn't the best time for a lecture, but the professor in him emerged.

"This is just an observation and I may be way off course, but including the four of you I counted ten people in this bar and eight cars in the parking lot. None of them were electric. I'm just speculating, but I'll guess none of you has a single photo-voltaic cell on his roof."

The question marks on their faces answered Derk's query.

"And, although I'm sure some of you probably recycle your empty Bud-Lite cans, I'll bet none of you composts your waste or has planted a tree in the past year. I empathize with you. The situation sucks, but until each of us becomes part of the solution we are part of the problem. We have ourselves to blame for this big mess. If you don't mind, I have a job to do."

"We understand," Estee said and dismissed her colleagues. "I'll get with you later." She got up and moved to another table. "Let's sit here, Dr. Bryan."

"One more round?" Bubba said, trying to change the mood. Sandy and Chris waved off his gesture and went into the main bar. Bubba followed.

She was about to say something, a retort Derk assumed was a gesture of support for her friends, but Derk opened his hands toward the beach and said, "What do you see out there?"

A tractor pulled a machine along the beach wisping up mounds of seaweed left by the storm surge. A man on a fork lift at a nearby marina separated the boats ruthlessly stacked upon each other. Up and down the beach people were engaged in various stages of repairs. There wasn't a smiling face among them.

"Despair," Estee said with a sigh.

"Exactly. I'm sorry I was so blunt with your friends, and as to your suit, in this political environment, I wouldn't be optimistic. But I need to talk with you about what you found," Derk said.

"I couldn't tell them," Estee said. "They know I found someone. It was in the news, but I couldn't give them any details. They don't need more bad news."

"Like what?" Derk asked.

She winced. "Did you see her?"

He nodded.

"You know if I told them, they would—" She paused as if she were searching for the proper word. "Well, they're guys and she was naked."

"Ask a lot of embarrassing questions," he said.

She closed her eyes and nodded up and down. "She was someone's daughter. Maybe even a mom."

Estee couldn't hold back the tears that washed across the tiny lines that extending from tired eyes. Those lines that tattled her true age. She was probably approaching forty.

Derk's attention was drawn to an animal inked onto her arm. She stood and did a slow one-eighty. With her back to him to him she lifted her shirt and exposed another tattoo. She turned and revealed one on her torso. He recognized each of them. One was a West

African Black Rhino. She also sported a Baiji White Dolphin and a Dodo, a Woolly Mammoth and a Passenger Pigeon. Each of them was extinct and each of these animals had become extinct at the hands of man. They had been hunted into oblivion while failing to adapt to a changing climate. Estee Sparks had transformed herself into a blunt reminder of man's ability to destroy everything in his sight. Derk thought he was committed to environmental justice, but this woman was in another league. Something monumental must motivate her.

"That's quite a statement," Derk said. "What happened?"

With a sad smile she exhaled and lowered her shorts to expose a small scar across her abdomen. "That's where they took Lincoln out of me. I got to hold him, baptize him and bury him."

Derk hadn't seen this coming.

"He died without my amniotic fluids which is what the plastic does to you. They're in everything. He had undeveloped kidneys, no bladder and no bowels." Anger filled with resolve as she spoke, "Did you know that average person consumes about five grams of micro-plastic every week. That's about the size of a small cigar. Every week!"

He recalled the time Code Enforcement denied his request to install a windmill on his roof. There was no good reason. It angered him, but she had lost a child. In her world this should not have happened. He wanted to console her but she closed her eyes and took a few breathes. In a few seconds for her demeanor changed.

"We go out and pick this stuff up from the beaches in truckloads." She tossed back her red hair and pumped out her chest bearing the plastic bottle with the red "X" on it. "I volunteer for Blue Skies/Clear Water. We drag the Gulf and come back with tons of this stuff: fish nets, rods, lines. We've found enough fishing nets to go around the Earth eighteen times. Plastic waste is killing the oceans. It killed my child. It killed our business, and it's probably going to kill me."

"What do you mean?" Derk said.

"My doctor says I have a bad liver."

"I am so sorry, Estee." He got up and opened his arms.

"Thank you," she said but refused his embrace. "I'm dealing with it. It hurts. It will always hurt, but I'm dealing with it."

"Is there anything I can do?"

"We're going out tomorrow and—" she said, but didn't finish her thought.

It was only a hunch, bit it seemed as if she was about to tell him something that she shouldn't.

"Do you mind if I ask you something?"

She closed her eyes and shook her head, "No."

"Where did you discover the body?" He returned to his seat and she followed his lead.

"I'm not really sure. We'd been in the Hypoxic Zone picking up debris and getting water samples. We didn't notice it until we got almost to the harbor."

"Where was that?"

"Apalachicola. We'd left out a net to collect plastic and anything else that shouldn't be there. You know this stuff comes from everywhere. It drifts down the Mississippi. Charters throw it overboard. Recreational boaters dump it into the water. The cruise lines are monitored but you can't trust them."

"We work with the Coast Guard to try to stop it," he said. "But where did it come from, the body? What direction?"

She turned and pointed west, toward the water. "Out there, but I guess it's your job to find out exactly where."

"Well, somebody's." He didn't think it was his job or the EPA's. His cases usually involved a decomposing corpse in swamp of toxic pudding or a golfer that ended up in a lake filled with industrial waste due to ruthless chicanery.

"I'm afraid I let them down," she said.

"Whom?"

She motioned toward the door that her friends had exited.

"Don't be too hard on yourself," Derk said. "You're doing more than most people. A lot more, I'd say." He pointed to one of her tattoos.

He handed her another business card. "Email me their names and their businesses and I'll see if there is anything that can be done."

During the remainder of their conversation, he learned that Estee had grown up in the Panhandle. Her family and most of her friends had been in the oyster business. She grew up working with her father and she knew the waters of the Gulf as well as anyone. It wasn't until he was half way to Tallahassee that he recalled a casual remark she made about the police response to the incident.

"I think they assumed that someone in the Panhandle dumped the body out there," she said.

The coroner had told Derk the police were checking every marina from Pensacola to Panama City.

"That body could have drifted from anywhere. The current in the Gulf runs from west to east," Estee told him.

Her words kept running through his mind. Located along the Mississippi River and down the west coast of the Gulf, from New Orleans to Houston, are some of the largest petrochemical plants in the world. Their raw materials, oil and natural gas, are the principal ingredients in plastic. Whatever encased the woman with the red nails, it appeared to be a form of plastic.

He called the director, "Sahith, did you know that the current in the Gulf flows from west to east?"

"No," he replied. "Why?"

"Do you believe in coincidence?"

Before his boss could reply, Derk said, "I don't."

Climate Fact:

Agriculture is responsible for 90% of deforestation. Mangroves and coastal wetlands hold up to five times more carbon per acre than tropical forests. The United Nations Intergovernmental Panel on Climate Change has determined that by legally protecting 30% of our land area from abuse and development is close to what the Earth needs to rebalance itself. Only 16% of land is now protected in some way.

What can you do about it? Do not support new development in environmentally sensitive areas.

4

Pendleton Danswirth had only walked from the parking lot to his suite in the Rock Hard hotel, but he was dripping with perspiration. Due to the record high heat index the Tampa Health Department had issued a warning for people to stay at home, but Danswirth had been anticipating this event for too long. He stripped, showered and put on a tuxedo in preparation.

He was going to reveal *GodNet*, a cell phone network made possible by launching a series of low orbit satellites. The service would be available to places of worship and their supporters. The organization financing *GodNet* would be controlled by Danswirth and his rich and politically connected friends. He was intoxicated by the scent of money he would make by merging faith with fossil fuels.

Deacons, pastors, elders, officers and some of the most fervent politicians in the country were gathered for what had been rumored to be a game changing announcement. The irony that he hadn't been in a church for twenty years never crossed his mind.

There had been rumors and doubters. A project this big wasn't easy to keep under wraps. Most of the gossip was among those who considered *GodNet* to be a fantasy of some religious nut. Who would send up hundreds of satellites to establish a cellular network to reach an audience that was not much bigger than Jonestown. It would have been considered a failed business model if anyone other than Pendleton Danswirth III had proposed it.

The project was his response to the climate crisis. He didn't need the heat index or health department warnings to convince him the planet was warming. Every kid who took a high school science class understood the principle at work. If you enter your home, lock your doors, seal the windows and light a fire it will become so hot nothing in the house will survive ---including you.

That's what was occurring on Mother Earth, and he knew it was due to the use of fossil fuels. He also knew that restraining the use of fossil fuels would become a big problem for him. His family owned one of the largest plastics manufacturing companies in the world, and natural gas, a fossil fuel, was the primary ingredient in every one of his products. His company's motto for fifty years, *Your Life is Better with Plastics*, was under attack from cities enacting rules to reduce single use and other forms of plastic products. The entire fossil fuels industry was on alert. He was confident someone would find a solution to this challenge. They always did.

Danswirth also knew that there were over seventy million people in the U.S. who considered themselves true believers --- people who are more concerned with dying in the fires of hell than burning up on Earth. He thanked his Aunt Virginia for dropping that statistic on him. Of course, it was during another one of her futile attempts to lure him back to God. She had always been the pious one in the family. She was proud of his success but always reminded him that something was missing in his life. In Danswirth's opinion, if there really was a God, he lost interest in the people of Earth a long time ago.

He enjoyed the lofty, over-inflated role his family had attained. At a PAC fund raiser held at his estate, he warned the industry Bigs and elected officials, "One day people will understand what is happening and demand a change. Our livelihoods, our lifestyles and our influence will come to an end. We must control the narrative."

Pendleton Danswirth's family was one of the richest in the world. They were lifetime Texans. His grandfather started as a wildcatter. His father added natural gas to the mix, and Pendleton moved the company into manufacturing. The Danswirth clan hobnobbed with presidents, sheiks and one per-centers. His estate was once featured on *Homes of Rich and Famous*. His friends owned islands and airplanes to fly to them.

"Our initial target," he said to those assembled, "should be the people who are more afraid of their messiah returning and condemning them to the fires of Hell than they are of burning up on Earth. *GodNet* will enable us to be in the pockets and purses of millions of believers with one simple message: *Fossil fuels good. Regulations bad.* And, we'll be the cheapest service on the planet." They would give away the phones.

He checked himself in the mirror one final time before making his entrance. He had memorized his lines and was in a haughty good mood.

In his suite were oil barons, gas frackers, casino owners, church elders and politicians, but as far as Danswirth was concerned Sacred Waldo Abernathy was the most important person in the room. His book, The Sacred Bible, had sold a zillion copies. His rise to fame was legendary among believers, and his followers were the audience to which *GodNet* would provide a direct link.

Danswirth would have dismissed Abernathy if he hadn't heard about the man from his aunt. Aunt Virginia quoted bible passages like Al Michaels knew baseball stats. She was a doting but severe old maid school teacher on his wife's side of the family. Her principal goal in life was to convert pliable young minds to believers before, "They get caught in the Devil's grip." She never missed a sermon at her church or a "God Bless You" whenever in his company. She was a long-time member of The Last Chance before Damnation Baptist Church. The church supported an outreach program with the purpose of guiding ex-cons back to the "righteous path." It was Aunt Virginia who encouraged Danswirth to talk with a minister from Last Chance about supporting the program, and it was this minister who convinced Danswirth to talk with Pastor Trout at the prison. Danswirth had been searching for someone to host a radio talk show he intended to call *Don't Back Talk God.* It was the success of that program that inspired him to develop *GodNet*, and it was this same preacher that alerted him to Sacred Waldo Abernathy, so named because Sacred's mother had decided that he was a gift to her from God, a Sacred gift.

According to the preacher the story of Sacred Waldo Abernathy went something like this. "Years of living in sin had taken its toll on Sacred's mother. The ultimate party girl was thirty-five and barely making ends meet as a bartender at a fleabag beach hotel when she found God. At least, that's what she thought when the handsome and charismatic Reverend Tom showed up in her bar. The Reverend was there for a break from a religious retreat with his choir master until she found out he was married. Sacred's mother hitched up with the reverend after he convinced her he could save her soul. After a couple of drinks, he persuaded her to summon up the sins from her past and suggested that the road she was on was paved with tar from Hell. Have you looked at yourself in the mirror he asked? Her tee shirt read *Last Bar before Hell*. After intense and intimate conversion therapy involving cocaine and a threesome, the glib Reverend Tom became her savior. He also became Sacred's father."

The preacher was not proud of Reverend Tom's work, but he was impressed with the preacher's linguistic skills. "I don't condone his methods, but the guy could talk his way into a meeting of the La Leche League."

He seemed disgusted with the Reverend's moral flexibility, but enthralled by Sacred's rise from the depths of despair. "When Sacred Waldo was born, Reverend Tom, wishing to protect his position in the church and to avoid costly alimony payments," the preacher frowned, "used the money he skimmed from the parish tithes to support Sacred Waldo and his mother after she agreed to tell no one about their affair. Not only did she agree, she developed a freaky relationship with the Almighty and immersed Sacred in every aspect of her obsession. She wasn't a nun, but she tried to join a convent— I'm guessing for the free room and board—but she was rejected when she showed up with Waldo in tow. The word is she unloosed a series of invectives upon parish sisters that was so vile that one of them had to be restrained from choking her to death with her rosary."

A rise to fame from this sordid account didn't seem plausible to Danswirth, and he peppered the preacher with questions, but the preacher's awe of Sacred was evident and he pressed on with the story.

"The name Sacred became an embarrassment for young Abernathy and subjected him to ridicule by *those whom have not been washed by the light of God* according to his mother. Young Abernathy rebelled at first and rejected the teachings of his faith," said the preacher, exhibiting some despair in regard to that shortcoming, "and, against his mother's wishes, he enrolled in a liberal arts college, referring to himself only as Waldo. Things didn't go well. He was confused in the secular world. You know," the preacher said disparagingly, "the world of sex, drugs and free will. In fact, so much that he dropped out of school in a haze of experimentation until his soul drifted. We almost lost him."

The preacher grimaced. "In one particular psylocibin induced high he envisioned himself living in an Eden like forest where he was able to fly and the fruits, that dripped from the trees, were filled with intoxicating nectar. Somehow, and I have no idea why, he misinterpreted this as a message from God. God does act in mysterious ways. Three days later Sacred responded to a want ad for a sales position with a company that sponsored wilderness tours. Within a week he moved from Texas to a remote part of the northwest."

The preacher paused and took a long, deep breath. "I know. It was hard for me to believe the first time I heard about him. Anyway, the job took place in a forest, but it certainly wasn't Eden. There he found that his best clients were hard core wannabe revolutionists. You know, gung-ho guys with tattoos, four by fours and guns who are convinced the government is coming for them."

The preacher laughed aloud. "If the government was really after them it would tie up their credit cards, but that's another story."

He continued, "So, he convinced the tour owner to lease a couple of Hummers and add weapons training to the outdoor adventure. Sales became so robust he was able to acquire something he never had, the material trappings of life. However, so much time in the bush with these rugged misfits in pursuit of unfulfilled dreams didn't fill the void in his own soul." The preacher pursed his lips and nodded with raised eyebrows. "He later confessed this in his memoir, *Life is Sacred.* He had become detached from God." A cloud of despair descended upon the preacher.

"After his mother urged him, '*Sacred, sweety, you need more discipline in your life,*' he tried to join the Army."

The preacher shook his head in disbelief. "Apparently because he knew so much about guns and living in close quarters with guys, but even that didn't work out. As a result of an incident involving weapons at the local Army recruiting station, the Sergeant in charge wrote two words on his application, Waldo Whacko."

Danswirth excused himself after a yawn.

"It's a convoluted tale but it gets better," said the preacher. "He returned to his mother's home, forlorn and severely depressed. He drifted down, so far that the Good Book got mired under a pile of empty beer cans and pizza boxes. Until the intervention!"

That got Danswirth's attention. "Intervention?"

"Yes, the intervention," said the preacher with a foreboding tone. "Under the threat of homelessness, Sacred's mother forced him to participate in something called, *Helping Hands.* His mother's latest reverend, and lover, matched poor souls cursed by social functioning disabilities, which included those suffering from Costco sized despair and the heartbreak of psoriasis," the preacher he quipped, "with other poor souls."

"In other words," Danswirth said, "Sacred had to become chummy with someone even more fucked-up than he was."

The preacher responded like a bobble head. "You're beginning to understand. Now, this is the good part. What began as an intervention resulted in a miracle and involved a half-crazed curmudgeon named Conover Converse. Conover, one of God's lost creatures, was teetering on the precipice of darkness when Waldo was assigned to intervene in his life. Now this was against the inclination of every fiber in Conover's body. Conover had become totally perpendicular to the benefits of interpersonal skills. He was always mad, and when he was mad, he threw things."

At this point the preacher became highly animated with his hand and arms. "Like beer cans and lamps and radios. One time he threw a tennis racket through his living room window from his Lazy Boy rocker and it hit the postman, John McEnroe style," said the preacher with a grin, thinking he had made another joke. "And Conover cussed. In fact, Sacred said that he never heard Conover speak an entire sentence without the word the F-word in it." He shook his head again, this time with sadness. "Anyway, he, Conover, had a bum leg from an injury in an industrial accident, and he got around with the help of a cane he crafted from a broken ball bat, a Louisville Slugger."

The preacher started to talk about playing baseball when he was a young man, but Danswirth cut him off.

The preacher went on, "Apparently, he was good at something. Anyway, to make things worse, his wife left him for a welder she met at the picnic put on by Conover's company."

Danswirth rolled his eyes.

"Sorry. I know it sounds bad, and it was. He survived on disability checks, braunschweiger sandwiches and reruns of Judge Judy. Sacred said he cussed at every verdict. It didn't matter who won."

"Okay, I get the picture," said Danswirth. His impatience was showing.

"I am surprised. You don't know any of this story?" said the preacher.

Danswirth shook his head. What he needed to know is how Sacred Waldo Abernathy had become a stepping stone to salvation for so many people, but the preacher was going on as if they were in the middle of a five-course dinner.

"Well, I must admit that this next part is real fire and brimstone stuff, but," he made a clicking sound with his tongue, "it will send shivers up your . . ." The preacher stopped when Danswirth pinched the bridge of his nose with two fingers.

"Okay, Sacred Waldo wasn't exactly a trained counselor so he resorted to something that came to him osmotically to assuage Conover's temper," the preacher said.

Danswirth gestured with frustrated hands, "And what was that?"

"He repeated bible passages, lines he recalled during his time as an altar boy." This made the preacher smile. "It's important that boys and girls, of course, become acquainted with biblical teachings at an early age."

Danswirth's eyes rolled again. The preacher picked up the pace.

"This only served to raise Conover's ire. One day, as Sacred Waldo was reciting an adage to mollify his own frustrations; you know, the one about God granting the patience to change only that over which we has control and the wisdom to leave the rest alone. Well, Conover went postal."

Danswirth's brows rose and the black in his eyes glinted like opals. Maybe the end was coming.

"The result was a streak of vitriol against God, and of course Sacred, that was so venomous it shook Sacred Waldo to his core, to his very soul." The preacher paused as if reliving the moment.

Danswirth gestured with his hand to continue.

"Conover's blasphemy apparently had an even greater impact upon God." The preacher's posture and voice changed. It was as if the words came from God himself. "As he sat in his Lazy Boy, spitting out pieces of a bologna through a four-lettered diatribe, a bolt of lightning penetrated the roof and cut his vulgar soul in half. There Conover Converse sat, smoldering, with a Miller Lite in one fist and the words *Fuck Jesus* on his lips."

The preacher said nothing for an awkward moment while Danswirth awaited the coda.

In a rapturous tone the preacher said, "At that very moment Sacred Waldo Abernathy was transformed. He put behind all of his past doubts and meanderings and committed to do the Creator's work as his life's work from that day forward." The preacher again waved his arms. "From that point on, whenever he felt the urge to stray, the image of smoke rising from Conover's unholy corpse brought him back to his senses. That was the day Waldo Abernathy realized that the name Sacred had become a blessing from God, and he set about informing others of his miraculous transition."

"Thank you, Reverend, for such an illuminating story," said Danswirth, exhaling deeply.

He had perused The Sacred Bible, but his only copy was used as a pedestal for an artificial fern that squatted next to his credenza. As far as Danswirth was concerned Sacred Waldo's interpretations were nothing but drivel. His ramblings about the benefits of slavery and the abomination of abortion and homosexuality were outright diversions from reality, although they became justifications for many willing to overlook their academic deficiencies. This was especially true about Sacred's endorsement of gun ownership. It ignored the reality that the rifle wasn't invented until the 15th Century and the handgun didn't hit the market until Samuel Colt and his partner, Samuel Hamilton Walker, came up with the Colt 45 circa 1846.

Each of these inventions occurred a century and a half after the birth of Christ.

It may have been entertaining in the way some appreciate slapstick comedy, but it was filled with historical discrepancies and outright fantasies. Why so many had embraced it was anyone's guess, but Danswirth supposed it was because Sacred gave credence to the idea that the creator would return within Sacred's lifetime and he would exact his wrath upon the non-believers. These were the folks Danswirth wanted to target. They were more worried about being condemned to Hell than being cremated by their own prodigal habits on Earth. If he could win over Sacred Waldo Abernathy *GodNet* would become a reality.

Danswirth mingled with guests while Waldo and his disciples distributed pocket-sized versions of The Sacred Bible entitled, *The Way to Rapture.* For twenty bucks you got an autographed copy while he put his hand on your forehead and pointed to the sky, "Your salvation is within reach." When people fell to Sacred's feet, Danswirth's dismay was countered by a twinge of envy. The Sacred Bible was a cash cow.

When the corpulent Sacred Waldo Abernathy settled into a large divan, he was accompanied by two middle-aged women with too many pounds and too much makeup. Dressed in matching white ensembles from Marshalls they greeted everyone with, *"Have you been saved?" w*hile they continued to hawk copies of Sacred's *Rapture* at twenty bucks a pop.

Danswirth Enterprises provided jobs for thousands of people and each one of them got a bonus after ten, fifteen and twenty-five years of service. He supported many charities and he financed a chair in economics at a local university. In return for the latter, he expected the professors to develop a curriculum kind to his specific brand of free enterprise, the hallmarks of which included lax labor and environmental regulations and low taxes. He had Senators' and

Presidents' private numbers in his rolodex. He deserved the respect that his success had earned him. What he didn't need was to be saved by Waldo or anybody else, so in spite of his admiration for the man the fact that he needed Waldo's support gnawed at him like indigestion. He popped two antacids just in case.

He waited for Waldo to extricate himself from the two voluptuous women with reproving stares. One would whisper into Waldo's ear, and he would whisper into the other's ear. He assumed they were surveying the room in an effort to guess who was there with someone other than his or her own spouse. Danswirth knew who they were, but he overlooked it. Since his wife had become ill there was the cocktail waitress in Galveston and a secretary at his San Antonio office, but they were only dalliances. If he were completely honest with himself, he would admit that his attraction to Angelina bordered upon obsession. Other than that, he had been faithful.

He seized his opportunity when the women arose, along with their artificial smiles, and headed for the restroom. Before he could reach him, Waldo began sharing small talk with a couple of suck-ups whose fealty to the faux-holy man bordered upon embarrassing, unless they were gay. He tried to erase that image, but he was too late. He circled behind Waldo as one of them became extra touchy-feely, which didn't seem to bother Waldo even when one of the man's hands dropped below Waldo's waste. Danswirth backed away in disgust.

Danswirth nodded to Murdoch Lundgren, owner of a media conglomerate that spanned two continents. Murdoch was sitting in a large red leather chair, one leg casually draped over the other, while pontificating on his favorite subject: *The dangerous rise of socialism.* That the world was actually experiencing a rise in nationalistic populism bordering upon fascism and that corporations were raking in record profits didn't matter to Murdoch. He was in the entertainment business and his newsroom was a stage. Danswirth Enterprises often advertised on his network.

Munching on Russian caviar while sipping Dom Perignon was Wayne Stevens, the principal in a resort hotel and casino mega-enterprise that dwarfed its competitors in both the United States and Macau. He seemed to be waiting, albeit anxiously, for a pause in Murdoch's emoting so that, Danswirth assumed, he could whine about the government's never ending racketeering investigations of his own operations. No one had proved it but everyone suspected that Wayne Stevens really did know where bodies were buried. The police were still searching for a New Jersey prosecutor who disappeared in the middle of a case involving one of Stevens' casinos. Danswirth sloughed off such matters. Rich people had problems. Danswirth had retainers at four different law firms to handle such inconveniences.

None of his guests seemed to matter when Princess Duval, wife of the owner of one the largest defense contractors in the country, entered the room. The alluring Princess, dressed in a long black evening gown, and he had, of lately, become regulars at political fund raisers. Speculation of their affair had yet to make the tabloids, but it was only a matter of time. Princess Duval was super model slim with long black hair. Danswirth knew for a fact that she camouflaged her mildly drooping cheeks with Botox, on both her face and her ass, which was a place Danswirth was frothing to explore. Not only was she a former beauty queen from a wealthy family, she had amassed a fortune on her own by financing charter schools. It was understood that she wanted to be Secretary of Education in a future administration. The only resistance came from those who knew that she nearly dismantled the public education system in her home State.

"Good evening, Mrs. Duval. So good to see you here" he said and kissed her on the cheek.

"Penny, my dear, this is your night," she whispered into his ear.

He fought off an erection that her pheromones always aroused. He took her hand as they worked the crowd. With Princess at his side, he was routinely interrupted. He tugged on her hand whenever anyone lingered too long. Country music played softly in the background, interrupted occasionally by a contemporary gospel number. Money and religion combined to make a powerful combination.

He stopped to thank the Colonel for coming. Among his oil baron buddies, Colonel Conrad Oglethorpe, founder of a successful fracking operation, was one of the most flamboyant. He was called Colonel due to his uncanny resemblance to the fried chicken king.

The Colonel was engaged in a *"who has the biggest dick"* debate with Spade Christenson. The topic was unclear. Danswirth knew it could have been anything or nothing. The only thing larger than Spade Christenson's ranch was his arrogance. Spade, with the boots, ten-gallon hat and bolo tie, was a branded Texan. He claimed he had a relative buried at the Alamo. It was convincing bar talk, but the truth was less noteworthy. He once confided to Danswirth that he had an uncle that was named after a horse, Travis, whose name came from William Barret Travis, the commander who died at the ill-fated Alamo in 1836. Spade's Texas ranch was half the size of Rhode Island. Danswirth had spent a weekend there shooting pheasants and talking about what to do when folks realized that burning fossil fuels were the main cause of global warming. "I own an island that is a thousand feet above sea level," he told Danswirth. "Why should I worry about global warming?

Colonel Oglethorpe's claim to fame was that his company's successful fracking operation had transformed America from sucking upon Saudi teats to an energy independent, free State. The Colonel's operation, with an annual income that exceeded the GNP of a small country, also resulted in the release of tons of methane. So much methane that the disaster clock from global warming was ticking closer to midnight than ever before. Natural gas, a primary component in plastic, made Danswirth's lavish lifestyle possible. He had decided long ago that global warming was someone else's problem. He had his own.

Danswirth winced when Princess excused herself to hobnob with Redding Thomas Anthony Hastings. Danswirth had not invited him. He camouflaged a scowl and acknowledged him with a raise of the brow. Hastings often showed up at this sort of gathering. Redding, Thomas and Anthony were each Hastings family names that dated back to the Puritans. As to his stuffed-shirt family heritage Redding's narcissism was only surpassed by his self-indulgence which included the eight-hundred-dollar Italian ensemble he was wearing and a two-hundred-dollar haircut. He had a nervous habit of shrugging his shoulders and cricking his neck. If it was Tourette Syndrome, Danswirth would have been sympathetic, but everything other than the tic was an act. Danswirth had heard from trusted sources that Hastings and his wife were members of a swingers' club. What goes on behind closed doors between consenting adults wasn't his business, but as the spokesman for the Family Values Council, Redding Hastings was a fraud.

Tonight, Redding mingled among the uber-rich with a copy of Sacred Waldo's bible clasped in his hands. Occasionally, he stopped to crank his neck, a nervous habit that made Danswirth wince, as if he had gargled with pickle juice. When Redding opened his arms to greet Princess Duval, Danswirth burped.

Of the guests gathered tonight, there were few that Danswirth would call close friends.

Many were acquaintances. Most were conveniences with connections. He was, however, not only inspired by them, he was confirmed by them. It was about power, privilege and freedom. These were people with the kind of wealth and power that most people thought perished with medieval kings and Russian Tsars. There were, at least, ten men in the room who could, at the conclusion of this event, fly every single person in attendance to a private island for a weekend of wine and frivolity. In fact, he had done that. If he wanted to ski the Alps, surf Jaws on the north shore of Maui or play golf with the President, he could do it. In fact, he had done all of those things. The freedom to exercise almost any desire was the reward and the addiction of wealth. It had become the defining force in his life. Only a few people achieved this status, and he was proud to be a member of the club.

Redding Hastings wasn't in the club and if he didn't have the attention of tens of millions of people Danswirth would have brushed him off like a bug on his lapel. And, there was the other thing. His invitation was clearly arranged by Princess Duval. Hastings was the long-time executive director of the Family Values Council which supported the privatization of education via charter schools, one of Mrs. Duval's favorite topics. He was also a frequent guest on a variety of conservative news programs where he repeated support for his distorted view of family values. Danswirth thought it would be easier to live your life in a straight-jacket than follow the mandates that the FVC had espoused over the years, but offending him could get him kicked out of Princess Duval's bed before he pulled up the sheets. In this league everything was about money.

Even Marshall Hucklebee protested when Danswirth suggested that Hastings be a guest on his radio program. "I know a con man when I see one," Huck said. It had yet to happen. Now he had to engage in small talk with this self-indulgent, effete fraud and ask for his support.

Danswirth was straightening his clip-on tie using a mirror across the room when a bell tingled and the lights flashed twice. He sidled over to the microphone, greeted everyone and thanked them for coming. Princess Duval stood to one side and applauded, encouraging others, particularly when certain guests were introduced. She knew the ones whose egos demanded attention. Then Danswirth asked Waldo to guide them with a prayer. At the conclusion, Danswirth held up his glass and joined the chorus, "Amen!"

Danswirth took back the microphone. "Now, if you would, please turn to face someone here that you don't already know and introduce yourself."

To encourage everyone, he turned to the person closest to him. "Hello, I'm Pendleton Danswirth. See how easy that is."

When he entreated his guests, "Come on, you're among friends," others followed his lead.

"What people of faith and industry can build together is almost beyond imagination," he said. He paused, closed his eyes, crossed his arms and looked to the heavens. "If it were not already in your dreams you are about to become part of history. Please join me in the ballroom for a special announcement." He motioned for everyone to head for the door.

Hands clapped, wine glasses jangled and Amens filled the room. It was revival tent electric. Danswirth knew it was the duty of this assembled crowd to spread the message, and he was about to provide them with the conduit. He smiled and shook every hand before moving to the main ballroom for his presentation. Princess Duval lingered nearby.

5

Pendleton Danswirth was intoxicated by the events of the evening. He had Princess Duval on one arm and an open bottle of champaign in the other as he approached his hotel room. Inside the suite he took a long swig from the bottle and then kissed her, deep and long. The Viagra was already kicking in.

"Whew!" she said, gasping for air. She raised her glass between them. "To you, Lord Danswirth."

He finished off the bottle and sat her glass on the coffee table. "Be thine queen tonight," he proclaimed and kissed her again. A torrid meshing of mouths and bodies followed by a frenzy of hands searching for lusher real estate.

Danswirth had been anticipating this moment of ecstasy for weeks. After his presentation Princess Duval entreated the crowd to imagine the possibilities of GodNet.

"We already have a 'Museum of the Bible' in Washington, D.C., right across the street from the White House. With a worldwide communication network, we can spread *the message* to everyone with a computer or a cellphone. This is a moment God has been waiting for," she juiced the attendees and received a raucous applause in response.

She was a dynamic woman with a gift for oration. He envisioned the two of them psyching up the faithful during rallies for the Crusades. That's when he popped the first Viagra.

As he unbuttoned her blouse, the scent of her hair and her breath on his neck ignited a lust he hadn't experienced in years. The acceptance of *GodNet*, followed by two tokes on a vape Marshall Hucklebee had slipped it into his pocket, had him soaring. He hadn't been this buzzed since the opium induced orgy with two Hindu women after closing the deal to manufacture plastics in India. The Indian deal opened the Asian market and allowed him to avoid the environmental regulations imposed in the United States. Tonight was even better. Two conquests in one evening. He felt invincible in the arms of Princess Duval.

Unknown to Danswirth or any of the attendees, earlier that day the Intergovernmental Panel on Climate Change and the EPA issuing this warning:

"The toxic waste from making plastic and its various forms, including Styrofoam, polycarbonate, polyethylene, polypropylene and others, threatens all of the aquatic life on Earth. Micro-plastic particles are present in almost every living person on the planet and fifty percent of the household water taps in the United States."

Later that week Danswirth Enterprises released the following response, "We can't help it if people don't recycle."

As her blouse came off, he loosened his tie and threw his coat over a chair. They pawed each other like two lions preparing to mate. As his hand drifted below her beltline it was apparent, she was ready, but suddenly, something held him back.

Now what, he thought? He kissed her again, on her neck and her ears, trying to relight the flame. As if a switch had been flicked off in his libido, he couldn't go there. Damn it! What's happening? He tried to step away from her, but she held him close.

"Come here," she said and pulled him onto the bed.

"Soon, baby, soon," he said as she tried to remove his shirt, but he offered no help.

"What is it, Penny? Tell me," she said.

Empathy and hurt swelled her eyes, but he let go of her and backed away. Mixing sex and business was risky. Once people signed up for the *GodNet* service he would have a conduit to millions of people. Until it was finalized by a vote of the Board, he couldn't do anything that may jeopardize his goal. He wanted her, and she wanted him, but he couldn't do it. Not yet. The splendor he had imagined would have to wait.

Princess Duval was having no such reservations, and the sildenafil phosphate tablet she had dropped into his champaign glass was working. She grabbed onto the bulge in his trousers and pushed him back onto the bed. At the same time a Randy Newman tune played on Danswirth's cell phone, "It's Money that Matters."

"What's that?" she said, startled.

"My phone," he said, reaching for his pants pocket. There he felt the wad in his pants which was building like steam in a boiler. He maneuvered to separate himself from her.

"My God, Pendleton. I can't believe this!" she said.

"Excuse me," he said, sheepishly, and answered the call.

"No, it's okay. I'm glad you called," he said to Emily Rasmussen, his long-time secretary.

He sat up in bed and listened but said nothing. After hitting Off on the phone he turned to Princess.

"Turn on the television."

"What is it?" said Princess.

He spotted he remote on a table next to the bed and clicked through the channel guide until he landed upon CNN. She began to say something but he silenced her with the wave of his hand.

"We have just learned that several offices on Wall Street have been sabotaged. Information is trickling in, but it appears that someone, or a group of people, has broken in." The announcer stopped, held up one hand and pressed a finger against his ear bud with the other hand. "Correction. We're getting word these weren't break-ins. People apparently showed up at the headquarters of several major corporations today and, you're not going to believe this, they dumped trash all over their offices. They wore hazmat suits as if they were responding to a call from someone about an Anthrax scare." He paused again and held the ear bud. "Our sources say that is how they got by security, and they walked out without saying a single word. They left only these." Pictures of a Woolly Mammoth, a Caribbean monk seal and a Dodo flashed upon the television screen.

"What's going on?" Princess said, covering her breasts with her arms.

"Wait," Danswirth said and held up his hand again.

"There's more," the announcer continued. "These are pictures coming from Houston and New Orleans."

Someone had taken a video with a cell phone. Trash was scattered about the office, on top of desks, on computers and all over the floor. Most of it was plastic debris.

"What to fuck! That's my office," Danswirth exclaimed.

"The pattern appears to be the same as it was in New York," said the CNN spokesman. "They were completely covered by hazmat suits so no one could recognize them. This time they left pictures of an Irish elk, a Saber-toothed tiger and a Pyrenean Ibex. How absolutely bizarre." The announcer shook his head in disbelief. "In other news, the Intergovernmental Panel on Climate Change charged the leaders of the largest economies in the world with playing lip service to their commitments to reducing global warming. You are playing Roulette with the planet, the Secretary General said."

"What's going on, my Dear?" Princess said.

Danswirth turned off the television, arose from bed and paced, back and forth between her and the closet.

"Okay," he mumbled to himself, a decision made, and tossed his suitcase onto the bed.

"Pendleton!" she said, more forceful this time.

He stopped throwing clothes into the suit case and put his hands on her shoulders. "I have to go to Houston. Would you like to come with me?"

Confusion shrouded her face as she noticed the bulge growing in his pants.

"I'm sorry. Twenty-dollars of Viagra gone to waste," he said soberly.

"Forty," she said with a guilty grin. "I put one in your drink."

Danswirth couldn't help but laugh. "I love you, too."

Climate Fact:

What you wear makes a difference. The fashion industry is responsible for 10% of GHG, 20% of water pollution and 10% of plastic waste. The average fashion garment is worn seven times before it is discarded. Less than 10% of clothing is recycled.

What can you do about it? Avoid polyester. Natural fibers feel better and last longer. Re-use and recycle.

6

In the past seventy-two hours Derk Bryan had nearly drowned, been in the hospital, slept with an astronaut, seen a dead woman in a plastic box and interrogated a gal who would qualify as a side show exhibit. It was a lot for a guy considering retirement.

Strangely, his entire body tingled. It was more than lust. The attachment, physical and mental, rivaled what he had ever felt with anyone, including Jenny, his dearly departed wife, a victim of cancer. Something about Susan Carlton was different. She had been able to stop thinking about her since the moment she got onto that airplane.

At the same time, he sensed that a relationship with Doctor Susan Carlton would be complicated, maybe even risky. With so much uncertainty he knew sussing it out with the reporters parked outside his Passe-a-grill condo wasn't a good idea.

He passed his home and headed for his favorite bar. The Top End offered the best draughts, the best grouper sandwich and best pool tables in Tampa Bay. Half way there he realized, even among friends, his favorite refuge would be too public. He turned around and went home.

His condo featured a great view of the Gulf of Mexico, proximity to the beach and living quarters above the garage. As he approached the remote actuated the garage door which alerted reporters and gawkers. He eased past their cameras and microphones into the garage, avoided his 1949 Panhead motorcycle and stopped short of the power wall being installed as battery backup for his rooftop solar panels. The mob was so thick one of television reporters jerked his cameraman just in time to keep the garage door from hitting his equipment on its way down.

Derk waited in the car for the rapping on the garage door to stop. After five minutes he felt calm enough to go upstairs. On the way he grabbed a cold beer. He kept a cooler in the garage that had been

53

given to him by a friend in exchange for building a custom motorcycle that was to be raffled off in a fund raiser for The Sanctuary, a wildlife recovery center.

He dropped his bag on the living room floor and plopped onto the couch. Moonlight, the only illumination in the room, was partially obstructed by the palms that swayed outside his windows. As he sipped the import he dozed off.

He was awakened by a knock on the door. He got up and checked the clock in the kitchen. It was past midnight. Three more knocks, purposely but not obnoxiously.

Only a single car, an aging Sebring convertible with a torn top, was on the street when he peaked through the upstairs window. It didn't belong to anyone he knew.

He turned on the lights and took a deep breath. His arm still hurt, and he was in no mood to talk with anyone.

At the door a black man in his early fifties with ash tinted hair stood in front of him. He had one really distinguishing characteristic. He smelled like the cologne counter at Macys.

"Samantha Card sent me," the stranger said.

The cologne, however, couldn't overcome his dissembled appearance and weary eyes, in spite of his attempt to present a happy face. Derk held the door ajar but not enough to encourage entry.

The stranger held out his hand. "King Carver, sir. I mean Doctor." He was fidgety.

The mention of Samantha Card might normally to enough for someone to gain entry, but Derk kept a firm grasp on the door handle.

"I understand your hesitation, sir. I would too if I showed up at your door, given my situation." The stranger was unable to stand still.

Derk held the door more firmly. "Situation?"

"Sir, I mean Doctor, can I come in? I really need to use the bathroom."

Derk recognized the guy was holding back what any man would recognize as a serious need to urinate. He opened the door and waved him toward the bathroom. "Second door on the right."

The stranger ran past Derk. A few minutes later he returned from the bathroom, calmer and less disheveled. His face was a little wet, not sweaty, probably from sloshing water onto it.

"I apologize, sir. Doctor." He pumped his fists in a show of frustration. "I've been waiting all day for you."

"In your car?" said Derk.

The gentleman nodded. Embarrassment shadowed his face.

Any fear Derk had of the stranger was overcome by his own exhaustion. His body ached and he was on the verge of collapse.

"I'm sorry. I can see it's really a bad time. Can we talk tomorrow?" He handed something the size of a business card to Derk. On the front was printed King Ardale Carver, Journalist.

"What's the Ardale for?" Derk forced himself to ask.

"Ardale is a family name, but I was named after Martin Luther King. My mother marched with Dr. King. What would be a good time to call, sir? I mean Doctor."

Derk shook his head. The whole professional title thing often led to awkward moments. "It's Derk. I gather you're a reporter?"

"Journalist, sir."

That answer, even though expected, sapped his remaining energy. He closed his eyes and shook his head. "I know what you want and I'm not interested." Derk made a motion to close the door that ignited the pain in his arm. "Ouch!"

"I'm sorry, Doctor Bryan, but that changed when you jumped out of that airplane."

He wasn't about to debate anything with a stranger even if Ardale had been sent by Samantha Card, publisher of the Bay Magazine. She had helped him resolve one of the most convoluted cases he had ever worked.

"Can you call me tomorrow?" he said to get rid of the guy.

"Sure," said the reporter.

As King Carver turned to go, Derk asked, "How is she?"

"Fine, sir, Doctor," he said.

"Do you need my number?" Derk said.

"No, sir, Doctor. I have it," the reporter said, already halfway down the stairway.

Derk went to his own bedroom for the first time in four nights and crashed onto his king bed.

7

The doorbell interrupted Derk's fall. He was tumbling through space, trying to catch someone, but she stayed just beyond his grasp. Smiling, her face showed no fear, but he was desperate—afraid he couldn't reach her in time—or that he may never reach her at all.

Then came the racket of power tools. He threw off the covers and jumped from his bed. The sun had barely penetrated the blinds, forming only faint slits on the dark floor. The neon from the bedside alarm clock screamed six fifty-five. The doorbell rang again.

"Oh my god, what's happening?" He ran one hand across his forehead and through his hair when he realized it was the battery installers. "Why on Saturday?"

Before the day was done, he would have a battery backup system that would capture all the energy his rooftop solar installation could produce, but at the moment he was too exhausted to appreciate it. A decade ago, there was a storm every four months that resulted in a billion dollars of damage. Now they occurred every three weeks, and he was tired of being without power. With the sleep deprivation of the past three days this was not on his mind. Nor was the reality that he had given the work crew a key to the garage and told them to fit him into their schedule whenever they could.

The doorbell rang again. As he pondered who would be at his door at seven a.m. he recalled the swarm of reporters outside his home last night. Without looking out the window he retreated to his bedroom and went back to sleep. An hour later his phone rang.

"Dr. Bryan, you might want to turn on your TV," said a vaguely familiar voice.

"Who is this?"

"King Carver."

"Ardale?" Derk said groggily.

"Yes, sir. You may want to—"

"Are you in that throng outside?" Derk interrupted him.

"No sir. You should—"

"Didn't I tell you to call me later."

"Turn on CNN, Doctor." The line went dead.

Derk hobbled around the bed in search of the remote. He winced at the shrill whine of a saw cutting something in his garage.

"A follow up on that amazing air rescue over the Colorado River," a female announcer was reporting when he turned on the television. CNN was replaying a video that someone had taken of Susan Carlton's fall and her rescue.

His stomach ascended to his tonsils with a bam! The dream, he thought. It was Susan. Panic! It was as if someone had pushed him into an empty elevator shaft. Now he was falling. Derk Bryan, the scientist, the guy who calculated the odds in every situation, wouldn't leap from an airplane with such a narrow probability of success. Yet there he was, in the video, spiraling through space. This time, unlike the dream, he caught Doctor Carlton before they fell into the river. Suddenly the television screen turned black as the power went off.

"No, no!" He ran to the kitchen, opened the door and shouted into the garage, "Hey, mi amigo, turn on the power. Ahora!"

"Lo siento. Thought you were out of town," said Juan Ortega.

Derk recognized the voice, but hadn't met the guy. "Please!" Within a couple of minutes, the television was on and the air conditioning was humming again.

"This is Doctor Susan Carlton's first public appearance since surviving the fall while on an expedition into the Grand Canyon," the announcer said.

Susan Carlton was wearing blue coveralls with a NASA patch on the breast pocket as she answered questions from reporters. The same woman Derk saw in the hospital lobby was in the background, armed as usual.

"I am fine. It was an accident. We are trained for this kind of thing," she said with the demeanor of a trained animal—almost emotionless.

"Was this part of your training?" a reporter asked.

She forced a smile. "I tripped, clumsy me, but we train for contingencies."

"Have you been in contact with Dr. Bryan?" Another reporter asked.

"No, but I've been told that Dr. Bryan is alright."

Did her voice break or was he imagining that?

"Thank you, Dr. Bryan. You saved my life," she whispered and waved. The smile was familiar but her eyes seemed regretful. Or, was he imaging that, too?

That she would be the first woman to land on another planet raised a flurry of inquiries. Was she concerned about being gone so long? Was she afraid of not returning? What did her family think? She answered all of the questions with ease but when the reporter repeated the inquiry about her family a man in uniform came forward.

"Doctor Carlton has no parents. She is an orphan. I am sorry, but Doctor Carlton must get back to her training. There will be time for more questions later. Thank you for coming."

Doctor Susan Carlton was intelligent, competent and courageous. As are most military types, she was in phenomenal shape. She was also gorgeous. A woman like this could be self-absorbed, demanding and arrogant, but she was none of those. The Susan Carlton, whose arms and heart had revived him, exuded femininity and vulnerability. Among the myriad reasons they connected so quickly were the circumstances. Now that he knew she was an orphan offered further insight. He understood the loneliness that comes with that. Since his mother and Jennifer died, he was alone. In her arms a giant void was filled. He felt safe. He couldn't say it was love, but he hadn't felt this way in a long time. He called her again, but the only response was a series of beeps.

Eager for more news he went to retrieve the morning newspaper. The Times must have covered the story. As Ardale had said they made the national news.

He left the television on while he went downstairs to fetch the newspaper. As he opened the garage door, cameras, neighbors and people he didn't know greeted him. Lights flashed in a flurry. Questions followed. Juan Ortega, the solar technician in Derk's garage, had to shield his eyes to block the flashes from the photographers.

Derk stopped for a moment, surveyed the throng and nodded but said nothing. He ran his hand threw his hair and proceeded to pick up the morning newspaper delivered daily by a carrier from the Times. He casually swished people back with his hands until he found it. The newspaper, folded and stuffed into a plastic bag before being tossed onto his driveway, was under the foot of a rather large, middle-aged woman wearing what could be described as an XL-sized yellow tent. The press badge around her neck barely camouflaged some remarkable cleavage. She held out a microphone as Derk approached.

"Doctor Bryan, what does it feel like to be a hero?" she said.

The crowd hushed. Derk looked to his left, then to his right and then he looked down.

When he looked up, with a smile he said to the reporter, "Madam, you're standing on my newspaper."

The reporter in the neon teepee repelled so quickly she lost her balance. As she toppled Derk grabbed her microphone but she landed upon two men behind her. As Derk helped her get to her feet, he collected the newspaper. With everyone upright again, he shrugged his shoulders, cranked his neck back and forth and returned to his garage. As the queries and flashes reached a crescendo, he turned to face her.

"I really don't know what a hero feels like. I did what anyone would do for someone in distress. I just hope that Susan, Doctor Carlton, is alright."

The questions continued, but his mind was elsewhere. He closed the garage door without answering and shuffled past a befuddled Juan Ortega. At the foot of the stairs Derk turned around. "I jumped out of an airplane. That's all."

He heard voices upstairs. Oh no! Someone had sneaked by him and was in his house.

"Ouch!" he said as he climbed the stairway. The sling was gone, but his arm still hurt when he flexed it. Three steps with each leap landed him in the kitchen.

He heard the voice again and ran from room to room but to no avail. He was sure that someone was in his house. A sigh of relief came when he realized he hadn't turned off the television. He hoped he would feel well enough after breakfast to put some miles on his bicycle. A ride up the beach road would help him get back to his normal routine.

A normal morning included a glass of orange juice while he perused the newspaper on the patio balcony. Then he would ride to John's Pass. The round trip took about an hour unless he stalled to watch the tourists on the beach walking hand in hand while collecting shells. Sometimes he would sit on the sand and try to sync his breathing to the rhythim of the tide as it chased the gulls back and forth on the shore.

Today he plopped onto the couch and wondered why Susan hadn't returned his calls. A myriad of reasons leaped out. Maybe she needed a formal introduction. He laughed at the thought. Even if she were of some orthodox faith, they were way past that. Cautious? Maybe, if she had been burned in a previous relationship. Aloof? She was anything but that. He dated Jenny for six weeks before they became lovers. To Susan the concept of time seemed ethereal. Every possible barrier between them seemed to have evaporated like the morning fog when the sun creeps above the horizon.

What about another guy? Huh! If anything, he was the other man in her life. She was training for a Mission to Mars. Besides, she hadn't mentioned a lover, a friend or given any indication there was anyone else in her life. Neither had he told her about his deceased wife, Jenny, or any past romance.

"Damn it!" he said to himself. "Get a grip."

Susan and he were two people brought together by extraordinary circumstances for what, most likely, was a single moment in time. Their past loves and everything else in their lives had become irrelevant in that moment—a moment when all either of them needed was in that room. As real as that possibility was, Derk didn't want that moment to end.

He stared at the cell phone on the table next to him, resisting the urge to call her again. He rested his head on a cushion and pretended it was her lap before drifting into a deep slumber.

***

He was awakened by the William Tell Overture, the ringtone on his cell phone. It wasn't Susan's number so he ignored it, still not ready for the day to begin.

The angle of the sun's rays coming through the window indicated it must be close to noon. He went to the patio, rubbed the sleep from his face and took in the beachside air. The stiffness in his knees was a two on a one to ten scale. That was his guide for riding, anything less than three. Today he would go all the way to Clearwater Beach and have a late lunch at Frenchy's Salt Water Café. The Cajun grouper sandwich with fries was his go to order.

Churning gears helped him separate the noise from the theme music. He had solved cases while on his bicycle. It freed his creative side and enabled him to piece together parts of a puzzle that each case presented. A recent case involved the death of a farm and garden supply owner whose truck crashed into Lake Manatee with a load of pesticides. During one of his rides, it came to him that there were no skid marks on the pavement. It was no accident and his murder turned out to be part of a coverup for a criminal enterprise operating within the Sheriff's office.

Solving cases wasn't the primary reason he cycled. Movement is the enemy of arthritis and overcoming arthritis had become part of his daily routine. He rode five times per week. He also had a set of weights, somewhere, that he kept promising to use, and he was in the process of giving up red meat. The science about red meat's contribution to joint pain wasn't clear, but two colleagues at the university told him they felt better after they gave up eating things that walked on all fours.

Every time he had lunch with his friend and colleague, Dr. Samson Mabazi, he heard about the consequences of red meat consumption.

"It takes three fourths of a gallon of oil to make a pound of beef and the methane that emanates from both ends of the cow contributes more to global warming than the exhaust from all of the gasoline engines combined," Samson would say.

He was sure that Samson thought he could guilt him into carnivore sobriety. That would be no conflict today. Frenchy's had the best blackened grouper sandwich on the west coast of Florida. He was salivating when the phone rang again.

"Good morning. Derk Bryan here."

"Do you know who *this woman* really is?" said the familiar voice.

"Ardale?" Derk said, disappointed.

"Uh huh."

"What woman?"

"Your sky diving buddy. I've been doing a little research on Doctor Susan Carlton. Did you know she had been selected first alternate for the Mars Mission?"

"Yes, Ardale."

"Did you know if she goes, she will become the first woman to walk on another planet?"

Derk listened but said nothing.

"She's Einstein-fucking smart. Has PhDs in biology and molecular engineering." King Carver paused, but when Derk remained silent, he continued, "Apparently, she's an orphan, as in given up for adoption. But,"

"But what, Ardale?"

"Most people call me King."

Derk wasn't sure why he kept calling him Ardale. For a reporter he was friendly, polite and respectful, but he was also annoyingly persistent. Derk had learned not to say anything to a reporter that he didn't want to hear on the nightly news.

"What do you want, Ardale?" Derk said.

"I think we should talk."

"I've already made a statement to the press."

"If I can find out this stuff about Doctor Carlton, so can anyone."

"Ardale, you're just fishing," Derk said and ended the call.

The next call was to Samantha Card.

✳✳✳

"Doctor Bryan, so nice to hear from you." Samantha Card answered on the first ring.

"It's been a while."

"Too long, but I doubt you're surprised to hear from me," Derk said.

"I guess you've met King Carver," she said.

"Ardale?" Derk said. "Yes, ma'am. I figured he didn't get my name by chance."

Sammy Card was the publisher of Bay Magazine, the one stop shop for local entertainment news in Tampa Bay. She had been wanting to do a story on Derk since he helped her expose the local sheriff after he turned the drug forfeiture laws into a profitable enterprise while partnering with a musclehead who ran a gay sex for hire scheme. It was a convoluted story that earned her a Pulitzer nomination.

"I see you're back in the news again, Mr. Indiana Jones of the EPA," she said.

That wasn't the kind of the publicity he sought. He preferred to focus upon the chaos that global warming was creating. "Because I haven't yet agreed to do a story for you, you sicced Ardale on me."

"He's polite and he needs a break."

"He's persistent and he's annoying."

"He's also a really good reporter."

"There's a lot of good reporters."

"And he's quite charming," she said.

"Yea, like a snake."

"Please, Derk, give him a break. As a favor to me. How about I buy you dinner?"

"Samantha Card, are you trying to ploy me with one of your order-in pizzas again."

"Professor, you could do worse than a fanatic, over-worked journalist."

"Whose kid is smarter than the two of us combined," he said. Samantha's daughter was bi-polar but had an IQ over 130. "I don't think I can compete. By the way, how is she?"

"Deciding among college offers and as challenging as ever."

"She's a great kid and she's lucky to have you."

"I know. She liked you, too."

"Okay," Derk relented.

"Okay what?"

"If I meet with him is there anything I should know?"

"I met him at a conference one time. He does his homework. He went to Iraq and Afghanistan with some youthful illusions and came back with a bag of bad memories."

"Who's he working for?"

"Freelance, looking to break a big one. By the way, if you let him do your story toss him some expense money now and then," Samantha said.

Derk gasped aloud. "You're telling me if I let him do a story on me, I have to pay him."

"I think he's living out of his car. You know I'd put him on my staff, but he needs the exposure of a national publication. He's that good."

"Oh, Samantha," he sighed. "I'll meet with him, but that's all."

"Hey, Professor, are you going to save anyone today?"

"Stop it. It was a stupid thing to do, but it worked out," Derk said. He heard another phone ring and a voice in the background.

"Sounds like you've got to go," Derk said.

He heard her say, "Sorry," and she was gone.

Climate Fact:

Almost one gallon of oil is used to make a pound of beef which makes the cost of your burger as much about oil as it is about meat. Petroleum contributes 25% to the cost of a steak dinner. The space currently utilized for meat and dairy production takes up 1/3 of the habitable land on Earth.

What can you do about it? Buy local foods, eat local foods and eat less beef.

8

Estee Sparks was awakened by the sounds of an engine revving and a man snoring. The snore came from the man lying next to her.

"What the fuck!" She sat up in bed. As she did, she awakened the guy on the other side of her.

She tried to extricate herself, but she was tucked between two very fit men in their twenties. A peek under the cover revealed she was still dressed. That answered her first question. The sulfite driven headache answered another question, and the sight of Jones behind the wheel of his camper brought her situation into focus.

She was one of four student volunteers that raided Danswirth Enterprises as part of Blue Skies/Clear Waters' RAP campaign, Rage Against Plastic. RAP raids had been planned throughout the east coast. They plan was simple but not without risk. Devise a distraction and get in and get out before anyone discovered the ruse. Once inside they dumped bags of plastic waste everywhere. Estee and her friends had penetrated the inner sanctum of Danswirth's corporate headquarters and made a big mess of the executive offices. Every kind of plastic waste from soda bottles to fishing lines were strewn onto the desks, computers and carpets. They were the discards of the very products that Danswirth manufactured. With their mission completed they spent the night drinking cheap wine, light beer and improvising catchy jingles to rap-rhythms that encapsulated their accomplishment. Estee felt more exhilarated in the past twenty-four hours than she had in the past five years.

Jones, along with her bed mates, Teddy and Fendru, had picked her up at her home in the Panhandle on their way to the Danswirth Enterprises office in Houston. After trashing the corporate offices, they celebrated on their back to FSU law school in Tallahassee. The camper reeked of cheap wine.

"Let the revolution begin!" Jones had said to raised glasses.

When the last of them was too drunk to drive they parked in a roadside rest area along Interstate Ten and fell asleep in Jones' camper.

Estee arose with a nasty headache and full bladder. When she couldn't slither between her bedmates, she climbed over Teddy. As she did, he turned, which tossed her onto the floor with a thud.

"Ah!" she moaned and looked up at Teddy, lying face down on the edge of the bed.

"Good morning, Estee. Can I pat the Mastodon?" Teddy said.

Among the display of extinct wildlife on her body was a Mastodon on her right thigh. Her gallery of the victims of natural selection always drew some unwanted attention, but Teddy was Hollywood handsome.

"I've got to pee," was all she said.

"Maybe when you get back?" Teddy said.

In the tiniest bathroom she had ever seen she relieved herself, splashed water onto her face and tucked her shirt into her shorts. That's when she noticed her shoes were gone. She also noticed a small blemish on her forehead reflected in the tiny mirror over the smallest sink she had ever seen. She looked closely. It was just a bit of skin discoloration, probably from the Sun, but she probed for other signs of wear and tear. Even though she was, at least, ten years older than Teddy, she had the body of a woman who still could still stop traffic. She took a final glance into the mirror and took a deep sigh before opening the door.

"It's not breaking and entering because they let us walk in," said Jones.

"And we didn't take anything," said Fendru.

"He's right, we took nothing," added Teddy.

All law students, they were assessing the consequences should they be discovered. Except for Jones, the others had on nothing but their undershorts.

"How about littering?" said Fendru. "We definitely littered. What's the rap for that?"

"Misdemeanor," said Estee. It was probably more than that. Was she rationalizing? Or was trying to justify her decision to dump trash in the offices of one of the manufacturers of the waste she had been untangling from wounded marine life for too long.

"Top of the day to you, me Lassie," said Jones. He wasn't Irish, but he was always entertaining.

His name was Jones, but he pronounced it Jonas with a deep Irish brogue.

"Good morning, Jones," she mumbled and shook her head, still trying to spin off the remnants of cheap Gallo while chastising herself for not knowing better.

At first, she had been reluctant to join them --- she wanted to be a lawyer and a felony was a certain disrupter on that career path --- but she was angry. This stuff they shoveled onto Danswirth's offices had disrupted her entire life. She couldn't prove it nor could any authorities because the damage caused by the plastic producers was insidious. It crept up on her like a cancer. She likened it to dripping water. One drop can't kill you but when it becomes a lake or an ocean you can drown in it. She broke the law but with good intention.

The agencies responsible for regulating the companies whose products killed her son weren't doing their jobs. She had to fight back. Going to law school was a viable path but it was long term. She wasn't ready to hear the Blue Skies/Clear Waters plan until her meeting with the EPA official. Dr. Bryan made it clear that too many people were complacent, the government moved at the pace of snails and the agency charged with keeping the air and water clean had been chopped off at the knees by the Supreme Court. Her friends had lost their businesses. She had lost her baby and her husband left her in the aftermath of the chaos. This was a real opportunity to ameliorate some of the anxiety that had accumulated within her over the years.

Although it came with risk the RAP campaign promised an immediate reward. Her accomplices had as much to lose as she did, but as youthful idealists time was on their side. She had less time on her side, but she was guided by the words of her father, "To achieve anything worthwhile in this world, you will have to get out of your comfort level."

This was the boldest thing she had done since turning her body into a billboard. That was not an easy decision. She had never found it difficult to get men's attention. She was an attractive woman. But this changed everything. She was like a flashing red light with a sign that said, *Stop and Look at Me.* And people did. She had to talk different and walk different than before. She had to be bolder and carry her herself with authority. The law degree would go a long way in that regard by increasing her vocabulary and her credibility. It didn't, however, satisfy her need for more immediate feedback. She needed them, the big plastics manufacturers, to feel her pain. It was a huge step for her to trash the office of a major corporation, but she smiled when she heard her father's voice in her head, "It's easier to get what you want with a kind word . . . and a gun . . . than with just a kind word."

She couldn't have done it without Teddy's encouragement. His reassuring voice boosted her confidence. "This is your weapon," he told her as they prepared for their caper. "Your daddy will be proud."

Fendru, now out of bed, was looking for something, "Has anyone seen my shoes?"

Estee look down at her own bare feet and scanned the camper. She shook her head and held out her hands, palms up.

"Where's our shoes?" Teddy said. Everyone looked at Jones.

"Good question," said Jones, looking at his shoeless feet.

"Nothing here," said Teddy as his head surfaced from under the bed. He was wearing only his underwear and one of the WWI gas masks they had donned for the raid. Fendru let loose a raucous laugh, louder than necessary, but it was infectious. Everyone joined in.

Estee was among friends. They had evolved from fellow students to acquaintances to friends, four people from different backgrounds. Her new friends were also competitors --- law school is a competitive environment --- and they were smart. They were wise enough to listen to everyone's ideas, even to Estee, the elder in the group. When they found that she worked in a law office and knew procedures, they looked to her for guidance. She took charge. The initial plan had them painting their faces, donning clown suits and carrying party balloons into Danswirth's office as their cover. That changed when Teddy went to his car and came back wearing white coveralls, goggles and a gas mask he picked up at an Army surplus store. When he laid out three more sets of makeshift hazmat suits, they had their ruse. The plastic waste was easy. Estee and the Blue Skies/Clear Waters volunteers had been collecting it for weeks in anticipation of turning it over to a local university for research.

From that point forward Estee and Teddy took charge. Teddy was affable, charming and totally committed. They were supposed to use fictitious names, but Teddy rejected the subterfuge. Estee used Estee because it wasn't her real name, but Teddy saw no need for acting as if they didn't know one another.

"If you move your mouth, it means nothing if you don't move your legs," Teddy said.

He once commandeered a True Green truck that was idling in front of a neighbor's house. He drove it to the True Green manager's home and sprayed the entire contents on his lawn, garage and house to test the claim that their chemicals were safe for humans. "I had my doubts," he said. The manager power-washed the home inside and out before placing it up for sale. "I think I proved my point," Teddy said.

"Are those new skivvies?" shouted Jones, watching in the rearview mirror. The bright red boxers fit him like he was an underwear model.

Handsome as he was, Teddy's wardrobe consisted mostly of previously fashionable garb acquired from Goodwill and second-hand shops.

"Are you making a lifestyle change or do you have a date?" joked Fendru.

"Only freshly milled cotton touches my personal parts." Teddy pirouetted to display his boxers against taut legs the color of a creamy latte.

"So, you're not against mass consumption," said Jones.

"I get new shorts. What's the big deal? You get a new suit every week. That's mass consumption, and we're burying ourselves in our own trash. We lived in harmony with the planet for two million years and in the past two hundred we're tampering with our own longevity. You can't be partially for conservation just like you can't be partially gay," Teddy said.

That drew a hardy laugh, but as serious as a knife in the heart, Kendru said to Jones, "Is that true? Are you gay?"

Jones turned and batted his eyes at Fendru. "How about you and I right here? What do you say, Fendru dear?"

"Oh, stop it," Fendru said. "I've never seen him with a girl. That's all."

"I've never seen you with a girl," Jones said. Fendru retreated.

Facing Jones, Teddy said, "Well, are you gay?"

Estee burst with laughter. Fendru and Teddy followed.

"I'm not gay," Jones said. "Hey guys, I'm not gay."

Teddy thumbed through a small rack of suits that fit Jones' style. Button down, slim cut tropical wool blends, probably custom fit. He gave little room as Estee slipped by him. Teddy was almost ten years younger, but she shuddered when their bodies touched. She hadn't been with a man for months, and her reaction of his porcelain body against hers was incendiary. He held eye contact with her as she passed.

"Just because you get your clothes from the throw away bin at Goodwill and I prefer a fresh look each day doesn't make me environmentally irresponsible," said Jones as he buckled his seat belt. "It wouldn't hurt you to move into the Twenty First Century."

"It's the Twenty First century that's killing us," said Teddy but he looked at Estee. The confidence in his eyes excited her. "At the pace we're on we're going to exceed the threshold from which there is no return. There's no more business as usual. We're playing roulette with life on the planet."

The profundity of Teddy's words silenced everyone. For a few moments the only sounds came from the engine and the road, the festive atmosphere having been replaced by introspection.

Estee felt guilty for celebrating any idea that they had accomplished anything important. They made a statement, but it wouldn't stop the machine. As Doctor Bryan had pointed out she didn't drive an electric car, most of her clothes were made from polyester and none of her friends had solar panels on their roofs. Was she nothing but a hypocrite? Danswirth's products killed her child. They made stuff with long term harm to the everyone's health, and they took no responsibility for their actions. But she was asking them to change before she took responsibility for her own actions. Teddy was correct, "You can't be partially for conservation." She and everyone else would have to change. It wasn't enough that she made her body into a documentary on extinction. That wasn't real change. She contemplated what she should do first. Where should she begin?

Maybe she should have called Dr. Bryan, apologized for ambushing him and asked for advice.

As these thoughts raced through her mind, she recalled her brief brush with motherhood and how it had led her into a downward spiral. Her depression became so bad her husband left. She had been angry for so long --- at him, at the world. It became too much. It took time, but after some deep introspection she stopped blaming him. She would have left, too. She didn't like herself.

"I need a beer," said Fendru, trying to break the pall.

"In the cooler," said Jones as he motioned toward a small refrigerator.

Teddy continued but in a somber tone, "We think everything is about progress. We must keep growing. We have convinced ourselves that some new technology will suddenly get us out of this mess. If we don't get off this consumption treadmill, we're going bury ourselves in our own waste." He took the seat next to Jones.

Jones alternated glances between Teddy and the road. "What good are you to mankind if you're still using an Atari computer? We need innovation and that means new things. That's not necessarily mass consumption. It's about people inventing and adapting to new and better technology."

"You're living under the illusion that our current system, based upon innovation and consumption, can provide us with the means to solve the climate crisis when it is that very system that got us into this dilemma," Teddy said.

"Teddy, are you a closet socialist?" Jones said.

"For the moment I'm going to overlook the fact that your family got rich from this system and that it is footing your bill for law school. You don't want to bite the hand that's paying the bills. The climate crisis isn't about finding new technologies. It's about evolving," said Teddy.

"Change or die, survival of the fittest. I get that, but's it's always been that way," countered Jones.

"Or in your case, the best dressed," said Teddy with a smirk. "Not just for the fittest, nor the few, nor the wealthy nor the elite white," said Teddy. "This is for the survival of the species."

"Good luck trying to convince third world countries that more is not acceptable. They don't have all the shit we've already got and we're telling them they have to cut back. Look, I grant you're thrifty. That's a good thing," said Jones, "and I know we have to repurpose and make better use of the stuff we produce. We're a prodigal bunch, but we can't recycle our way out of this crisis. There's too many of us. We need breakthrough technologies."

Teddy threw his hands into the air and turned to Fendru and Estee. "He really doesn't get it. He thinks we can push a few buttons and get out of this mess." He turned back to Jones. "You're not wearing those suits to the lab. You're going to a fashion show to defend the very folks we're trying to stop."

"No, my friend, I'm going into environmental law," said Jones as Fendru stepped behind them with a beer in hand.

Fendru tried to change the subject. "Is it true you sold a 1967 GTO? Three hundred and eighty-nine cubic inch V-8 with a Carter AFB 4-barrel carb?"

Teddy looked as Fendru with dismay. He was changing the entire vibe. It was true but, other than a nod of confirmation, Jones said nothing.

"Why?" asked Fendru.

"My grandfather bought one of the originals. Took me for rides in it when I was a kid. Said he would give it to me when I completed law school. He died last year and I got the car. Sold it to an auto museum in Indiana. It paid for my second year of law school."

Fendru shook his head in disbelief. Glumly he said, "Wow. It was a classic."

"A real gas guzzler," said Jones.

"I'm sorry," Teddy said to Jones.

"For what?"

"What I said about your family. I didn't know you were paying for law school," said Teddy.

"When you get off your high horse, maybe you can start being a lawyer," said Jones. "We have a Supreme Court that was stacked by presidents who received a minority of the vote. That's dangerous to our democracy and our environment. And I just dumped enough garbage onto someone's office that will make the evening news. Does that tell you what side I'm on?"

"Holy shit!" said Fendru as the beer squirted like Old Faithful when he popped off the top.

It hit Jones in the face. He swerved to miss a car changing lanes without using a turn signal.

"Fuck wad!" He shouted with an angry Irish accent.

Fendru tried to stop the beer by putting his mouth over the opening, but he was showered with foam. Teddy shielded his face and dipped below the seat to escape collateral misting.

"Voila," proclaimed Teddy, as hit hand hit something with laces. Dripping wet, he held up a pair of shoes and then another. A collective sigh filled the camper.

Wiping lite-beer from his face, Jones laughed. "We got shit-faced last night, but I think we made a statement. Cheers, everyone." He held up one hand to mimic a toast. High fives followed.

The air of enthusiasm boosted Estee's spirit but also summoned some nostalgia. She folded up the sleeper sofa, plopped down and flashed back to her younger days. She had to go back to her late teens and early twenties to resurrect her last days of innocence and bliss. She didn't yearn to relive her twenties, but her younger friends encouraged her to feel that life can feel good. The disappointments, the failed marriage, her lost child and the strain of changing careers had taken their toll. She was always tired and under the camouflage she was aware that her youthful body had begun its inevitable decline. Her friends, all younger men, were fun and she could still keep up with them. Deep inside she took a moment to revel. She felt appreciated, connected and relevant.

As the miles passed, Teddy and Fendru buried their heads in their law books. Estee replayed the previous day. What stayed with her was the reaction of the employees she had encountered. They cooperated as she and her hazmat clad clan entered the building, seemingly unsurprised by their appearance. No one panicked. It was as if they were extras in a remake of Contagion. They worked for a company that produced some of the most insidious chemicals on the planet. Some of them, PFOs and PFAs, had become known as forever chemicals because they remain in the environment for an eternity. Over time they broke down into the microparticles that were being digested by almost every living creature as they made their way up the food chain. They were destroying the matter on which life depended. In the process they were compromising the oceans' ability to absorb carbon. Along with the burning of fossil fuels, the contribution of these chemicals to global warming had put us on a path to disaster --- something scientists refer to as an extinction event. There had been five others long before humans dominated the planet, but a new one was emerging that scientists were calling the Anthropocene era ---- man-made. We are creating the conditions for our own extinction. In the offices where she scattered the bottles and the plastic rings that held the six packs together, the discarded lines and old fishing nets, along with a collection of marine debris that she had dragged from the water during a recent scrummage, she knew she was despoiling personal spaces. She had toppled the photos of spouses and children and smeared baby-doo on their hopes and dreams. That bothered her. As a rule, she didn't seek out trouble. She'd gotten only one speeding ticket in her entire life. What justified her action was simple. These were highly educated adults and they either knew what they were doing was dangerous or they were too complacent to contemplate the consequences of their work. They should know better.

She returned a smile when Teddy winked at her over his law book. Jones was all eyes on the road. She felt safe, but she couldn't help but cringe. Jones had brought several large packages of disposable diapers --- his father worked for a consumer products company --- and dropped them onto a sheet of plastic at a roadside park on their way to Danswirth Enterprises. Then he dropped his pants and took a dump in the middle of the pile of disposable britches. Fendru and Teddy did the same after using the toilet in the camper. They had to seal it in an insulated box because the aroma was worse than a public outhouse on a construction site. Boys will be boys.

Leaving the pictures of the extinct animals was her idea. Hopefully, the message was not so subtle that some young, up and coming, executive wouldn't figure it out. Those young folks, and their children, were going to live their entire lives dealing with the consequences of their company's actions. Maybe, just maybe, what she did would motivate them to stop polluting every drop of water on the planet. In case this action wasn't enough, there were rumors that bolder action was being planned. What could be more in your face than what they had already done? Watching Teddy, calm and confident, was more than enough to overcome her anxiety. She laid her head on his lap and fell asleep for the ride home.

9

Seconds after saying good-bye to Samantha Card, Derk's cell phone rang.

"Oh my god!" Derk said upon seeing the caller's face on his screen. He had forgotten to call Samson Mabazi. "Hello, my friend, how are you?" Derk answered.

Derk had known the archaeology Professor for years, but since Samson took the teaching job in Uganda, they hadn't seen each other in months. They were going to remedy that absence by exploring the caves of Lascaux, and their excursion was scheduled for the next weekend.

"I'm fine, Dr. Bryan, but I am not the one jumping from airplanes," said Samson in a Ugandan accent. Although they were friends, Samson always respected Derk's professional status by referring to him as doctor.

"We were about to go into the Grand Canyon when she fell. I don't know what got into me. I just jumped."

"Then you're okay?" Samson said.

"It only hurts when I breathe," Derk jested. "Did you know that the water level in the canyon is the lowest it's been in human history.

"I heard that."

"Samson, I had the chance to look back in time. Next thing I know I'm doing the Ironman dive," Derk said.

"Then you are okay," Samson repeated the inquiry.

"Oh," said Derk. "What you really want to know is if I'm going to be able to hike those caves," said Derk.

The caves of Lascaux, in southwestern France, were only two hundred and fifty feet long and fourteen feet below the surface, but they told a story that took place far in the past. That is why Derk and his colleague wanted to see them. The caves allowed entry only to select visitors. Samson and he were fortunate to have been chosen, and there were no refunds.

Derk had been looking forward to that trip. The images painted on the walls of Lascaux, mostly of large game animals such as bears, deer and bison, were one of the first surviving forms of human art. These images told a story that was critical to the survival of early humans. Humans depended upon large animals for food and skins. At the same time, humans were prey for these creatures. It was this juxtaposition of humans to the wildlife that had dominated most of human activity on the planet. They depended upon each other. Samson, a devoted vegetarian, kept urging Derk to swear off red meat, but the story on the walls in these caves made it clear that humans were not vegans. Animal protein was essential for the mental and physical development of humans. We needed their meat to grow bigger, stronger and smarter. Derk wanted to know if he could feel anything close to what early men experienced while living in those dank, dark caves twelve thousand years ago with a kill or be killed mentality.

Before he would confirm the trip to Lascaux he needed to find out where Ardale was going with his questions about Doctor Carlton.

"This old fiddle can still play, if that's what you're asking?" Derk said. He deferred a thumbs up or down decision until later.

"We could postpone it if you need to," said Samson.

"And miss French cooking and some Haut-MeDoc!" Derk said. "I'm really looking forward to this trip and seeing you, but I have to tell you, Samson, there may be a complication. Dr. Carlton, the woman who fell from the airplane, may need my help. Could you give me a couple of days."

"It's a woman," Samson chuckled with his African accent. "Aren't we fickle."

"I'll know more tomorrow, my friend. I hope we can make this happen."

"She must be special," said Samson.

"I'll call you tomorrow."

***

By five o'clock the last TV film crew tired. Derk called King Carver.

"If you want to talk, meet me at the Caddy in thirty minutes," Derk said. He hoped the tourists on the Boardwalk at John's Pass wouldn't recognize him.

"Can you make it six?" Ardale asked and Derk concurred.

Derk waited in his car in the parking lot of the Boardwalk. Ardale's convertible announced itself with two burps of bluish black exhaust. After a couple of rattles, the internal combustion engine shut off.

Ardale got out and glanced up at partly cloudy skies. He tried to pull up the top on the old Sebring, and in the process dropped something behind the seat. After a couple of attempts to recover it, he shrugged, waved a dismissive hand at the old clunker and headed toward the restaurant. A slight limp and a legal notepad accompanied him.

Derk intercepted him half-way there. "Get us a table in the back," Derk said as he pulled a Panama hat over his eyes. To complete the disguise, he had donned swimming trunks, sandals and a goatee.

Instead, Ardale took a seat at the end of the bar. Fortunately, Derk recognized no one and no one came over to say hello. Even so, he kept his hat on and tucked his chin to his chest.

Without looking up, he said in a distorted tone, "Order me an iced tea, and get whatever you want."

Ardale waved at the bartender. "Iced tea," he said in a normal voice. He ordered nothing for himself.

Derk covered his face with one hand and whispered, "Try to keep it down and have a drink on me."

"What's up with the disguise, Doctor?" was Ardale's response and said, "I'll have the same," to the barkeep.

"They have a full bar here, Ardale," Derk urged, disgruntled by being so exposed. "Get what you want. It's on me." He shielded his face with one hand.

"That wouldn't be a good idea," Ardale said while searching each pocket.

Ardale summoned the bartender. "May I borrow a pen?"

Realizing that Ardale was content with his seat at the bar Derk said, "Samantha said I could trust you, but who are you working for? Who am I talking to?"

The barkeep slid a pen down the bar top. Ardale clicked the pen to the writing position and laid it upon the notepad.

"I'm a freelance journalist. I sell stories, and what's up with the hat and the voice?"

"Under the circumstances I think it's better that I keep a low profile," Derk said.

"Is that your investigator side in action?"

"Who are you really?" Derk said, returning to his normal voice.

""You know . . . USA Today, Business Week."

"People Magazine, National Enquirer?" said Derk.

"That's not my target audience."

"You have a target audience?"

"Hard news, human interest, satire, irony and hypocrisy."

"Which am I?"

"Relax, Doctor Bryan. I'm a writer, not a proctologist."

Suspicion always lurked within Derk's milieu, but he trusted Samantha Card. "Samantha said you were a good reporter but something happened to you."

"I'm tainted."

"Tainted?" Derk said. "How about warped?"

"Contaminated. Damaged goods," said King Carver. The topic agitated him.

"The drink?" Derk pointed to the iced tea in front of the reporter. "You're an alcoholic."

King Carver sighed. "Something like that," and he changed the subject. "So, how's the suit with the county going?"

"Suit?" Derk said.

"You wanted the county to approve your gray water plans," Ardale said.

"It's just wastewater from showering and washing clothes," retorted Derk. "How did you find out that?"

"And the current plumbing codes prevent it?"

"All I want to do is spray it on the lawn. We're squandering millions of gallons of water in the midst of worldwide droughts," Derk said. He made a gesture with his hands. "What's this have to do with Dr. Carlton?"

"What do you really know about the Doctor Susan Carlton?"

"I thought we'd gone over that."

Their conversation was interrupted when the bartender placed menus in front of them and waited for their order.

"Give us a minute," Derk said in his disguised voice.

Ardale couldn't hold back a chuckle. He waited for the barkeep to get out of earshot.

"I did a little research. In spite of the degrees and the accolades there is no evidence that Susan Carlton ever existed, at least, prior to NASA," Ardale said. "Don't you find that a little strange?"

His hair needed cutting, and the wrinkled white oxford shirt was missing a button on the collar. In spite of his appearance, his speech was articulate, hinting no signs that he was inebriated or that he had ever been a drunk. He had also toned down the cologne.

"Why are you telling me this?"

Through a straw King Carver took a swig of his tea. "This is just a theory but ---"

Derk interrupted him. "Ardale, what do you really want? You want a story about Doctor Carlton, you should ask her. You want a story about me, then . . ." He didn't finish his thought.

"Doctor Bryan, don't you think she's hiding something?"

"What? Why?" Derk said. At the same time, he wondered why he was defending her with such insistence.

"What happened to the two of you after the fall? Where did you go?" Ardale said, all diplomacy aside. "How does someone fall from an airplane and bounce right up without a scratch on her? Your arm was in a sling and it hurts when you breathe."

Derk waved to the bartender, "Check, please." He slid off the barstool, threw a twenty on the bar top and left.

Climate Fact:

The trucks and cars we drive are responsible for 20% of greenhouse gases.

What can you do about it? Drive an electric vehicle and make driving more fun again.

The chief financial officer, the director of security and Pendleton Danswirth's administrative assistant were waiting for him when he arrived at his Houston office, but the ghost of a two Viagra erection was still competing for his attention. He wanted Princess by his side, but she had an appointment in Florida with the superintendent of education. They were devising a plan to subvert the prohibition against the use of tax dollars for parochial schools. Once the law was changed her company would fund a slew of new charter schools and rake in millions in the process.

Danswirth's secretary, Emily Rasmussen, met him. "We'll have to meet in Henry's office because your office is a bit soiled." She covered her nose as she said it.

"I've got to see this," Danswirth said, pushing through the assemblage.

"Holy shit storm!" Danswirth reeled backward from the aroma. His office reeked of dead fish, detritus and human waste. A couple of guys wearing gas masks were removing the furniture and tossing the dead fish, all impaled or enwrapped by plastic in some form, into large bags.

"Who did this?" Danswirth said. The veins in his neck pulsed.

"They wore hazmat suits. One of them said there was a leak in the building and that everyone had to evacuate," said Henry Staltzman, a wiry man of sixty and Danswirth's director of security.

"Did they take anything?"

"Not that I could tell," said Emily. She stood in the doorway with one hand over her mouth.

Under his desk Danswirth noticed a souvenir baseball signed by every member of the Astros' World Series team.

"Oh gross," he said when his fingers gripped the ball. He tossed it into the corner. "Anybody have a handkerchief?" he said, holding out his hand stained with excrement. "Who did this?"

"The police don't know yet," said Henry.

"What's the damage?" asked Danswirth.

"Forty thousand is our best guess," said Benjamin Eagleheart, CFO. He was one seventh Crow and the only indigenous American on the corporate roster.

Danswirth scoffed and shook his head. "What the fuck is this about?"

"They left these," said Eagleheart as he handed Danswirth some pictures with animals on them.

"What are they?" said Danswirth.

"Extinct animals," said Henry.

"Extinct?" said Danswirth.

"Yes. That one's a mastodon." Eagleheart pointed to one of the pictures.

"A mastodon?" said Danswirth.

"It's kind of a big, hairy elephant," said Eagleheart. As they walked toward Eagleheart's office the finance director flipped open his cell phone to show Danswirth photos of the Mastodon. "It's extinct. The last ones died eleven to twelve thousand years ago from over hunting and changes in their climate."

"Why were they left here?" said Danswirth.

"They weren't just left here," said Henry. "We got a call from Bill Edwards at Plasticom. The same thing happened at his office."

"And Plasticware," added Eagleheart.

"Eight offices, including ours," said Emily Rasmussen.

"On the same day? No way! This was an organized attack. What did the police say?" asked Danswirth again.

"You have a call, sir," said a young woman holding the phone for Danswirth as they reached Eagleheart's office.

"Can it wait?" said Danswirth, trying to grasp the message that someone or some group had left for him.

"Sir, I think it's your wife."

* * *

That Shirley Maxwell Danswirth was alive was a miracle to most people. She had been in a coma for weeks. Therefore, it was a total shock to her maid when Mrs. Danswirth sat up in bed and asked for a piece of raspberry rum cheesecake, her favorite dessert.

"I was famished," she said to the maid as she devoured the cake.

The maid was flitting about, unsure of what to do next, when Mrs. Danswirth suggested she draw a bath. She was going to bathe and put on some makeup for the first time in weeks.

"I'd like to put on that new dress I got from Anne Taylor," said Mrs. Danswirth.

Dorothea, the maid, brought her the dress and a bag that had been left in the garage.

"Dorothea, what's in this bag?" she asked.

"I thought it was odd for you to leave clothes in the garage so I brought it upstairs."

"Thank you," she mumbled as she removed a woman's dress, size five --- she was a seven --- and a blouse with a Palm Beach label that was also too small for her. There was blood on the dress and on a pair of silver earrings with a matching necklace upon which was engraved: *Angelina, forever yours, PD3*. PD was the name only a few people called her husband, intimately close people, and neither the clothes nor the jewelry belonged to Shirley Danswirth.

"You can tell Angelina that you're only half as rich as she thinks you are. I'm going to divorce your ass, take half of everything you own and make your life a living hell, PD," his wife said and the line went dead.

11

Estee hadn't been home more than twenty minutes when she got the call.

"The Coast Guard hauled in a dead whale yesterday," said Chris, glumly.

"Tell me," Estee said.

"All I know is that it was caught in a net," Chris said.

"Was it a Ricei?"

"I'm not sure." He paused, awaiting a response. "I just thought you'd want to know."

"Thank you."

"How was your trip?"

"Just got home. Exhausting." Her cover story for the weekend was that she had attended a conference for paralegals.

"Sorry. Wanna talk later?"

"Can I call you?"

"Okey-Dokey," Chris said.

She would call back, but it would be later than Chris expected. He seemed to want more from their relationship than she could provide. They were friends, but since his divorce he was an emotional wreck, and she didn't date anyone who said, "Okey-Dokey."

She was tired but the Coast Guard station in Carrabelle was only twenty miles away. And if it was a Ricei whale it was on the same path as her deceased child. Anything she could do to prevent the slow decline toward extinction for the Ricei was motivation for joining the action oriented Blue Skies/Clear Waters organization. The time for letter writing was past. She showered, dressed and left as soon as she could.

Sighting a Ricei was rare. She had seen a live one only once, not long after her son died. It was at a marine sanctuary where it was being nursed back to health. The whale had lost its calf was due to plastic ingestion. Estee looked the giant mammal in the eyes and shared an emotion that only grieving mothers could appreciate. She had felt a kinship with the Ricei ever since. They were mothers counting upon the same ecosystem for their survival.

There were less than one hundred Ricei whales left on the planet—probably closer to fifty. Estee had watched their decimation with bitter sadness. The Ricei, named after Dale W. Rice who first wrote about it in the sixties, was the largest mammal in the Gulf and the only whale indigenous to the Gulf of Mexico. An adult could reach forty-one feet and sixty thousand pounds. They lived on small fish and invertebrates by straining them through hairy plates in their mouth called baleen. Like every other creature in the Gulf, the Ricei depended upon clean water for its survival. Its fate was in the hands of humans so Estee had been doing her part by cleaning up the water. The thought that another had died chilled her.

From Apalachicola she took Route 98 to Carrabelle. Half way there she realized she hadn't eaten since their raid on Danswirth the previous day, and it was approaching two in the afternoon. The white sandy beach that hugged the shoreline of the Saint George Sound was one of the rare undeveloped parcels of the Panhandle, due to its location in Tate's Hell State Forest, so her dining options were limited. With hunger-pangs setting in she stopped for a Ginger-Pineapple Kumbocha and a couple of bananas at a gas station in Carrabelle. Except for an occasional oyster she had gone vegan after the death of her child. She finished off the Kumbocha in the parking lot of the Coast Guard station.

The Coast Guard was familiar with Estee, due to the years her family had run an oyster operation in the Gulf, and more-so recently since she had become a volunteer with Blue Skies/Clear Waters. The volunteer crews dredged up marine waste, plastic debris and all sorts of pollution. With mounds of dead marine life strangled by marine waste they would hold a news conference in front of the Coast Guard to protest that the agency wasn't doing its job. Estee had become a local spokesperson.

"They're not enforcing the laws against illegal dumping. If they send some people to jail this will stop," she told reporters. She had organized homeowners who live on the water to tell their accounts of manatees being run over by speed boats without enforcement. This story riled up both the boaters and Florida Wildlife Commission when it was reported in the U.S.A. Today.

From his toothy smile and exuberant demeanor Estee could tell that E. Howser, the Seaman on desk duty, was new. She leaned over the desk with a flirtatious grin and her cleavage at the seaman's eye level.

"Sailor, would you please tell Commander Stewart that Simone Theresa Sparks is here to see him."

The young man in crisp whites, mesmerized by the Dodo imprinted above Estee's left breast, responded, "Uh, yes, Ma'am."

As Estee stood upright the desk clerk's eyes followed the extinct fowl.

"Impressive," he said with a nod and a smile. "I think he's busy but I'll check. You're name again?"

"Just tell him Estee's here." She followed down the hall.

"Excuse me, Sir, but there's an S. T. ---" When he turned around, she was directly behind him.

"Estee Sparks, Commander," she said and slipped by the desk duty clerk.

As the sailor tried to block her entrance, Commander Stewart waved him off.

Before dismissing himself, the duty clerk looked back with an eager grin, "If there is anything else I can do for either of you, please let me know." His eyes ricocheted from the dodo to hers.

"That will be all, Seaman," the Commander said sternly, but he didn't get up to greet Estee.

"I should have expected you. I'd have taken one of those vacation days I've earned," said J. Cody Stewart as he motioned her to take a seat.

Stewart was a twenty-four-year veteran of the United States Coast Guard. He was once rugged handsome, but time had etched furrows into his sunbaked face, and the size of his waist-line suggested he had dined at too many buffets. Estee had also come to understand that behind the formality that his office commanded was someone who shared her concerns. He had spent his life on the water and was not aloof to the threats.

"And miss me. I'm always the highlight of your day, Commander."

"The highlight of my day is a twenty-year old scotch, Miss Sparks."

"It's a Ricei, isn't it?" She used the generic name for Rice's Whale.

His confirming gesture was sympathetic. He was close to her father's age. She respected him, but that didn't change her attitude when it came to protecting the Gulf habitat. This creature was on the verge of extinction and the Coast Guard wasn't protecting them.

"Male or female?"

"Not quite sure."

"So, it's female."

He sighed as his head drooped. "Probably."

Female. He had confirmed her worst fear. The Commander was aware of the consequences and the ire this would ignite in Estee and others.

"I'm not your enemy, Commander. We need these whales to survive," she said.

Commander Stewart rose from his desk and ran his hands through ashen streaked hair. "I know." He sighed.

From the window in his office, they could see the crew from NOAA finishing the autopsy. The rare mammal, Estee guessed to be thirty-five to forty feet, had been laid out on canvas under a boat hanger. A long, rugged gash marked one side of the whale.

"It got caught in a net and there's no way to tell whose it was," Commander Stewart said without turning to face her. "And it looks as if something rammed her. See the penetration below the pectoral fin."

Estee moved closer until they were standing next to each other.

"A propeller?" Estee said. She was familiar with the sight of manatees that had been stuck by propellers. It had become more frequent with the growth of Florida's boating population.

"What's that?" Estee pointed toward a pile of rubble lying next to a couple of plastic boxes.

"They put the organs in them. NOAA analyzes them for toxins and pollutants in the water."

"No, that!" She pointed to a wad of plastic larger than a basketball.

Commander Stewart went to doorway and shouted to the officer on desk duty, "Seaman Howser, could you tell Doctor Frederickson I'd like to see him."

Within a few minutes a slender, bespectacled man of forty, wearing white coveralls and rubber boots, appeared in the doorway of the Commander's office. An N-95 face mask tugged his neck.

"You wanted to see me, Commander?"

He pointed to the wad of plastic brought to his attention by Estee. "Sorry, this is Estee Sparks. She is, well, interested in whales."

Estee started to offer her hand but had second thoughts. It wasn't the aroma of dead fish that smacked her in the face. Those hands had been inside that dead whale. The thought of touching it turned her dark inside.

"What is that?" The Commander repeated.

"Plastic, sir. Food wrappers, zip lock bags, all kinds of stuff. It lacerated her intestines and blocked digestion. Our guess is she was starving, became weak and ended up in someone's net. Then a watercraft finished her off."

That Commander nodded his understanding but Estee was less than satisfied. The marine biologist noticed.

"Oh, there's another thing. She was pregnant," said Doctor Frederickson, his expression distorted by that revelation. He donned the mask as he left the room.

Estee resisted a Def Con one outburst of rage, but she couldn't hold back a tear. "Mind if I take a look?"

"I'm sorry, Ms. Sparks. I really am," said the Commander. He started to put an arm around her, but she hemmed and hawed, then left for the yard. "Be careful, they're still cleaning up out there."

Just outside his door she picked up a pair of white rubber boots and held them up for the Commander to see. "Brought my own." She forced a smile.

She took a mask from her pocket. Even though she had been around fish processing operations for most of her life, the aroma of dead fish baking in bright sunshine could be overwhelming.

"But of course," he said, followed by a laugh.

A couple of NOAA representatives hosed down the area while she circled the whale, feeling both awe and anger. She knew as much about whales as a New Yorker knew about Macys or Central Park. They were social creatures, swam in pods and could communicate with each other up to ten thousand miles using ultra-low frequencies. Their bodies looked like rubber but they were thin skinned and soft to the touch. They enjoyed close contact as much as humans enjoyed being hugged. They were so much like us. She often wondered why people didn't realize that we needed each other for our mutual survival. Even though this Rice's whale was four hundred times her size she felt a kind of camaraderie with it. Each of them, the whale and she, made its living from the bounty of the sea. Each of them had been mothers and each of them had lost a child due to the abuse of its ecosystem. The loss resurrected a nagging ache in her soul. She wanted but was afraid to have another child. This dead Ricei would have no more, and since Rice's whales could take nine years to reach sexual maturity, and only reproduced every two to three years, this was a Titanic loss to the species. Estee was thirty-seven but she might live longer than the last Ricei whale.

As she encircled the once magnificent mammal one eye seemed to follow her. Reddish-green in color, which she found ironic because whales are color blind, it pursued her with silent agony. It certainly aroused an agony in Estee. Maybe it was her imagination but was that look a cry for help. Death chilled her. She shuddered.

She didn't know why she was surprised when she saw the pile of plastic waste pulled from the whale's digestive tract. It was much like the junk they used to litter the Danswirth offices. This stuff didn't belong in the ocean. One piece could kill a thirty-ton whale. She was happy she had raided Danswirth's office. She didn't know what was being planned by Blue Skies/Clear Waters, but she had an idea of her own.

As one of the Coast Guard crew moved a forklift into position to haul away the remains she shouted, "Hey, stop, stop, stop," and she held up both hands.

The gashes under the pectoral fin were familiar. "Doctor Frederickson, she was hit by a propeller. Right?"

"Yes. It's right over here." He showed her a blade of a propeller his crew had removed from the whale.

"May I take a picture?" She snapped a couple of shots before the doctor nodded his approval.

She turned toward the sun that was beginning its descent over the Gulf of Mexico, removed her gloves and brushed back her hair. She took a deep breath and prepared herself for what she had to do next. Hutchin's Marina would be closing in one hour.

Climate Fact:

One serving of apple sauce contains 37 different chemicals. Our food is filled with pesticide residues that both the U.S. and Canadian governments say are causing brain and liver damage, in addition to birth defects and lower IQs in children.

What can you do about it? Eat organic. Pesticides don't taste very good!

12

Derk grabbed a beer from the cooler before climbing up the stairway from the garage to his second-floor condo. Given his challenged knees, a condition two MDs and three PhDs told him was natural for a man of his age, he was smugly pain-free. Every mile on his bicycle and every leap up the stairs proved their tweed coat opinions were premature. He pulled a chilled glass from the freezer, took a seat at the kitchen bar and booted up his laptop to begin the search.

An hour later the beer was warm and the trail from Susan Carlton, regular citizen, to Susan Carlton, PhD was as cold as yesterday's lunch. There was nothing that wasn't connected to NASA. NASA highlighted her gender, first woman expected to land on another planet, and how her credentials were unique and critical to creating an environment that would support life on Mars. Other than what was available on the NASA website and some related news articles Derk found nothing to indicate that Susan Carlton existed prior to joining NASA.

He took a bathroom break to contemplate his next move. When he returned it was so dark the only illumination in the room came from the computer screen. The end of Daylight Savings Time was approaching. He stroked a hand through his hair. His routine was synchronized with the rotation of the Earth around the sun. His bicycle rides, walks on the beach and the times he spent sitting on the patio balcony reading the morning newspaper were planned so that he could catch the solar rays. He was an admitted sun junky. Recently, though, he had been thinking that if the sun didn't shine as much as it did in Florida, there was little reason to live here. The traffic was stifling, the hurricanes were a constant threat, the cost of insurance was excessive and his local pub was becoming too gentrified. He put up with it mostly because, not only was he addicted to the sun and the waves, he was a hopeless romantic. The glow of neon after dusk brought back memories of warm summer nights. While the heat added an extra layer of lubrication, it also made him feel less inhibited. It helped him get out of his head and into his body, something Jenny had helped him do whenever his tensions approached the red zone. The beach was a place to fall in love. He wasn't sure if Jenny fell in love with the beach or him first. What he knew was how connected to the water he was. It would be difficult to leave. He would miss their walks. For a moment he pictured Susan and he, walking hand in hand, as the sand gave way under his feet and squished between his toes.

She had to have a life before college, but there was no birth certificate, no marriage license, no court record, no Facebook page, no home address. He found nothing, zero, nada. He had worked in government long enough to know that every person trying to hide something, even a spy, has a history and, with diligence and ingenuity, it can be uncovered. Curiosity and suspicion were assets for an investigator and much of time things were not what they appeared to be. In this case, what Ardale had been trying to tell him was exactly what it appeared to be. Doctor Susan Carlton was hiding something. In fact, she was hiding a big piece of her life. He wondered what could be that dreadful or that threatening?

He was hungry, but his fridge was empty. In no mood to cook or go out, he ordered a Greek salad with extra anchovies from a local deli before returning to his search. This time he punched in King Ardale Carver. There were a number of articles by him and stories about him and then there was a big-time gap during which nothing appeared on him. He had been an accomplished, award-winning journalist, then nothing. His courage as a reporter, while embedded in a war zone, was documented as were the controversies he spurred. Except for one story, little mention was made of the drugs and his fall into oblivion. The controversy was well documented. It arose from his effort to compare the restrictions on women in the middle east, fostered and enforced by religious fanatics, to the anti-women agenda of the Christian Nationalists and the rise of political power of the Evangelicals in the United States. The stark comparisons provoked responses from some that were so vitriolic it was as if Ardale had pissed off God himself. Assignments tapered off as many papers spurned him, but it was more likely due to his addiction to pain killers after an IED nearly crippled him while he was riding in a military jeep in Afghanistan. The last story or post about Ardale was five years old.

Based upon two brief encounters it appeared to Derk that Ardale was on a mission to become relevant again. Susan Carlton was on his radar, and Derk had to warn her. He knew the why. He felt protective. But how? She wasn't returning his calls.

People hide things out of fear, either the fear of loss or the fear of discovery. Like money under the bed being stolen or secrets once camouflaged being exposed by the light of day, the results could be painful. Hiding money or wealth obtained illicitly often involved dummy corporations and offshore accounts. Hiding one's identity was associated with recrimination, loss of reputation or fear of bodily harm. Fear of bodily harm? What had Susan Carlton done and to whom?

13

When Danswirth returned to his office the aroma of fresh carpet and Glade served only to remind him of the intrusion. That his inner sanctum had been penetrated so easily suggested a vulnerability he had never before experienced. Emily Rasmussen greeted him with a stack of calls from the heads of plastic producers all over the country. The common denominator among the victims was dead fish, plastic debris and pictures of extinct birds and animals. They were worried about their public image and wondered what they could do to prevent such a reoccurrence.

Danswirth did a search of the pictures left in his office. Each of the animals was gone forever, driven to extinction by a combination of a changing climate to which they could not adapt and, often, over-hunting by humans. This was not the act of one disgruntled former employee or a tree hugging zealot. This was an organized effort directed at the plastic producers. They were sending him and others a message. It was an attack on his industry and his empire.

Within an hour he had assembled his public relations team in a suite of rooms at the hotel across from The Galleria. He tossed the photos of the Dodos, the Mastodons and the pigeons onto the conference table where his team was seated.

"Make no mistake. This was an organized effort. We're under attack and we have to act now!" Danswirth demanded,

Before the day ended, with coordination of the Plastic Producers Association, his team had crafted an ad campaign to sway consumer support for what was increasingly being recognized as one of the most ubiquitous and environmentally disastrous industries on the planet. The Campaign was entitled, *Your Life without Plastic*, and would highlight the inconvenience and added cost for moms and dads trying to use everyday household products in their pre-plastic versions.

The TV ads had fathers struggling with dinner preparation while food burned in non-coated pans. This was followed by women complaining while laboring to scrape the pans clean. This was to be a sure Clio winner if Teflon were to be named one of the basic food groups.

Another ad highlighted frustrated cooks holding up pans scratched by metal utensils while a cannister of fresh, clean and colorful plastic spatulas and ladles danced merrily to a lilting melody.

In another ad, a child dropped a glass of chocolate milk on the floor and cut himself while crawling through the broken shards. The sobbing was heart tugging, especially for those prone to crying over spilled milk.

Another featured a young father, in an overly dramatic fit of repulsion, holding up a cloth diaper dripping with baby-poo while his smiling wife rescued him with a stack of friendly, artificially aromatic disposable diapers.

There was a lengthy debate over an advertisement that involved a woman who cut off part of her finger while handling a non-plastic storage container. At the sight of her finger lying in her own blood she fainted and hit her head on the counter top before crashing onto the kitchen floor. It was the kind of drama that opened a horror movie. As the camera zoomed in on the hand gripping the broken jar the following message appeared on the screen: *Your Life without Plastic*. It was gaudy, ghoulish and reprehensible but to the point.

All of this evolved from a team that seemed more like a group of socially impaired teenagers than grown men with advanced degrees. The idea for the campaign arose as they whittled down a list of common plastic items previously made of other materials and ranked them from one hundred to ten. One hundred was deemed the most ubiquitous item, the one that would wait until last if you had to give it up. The goal was to illustrate that *Your Life without Plastic* would be filled with drudgery and danger. Of course, each advertisement concluded with a statement urging people to recycle.

The recycling tag was the brainchild of Howard Havelschmitz, whose creativity, up until then, was considered to be just above a stapler.

He jested, "If we add a recycling tag to the end of each ad and have the PPA run them, we won't have pay for air time because they're Public Service Announcements."

The next day Danswirth promoted him and gave him the use of a company car for a year.

Three months after the campaign, Eco-Magazine would lambast the *Your Life Without Plastic* ads as nothing but greenwashing. In that story E-Mag would report that, "The amount of recycled plastic since the PPA campaign began remains at a stubbornly low nine percent and, at the present rate, the weight of all the discarded plastic in the oceans will equal the weight of all the fish by 2050." No television station aired this pronouncement even once.

Climate Fact:

The lights, phones, computers and appliances you leave on while not in use contribute to global warming and add 25% to your home's utility bill.

What can you do about it? Turn off idle lights and appliances.

14

On his way home Danswirth's neurons were more tangled than a ball of twine. Within three days his life had gone from a Royal Flush to a nine high. To top it off his wife had awakened from a coma and decided to toss him into a shredder.

He once loved Shirley, but they were long removed from the romance of courtship. She used to be fifteen years younger than him. Now she seemed fifteen years older. It wasn't just the tumor in her brain that changed her mood as often as the wind shifted directions in east Texas. She seemed to have settled, become content with the trappings of wealth, while her zest for life dissipated. Fizzled out would better describe it. They still went out occasionally, hosted some dinner parties and traveled to Europe annually, but even that had become obligatory. He wasn't sure if she had lost interest in sex with just him or with everyone, but Danswirth needed someone to, at least, try to keep up with him. He strayed before her illness, but he kept it in the closet. He wasn't particularly proud of that, but it didn't cause him any loss of sleep. After she fell into a coma, he got sloppy with his affairs. How was he to know? The neurologist said there was only a one in ten thousand chance she would live, let alone awaken. The tumor in his wife's brain rested upon such a sensitive place they could not operate without turning her into a rutabaga. "It's only a matter of time," the doctor said solemnly. Now, after being in a deep sleep for weeks, she woke up with a shrew's temper.

Although it was past midnight when he arrived, she was in his bedroom prodding the maid, Dorothea, to remove Danswirth's clothes from the closets and dump them onto a pile in the hallway. Shirley Danswirth rocked slowly in a chair while sipping a cup of Jasmine tea. She was wearing a dress Pendleton had not seen before. Her hair had been neatly coiffed, but her make-up appeared to have been applied by an epileptic. Her smile was frail and severe.

"Dorothea, that's not necessary," he said. "She's not in her right mind."

"Hello, Pendleton," his wife said calmly. "Where have you been?"

Turning to Dorothea, she said, "You don't need to fold them. Just dump them." Dorothea was being careful not to wrinkle his suits, the ones she had been ordered to throw into a pile in the hallway.

"At a Believers' conference in Tampa, my dear," he said. "Everyone prayed for you." He attempted to kiss her on the forehead, but she brushed him away.

"Pendleton, sweety, you don't any more believe in God than I believe in the tooth fairy. What were you really doing?"

"It's late. Maybe I should retire," said Dorothea. During the week she had her own room in the Danswirth home, a giant estate home on the outskirts of Houston. Unless she was needed for a special event she went home for the weekends. It was a week night, but the tension was building like steam in a boiler.

"Sure," Danswirth said. "Thank you for taking care . . ."

Shirley Danswirth interrupted him, "No Dorothea, keep going. Mr. Danswirth won't be staying here tonight."

Danswirth shrugged and forced a smile as he looked at Dorothea. "It's okay. You can go. I'll look after her."

"Dorothea, would you please call 911. Tell them there is an intruder in the house," said Mrs. Danswirth with the serenity of someone pausing in the middle of her knitting. She had slipped one hand into her robe and wrapped it around something. Whatever it was, it was pointed in her husband's direction.

***

Danswirth slept in the guest quarters above his five-car garage. At least, he tried. He tossed and turned until dawn wondering how and when he could search his wife's bedroom. Angelina's blood-stained clothes and the jewelry he had given her, had to be there. He had left them in a bag in the garage, but it was gone when he looked for it. Recovering those items wouldn't resolve all of the problems his wife presented, but getting his hands on those particular items would neutralize an eminent threat. What had happened to Angelina was an accident, but he feared not everyone would see it that way if the dress and the jewelry were to become public. He needed a cup of coffee.

He dressed without shaving and showering, then tread stealthily along the causeway that led from the garage to the rear of the house. He had to break into his own kitchen.

"What the fuck!" he shouted when he tripped over a pile of clothes that had been tossed haphazardly outside the kitchen door. Upon recognizing the blue blazer his country club had given him for sponsoring the club championship he groaned. It wasn't a green jacket but he was as proud as if it had been. "Damn, that's mean! I once loved her."

It was early so no one was up yet, probably because Shirley had them stay late packing up his entire wardrobe. This may not have been her intent, but she loved to give his old clothes to the homeless shelter. It made her feel charitable.

Among the pile was a nine-hundred-dollar Armani suit which resurrected the memory of his wife's attempt once to donate one of his favorite suits half-hidden in a pile of his clothing.

"You're thinking someone at the homeless shelter has an interview with Dell or Chase? If you really want to make a difference, give five million dollars to establish a chair at the university."

His cronies had been funding business schools for years in order to influence the kind of free enterprise they thought should be taught in American colleges. That included low taxes, low regulations and maximum freedom over labor.

Fortunately, the back door was not locked. In the kitchen he found the remains of yesterday's brew still in the Mr. Coffee. He poured it into a cup and set the microwave at a minute and a half. As he waited, he heard a commotion upstairs. Moments later he collided with Dorothea who had bounded down the stairs into the great room.

"Call the doctor. Call the doctor," she shouted.

"What is it, Dorothea?" he said.

As the maid picked up the telephone in the hall, she said, "She's not breathing, sir. She's not breathing."

He ran up to his wife's bedroom, but she wasn't there. In his bedroom he found her slumped in the same chair where he left her last night. Her pulse was faint and her breath intermittent, but she was alive.

He tried to sit her up straight but she slumped again. He propped her up in the chair with one of his pillows, then another, but she collapsed like a deflated balloon.

He was pressed for time. The paramedics would be there soon. He rummaged through his chest of drawers, the armoire and quickly sashayed through his nearly empty walk-in closet. He did not find what he was looking for. He was on the floor looking under the bed when the emergency crew arrived.

"I was looking for her inhaler," he said as he jumped to his feet. "She had been in a coma but awakened last night. Now she's gone again." He displayed as much empathy as he could, given his attention had been distracted by another task.

The paramedics could resuscitate her no further. She had digressed to the vegetative state in which she had survived for the past six weeks. They secured her to a gurney and took her to the hospital. He asked which hospital and told them he would be there soon.

Before leaving he asked Dorothea, "I left a bag with some clothes and a necklace for my wife somewhere here last week. Have you seen it?"

"Oh, yes. It was in the garage. I gave it to your wife. I hope I didn't spoil the surprise. Is she going to be okay?"

"No, I mean I don't know and no, she was definitely surprised."

He left the room, but immediately returned. "Dorothea, please put my clothes back into the closet and take the rest of the day off."

He went to his wife's bedroom and searched every nook and cranny before collapsing onto her king-sized, adjustable hospital bed. Furious that he had misplaced the kind of evidence that got people twenty-five to life, he found himself staring at a stain on the ceiling that resembled a Rorschach test. Why hadn't he noticed that before? Was it a leak? He allowed himself a sigh as he ran his hand through a full head of hair. He hadn't been in her bed for months. It had the aroma of expensive shampoo and sloughed skin. It aroused him and repulsed him at the same time. Although he was an adventurous guy in bed, Shirley had lost all zest for satisfying his primal urges.

"It's man's prime directive to spread his seed," he said after she rejected one of his advances. "I didn't create this. I'm just living with it and if we don't do this, no more human race."

Those were not the words of a loving mate and he sometimes regretted that their relationship had regressed so far. She never got on top so he never noticed the stain.

He wanted to love her, but now she oscillated between half dead and manic. He wondered how his marriage had turned to mulch, and he wondered where in the holy-fucking universe had Shirley hidden the jewelry and those blood-stained clothes.

15

The Coast Guard probably wouldn't pursue the death of one Ricei whale, but Estee Sparks would. The last best guess about the number of remaining Ricei whales was close to fifty. Now it was forty-nine, and because its unborn calf had died with her, there may never be fifty again. She didn't have room on her body for a tattoo the size of a Ricei whale. She was going to find whomever killed that whale and make him pay for his carelessness.

She had been around marine craft since she could walk. She had ridden in every kind of boat from trawlers to cigarette boats to jet skis. Each used a specific type of propeller. Commercial propellers were designed for efficiency and durability. The propeller that killed the Ricei whale came from something that was designed to go fast, really fast. Looking closely at the picture she had taken she noticed the letters PD3 engraved on the prop—suggesting it was a custom job. That meant it came from a shop that specialized in props. PD3 might be the shop's name, but she suspected it was more likely the designer's initials. One other possibility was that those initials belonged to the person or company that owned motor and the boat to which the propellor was attached. She knew a guy who might know.

Aloysius Hutchins and his family had run Hutchins Marine Repair for three generations. If anyone could identify that propellor, it would be Big Al. He had worked on engines for, at least, twenty-five years, ever since quitting his job with the Sheriff's office to take over his father's business. While interrupting a convenience store robbery he took a bullet in the leg that relegated him to a desk job. He still walked with a limp. He took early retirement, along with a pension, to operate the family business. One of the Hutchins had worked on her father's boats since she was a kid.

"Rats!" She sat in her car as the phone at Hutchins Marine Repair rang without an answer. It was now too late to get to his shop before closing. She was tired and hungry so she headed home. Five minutes later her cell phone rang.

"This is Al."

"Al, it's Estee Sparks."

"What can I do for you?" he said as if the name meant nothing to him.

"S. T. as in Estee, Chester Sparks daughter."

"Oh, yea. How is Chet?"

"He died last year," she said.

"No way. I'm sorry. I wondered why he didn't pick that part he ordered. Anyway, I've got to go."

"Al, wait. Is this your cell number?"

"Uh-huh."

"If I send you a picture of a propellor, at least, a piece of it, can you identify what it was on?

"I don't know. I've got this old Mercury spread out on my bench and I promised a guy I'd have it together tomorrow."

"Please, Al. It was on a boat that killed a Ricei whale."

"A what?"

"A whale, Al, a Ricei whale."

"A whale? Okay, I'll try. Bye."

"Al! Is this your cell phone?"

She heard the cell phone drop to the floor. She waited but he didn't return to the line. She hadn't seen or talked with Al Hutchins for several years. Senility seemed to be creeping up on him. She had seen it accelerate in her father until his business shriveled up. She doubted she would hear from Al again.

Climate Fact:

By 2050 the weight of the plastic discarded into the oceans will be equal to the weight of all the fish in the ocean.

What can you do about it? Install a home water filter and stop using single use plastic containers.

16

"NASA," a female voice answered.

"I'd like to speak with Doctor Susan Carlton," Derk's anxiety peaked as he made the call.

He spent part of the morning separating his clothes into two piles, one with polyester and one without. Three shirts, four pairs of shorts and a couple of pairs of Levis were all he had that were made from natural fibers. Bummer! Some of his shirts made with poly, a fiber spun from petroleum, had been his favorites. He was in the habit of giving every purchase he made a rating as to its addition to his carbon footprint. Now he was critiquing past decisions. It wasn't just about his ward-robe, it was about everything he did in his life. When it came to reducing one's own carbon footprint, he was black or white about it. One was either going to be part of the problem or part of solution. When Thwait's Glacier on the west coast of Antarctica, a slab of ice the size of Florida, breaks off sea levels will rise from eight to sixteen feet. He will be dipping his toes into the water while sitting on his patio. Everything counted. No more polyester.

"One moment, please," said the NASA voice.

He had recently ordered a wallet made from plant fibers to replace the old leather one. The new TomTex wallet was made from Chitin, one of the building blocks for crustacean shells, mushroom cell walls and insect exo-skeletons. It is one of the most abundant biopolymers on the planet, and it comes with a low carbon footprint. He was skeptical about this so he did a little test. He put some Chitin into the toilet bowl and added a cup of dirt to the water. The dirt attached to the Chitin and fell to the bottom so it could be flushed away. Since Chitin is biodegradable and the wallet came with a money back guarantee, he ordered one. It was yet to arrive and he wondered what it would feel like sitting upon a bunch of crushed sea shell.

He glanced around his condominium in search of other carbon reducing options. All of the lightbulbs were LEDs. His appliances were Energy Star rated. He recycled almost everything. As his survey reached the refrigerator, he felt his stomach growl.

"You called about Doctor Carlton?" said a deep male voice.

"Yes, sir. I'm . . ." he said.

"She gave a statement a couple of days ago."

"I'm Derk Bryan. May I speak with her?"

"She's in Mars Mission mode and unable to communicate."

"As in off the planet?" said Derk.

"As in unable to communicate."

"Major," Derk made up a title, "this is Doctor Derk Bryan and I'm the guy who jumped out of an airplane to save her life."

"It's Colonel and I know who you are, but she's unable to communicate."

"Sorry Colonel. Can you tell me when she'll be able to communicate?"

"Anything having to do with the Mars Mission, you need to talk with Media Relations," the Colonel said and the line went dead.

He called back.

"NASA," answered the same female voice with the same dronish tone.

"I'd like to speak with someone in Media Relations," he said.

"Regarding, sir?"

"Doctor Susan Carlton."

"Please hold."

Moments later the Colonel was back on the line. "Doctor Bryan, I told you to call Media Relations."

"I did and they connected me with you."

"I guess no one else is available. Doctor Bryan, what can I do for you?" the Colonel asked with a polite but severe retort.

"I'd like to know how Susan, Doctor Carlton, is doing?"

"She's quite well and we thank you for that. What you did was courageous. When she is available, I'll be sure to let her know you asked about her."

"Thank you, but you have no idea when that will be?"

"Sorry, Doctor Bryan, but I don't. She's involved is extensive training."

"I see," Derk said, contemplating his next words.

"Is there anything else?" the Colonel asked.

Derk hesitated. What he wanted to say he wasn't going to share with a stranger.

"Sorry, Doctor Bryan, but I have to get back to . . ."

"Tell her there's a pesky reporter asking some interesting questions about her past. She knows how to get in touch with me." Derk said and paused before adding, "Can you do that, Colonel . . . when she's available."

"Of course, Dr. Bryan." Then he disconnected.

***

On his way for lunch at the Top End, Ardale called.

"Do you know where Doctor Carlton is stationed?"

"She's at NASA," Derk said.

"Do you know where, exactly?"

"No, but you're going to tell me."

"I can't locate her at any NASA facility. Nor is she affiliated with any university, certainly, not in a teaching capacity."

"You've obviously checked but why?" Derk said.

"One of you is an article. The two of you are a story," Ardale said.

"What if I don't want to be a story?" Derk said.

"Doctor Bryan, why don't you want the acknowledgment for what you've done. You saved someone's life, and it was the life of someone critical to the ongoing advancement of the human adventure," said Ardale.

It was the most sincere thing Derk had heard Ardale say, but the scientist in him responded, "Human adventure. What are you talking about?"

"You of all people should know that not everyone evolves at the same rate. There are leaders and there are followers. We need big ideas, like space travel, that require new technologies. Some ideas are costly and don't pan out, but some of them transform us. You, a guy who is Earthbound, saved the life of one of those people who is not. That's a story a lot of people want to hear about," said Ardale.

Derk chuckled. "The philosophical reporter speaks, but that's already old news. The real story is I don't want to accept that we have become so pessimistic about our chances of survival on this planet that we're building space ships so we can go and fuck up another planet. Excuse my frankness."

"So, you think the Mission to Mars is a mistake?"

"I see something amiss; I analyze it. I assess the options, the probability of success and then go about solving the problem. Left-brain stuff. This discipline sends me messages that to survive my life depends upon the quality of the air, the soil and the water right here on Earth. Frankly, life on Earth is fun. I like my life here. I can do work that I like, live on the beach and meet beautiful women with brains. I can't do that and neither can anyone when we're running from droughts, floods, fires, famines and hurricanes. I can add gunfire to that list since it's become one more public health issue we're not confronting. But I understand the desire to relocate when life here becomes one crisis after another. However, when your home is on fire, long term planning is irrelevant."

"So, the planet is on fire and you think we're wasting time and money by going to Mars," said Ardale.

"I think our priorities are out of whack. We're wasting time squabbling over things that are irrelevant if we don't start living in harmony with the other living things on this planet. What do you think?"

"I'm a reporter. My opinion is not important here. What would you have us do, Doctor Bryan?"

"I'm sorry, Ardale, but being neutral puts lives at stake. We're all in this one together," said Derk. He didn't like feeding Ardale a story, but Ardale's question required an answer.

"For the two hundred billion it will cost to get people on Mars we could plant enough trees to cover North America and put solar panels on four million homes. It would be a start to making this place livable again. Do you know what happens when the Earth warms another couple of degrees? Think Mad Max, The Day After Tomorrow, Soylent Green. That will take us from chaos to unlivable. Now I'm not a doom and gloom guy because," he paused as he summoned the optimism that his mindset required, "I believe we can do it. We did it before. We rebuilt after the 1929 stock market crash, after the Great Depression and after World War II. We changed our banking laws and instituted public health insurance. We enacted social security, provided subsidized housing and even set in motion the funding for public arts. In the 1950s we constructed the national highways. In the 60s we sent men to the Moon. These were big ideas. They required transformations in our politics and our view of the connectedness of everyone. We can do it again. All this crisis really takes is the will to survive."

"Do you think we have the will to survive?" said Ardale.

"Frankly, I've been asking myself the same question. I guess we're going to find out." He paused before entreating Ardale, "If you really want to do a story, why don't you publish a list of ways that average people can stop this."

"Like what?" Ardale asked.

"How about I make a list and you publish one of them each week?" Derk said.

"It's that easy?"

"Ardale, do you have faith in education and the value of learning?"

"What do you mean?"

"You take your car to a mechanic when it breaks?" Derk asked.

"Sure.".

"You go to a doctor when your leg breaks?"

"Where are you going with this?"

"It's time we began listening to scientists. They know what to do. I can tell you five things right now that would turn this thing around. It's the will to make it happen that is the unanswered question? You still have connections, don't you? How about it, King Ardale Carver, can you do it?"

"Do you think people are ready to hear it?" Ardale said.

"I read your series on the cost that religion has placed upon the people of the middle east. You compared it with the rise of Evangelicals in the U.S. Heady stuff. You want a story, look into the connection between the fossil fuel interests and religion in this country. Anyway, please stay away from Doctor Carlton for the time being. I don't think she needs or wants the attention. Now, if you don't mind, I'm going to have lunch," said Derk.

17

Reverend Huck was in the middle of an interview with Senator Crux when Danswirth interrupted.

"I can't talk with you now. I'm on the air," Huck whispered into his cell phone. He was sitting behind a microphone in the radio studio of his double-wide. It was eleven a.m. He had donned his fake preacher clothes just for the occasion while he nursed a strawberry daiquiri. His headphones were tilted precariously on his head from repositioning each time Crux shifted his weight in his chair.

The Senator, known for his pearl buttoned shirt and signature bolo, was a regular subject of parodies on late night television as a result of his views on everything from equal rights to religion but more importantly for Daisy, the pearl handled Derringer he kept tucked in his boot. That's what made Huck so nervous. The gun misfired one time during a TV interview and took out a camera.

"Did you get rid of the boat?" Danswirth said.

"I'm with Crux. Third time this month. Is there a fucking election coming up."

"Did you get rid of the boat or not?"

"More or less, but I need to call you back."

The Senator, who usually called in from his Washington office, was on a State wide fund-raising tour and preferred to do the interview in Huck's studio. He was answering Reverend Huck's question about proper the relationship of religion to government in the United States.

"I don't think the Constitution was written with the intent of leaving God out. It's right there on our money: In God We Trust. Is there anything more sacred than the U.S. dollar?"

Reverend Hucklebee was no scholar of Constitutional law, but as far as he could tell, the Senator was just making stuff up. Every school kid was aware of the separation of church from State. It's in the First

Amendment to the Constitution. Huck seldom questioned the list of guests chosen by Danswirth because some of them generated sizeable donations. He came to notice, however, that they had one thing in common. They didn't care much for that "separation" clause and when it came to fossil fuels, they shared the same opinion as Senator Crux, "God wouldn't have made fossil fuels if he didn't intend for us to use them."

"Praise the Lord," Reverend Huck said as he watched the donations roll in, fifty-four thousand three hundred and seventeen dollars since the program began. Religion and politics do mix well.

"What's that, Reverend?" said the Senator.

"Praise the Lord," Huck repeated aloud. "It's been a pleasure having Senator Crux with us this morning. Senator, before we close, would you be so kind as to lead us in today's prayer."

This was the part of the interview Huck liked the most. Each week he asked his guest to say a prayer on behalf of someone in his listening audience. It was always someone suffering a grave illness or a family tragedy and always someone in desire financial straits. The name was selected from a computer-generated list of past donations. Only the first name and the person's home state were mentioned on air. Huck claimed that a percentage of that day's donations would go to the person in need. It wasn't much, maybe five percent, but it always spiked donations. The few minutes after the prayer ended had become the most profitable ten minutes for the entire station.

The Senator led a short prayer, and to Huck's relief, departed for another appearance. Huck sat back in his chair, took the last slurp of his daiquiri and forced a smile. Another step closer to Key West!

"Oh no!" He slumped forward, recalling he had to return Danswirth's call.

He had taken care of the boat. That's all his boss needed to know. He would leave out the part where he used the boat to make a quick five grand by ferreting some illegals from Mexico to south Texas. In the process he broke the propeller, damaged the drive shaft and almost drowned after hitting something in the water. The boat stayed afloat but he and his passengers were tossed overboard. Two of them were lost in the dark, unable to get back onboard. Close to shore, the others overwhelmed him and took the money. He called the marine shop that was his destination. Someone from Bud's Marina towed the boat back to the marina for repairs. Huck told the owner to do whatever he wanted with the boat. The owner of Bud's Marina seemed to understand that he would not return.

Huck held the cold glass against his burnished cheek, still tender from last night's tussle, and looked at the plastic Jesus on the floor.

"What the hell else could go wrong?"

Climate Fact:

Agriculture is responsible for 90% of deforestation. Mangroves and coastal wetlands hold up to five times more carbon per acre than tropical forests. The United Nations Intergovernmental Panel on Climate Change has determined that by legally protecting 30% of our land area from abuse and development is close to what the Earth needs to rebalance itself. Only 16% of land is now protected in some way.

What can you do about it? Do not support new development in environmentally sensitive areas.

18

The more Estee thought about the Ricei splayed in the yard at the Coast Guard Station the more furious she became. The whale and its child, starved by man's arrogance and finished off by his negligence, could never have imagined such cruelty. Like an apparition summoning her, the expectant mother was begging her to: "Help me."

"Teddy," she said, "we have to do something."

"Estee, nice to hear from you," Teddy whispered.

"They had a Ricei whale laid out in the yard, dissected like a lab animal," she blurted out.

Teddy tried to interrupt her, "Estee."

"It was pregnant, Teddy. They killed her calf, too."

"Estee!"

"Suffocated the mother and then ran over her," she added without taking a breath.

"Estee!"

"Yes, sorry."

"Tell me what happened," Teddy implored her in a hushed tone.

"It's difficult to hear you," she said. "Can you speak up?"

"Sorry, I'm in the library. Give me a moment."

"Are you in the law library?" She heard the shuffling of a chair and footsteps.

She felt the pressure of her studies. If it weren't for the Ricei she would be buried in the law books. Her current class involved case preparation and courtroom procedures. Fortunately, as a para-legal she was familiar with them.

She heard him say "Excuse me" a couple of times before he came back on the line.

"Okay, are you still there?" he said.

"Yes, am I bothering you?" The pause had given her a chance to consider that he was a law student and a law student's life is lived in the library. Volunteering for the trip to Houston was a sacrifice. Most students wouldn't have done it. Most couldn't have done it.

"Estee Sparks, you will never be a bother." He was as charming as he was handsome. If she were only a few years younger.

"They're not paying attention. Can you get in touch with the others?"

"What do you mean? What others?"

"The plastic producers. They're committing ecocide. They're murderers. Call Jones and Fendru and ask them to join us."

"Join us where? Estee, slow down,' he said.

She took a deep breath and regurgitated her encounter with the Ricei whale.

Before Teddy could respond she said, "We need to act now!"

"I know, Estee. Everything is connected. We have one giant ecosystem, and we're killing it," he said, "but what are you talking about?"

Teddy told her that after obtaining his undergrad degree he travelled. He had seen the degradation first hand: the depletion of the glaciers in Greenland, the snow caps of the Himalayas and the desertification of the southern Mediterranean countries. In addition to a hard body Teddy had a 3.90 GPA and the closest thing to a photographic memory she knew. She didn't think he knew it, but he took her breath away. Most important, she trusted him.

She laid out her plan. "It won't take much time, but we need to do it now. Please come with me."

"You're not seriously thinking about doing this on your own?" said Teddy.

"I'll cook dinner for you at my place when we're done and go over trial prep," she said.

"Okay, okay, I'm in and I'll tell the others," Teddy said. "Estee Sparks, you're a bad influence on me."

"Hopefully," she whispered.

19

Derk's conversation with Ardale was troubling. Why he was trying to protect Susan Carlton? She could take care of herself especially with armed guards from NASA by her side.

So, what was going on? From the moment he leaped from that airplane he had a notion, a gnawing sensation in his soul, that something in his life had changed. Be it love, lust or something else he had become entangled with this woman, and he felt a need to protect her. He wolfed down a grouper sandwich at the Top End and hurried home.

He would verify what Ardale had told him. A student's transcripts are only available upon request by specified agencies upon approval by the student, but PhDs are public record. He opened a public records website and keyed in his own name and particulars. In an instant his doctorate in anthropology showed up along with the year and university he attended. When he did the same for Susan Carlton, nothing came up. He did it again State by State. Still nothing.

He had spent less than twenty-four hours with Susan Carlton, but nothing suggested she went to school outside the U.S. Her accent was not foreign, and her command of English was flawless. In spite of this there was no record of her attending any college in the United States. It was unsettling how often Ardale was correct.

Thirsty, he went to the refrigerator for a beer. Nothing. He looked down and his toes were in plain sight. The five extra pounds he wanted to lose were gone, just in the past week. He opened the freezer. Other than a turkey breast, a prepackaged container of spinach and artichoke dip and a frozen pizza there was only a small plastic sandwich bag with enough pot to make one or two joints. He couldn't help but laugh aloud given the irony of the situation. Several months ago, they were celebrating the acceptance of Derk's proposal to make the university carbon neutral by 2035 when the disc jockey at the campus radio station, JJ Feever, slipped it into his freezer. Three weeks later JJ gave up pot and went on a spiritual sojourn to Tibet. No one saw that coming! Derk took the pot out to thaw and stuck the spinach dip into the microwave.

As he waited for the timer to ring, he thought some more about Doctor Carlton. The look in her eyes, after the call from Sahith, was unforgettable. She didn't want to leave him. She had a tear in her eye when they kissed goodbye. Then came the knock at the door and the female voice commanding her to return to the base. It was the same woman he saw escorting Susan at the hospital and the same one standing behind her at the news conference. She was training to go to Mars. Why did she have an armed guard escorting her everywhere?

Back to what base? Is that where she was being taken when he intercepted her in the lobby? Where was she stationed? Was it a NASA facility? Where did she live? Was it close to the base? Where do they train for a mission to Mars Mission? After coming so close, he was astounded by how little he knew about her.

He went to his office and rummaged through some papers until he found the receipt for the trip to the Grand Canyon. It was sponsored by The Institute for Archaeology in Boston. He called. As a long-time member he persuaded the events coordinator to give him the contact information for Susan Carlton. It wasn't what he expected. A company by the name of Advanced Bio-Technology had paid for her trip into the Grand Canyon, the same trip he had taken.

He did a Google search for Advanced Bio-Technology. ABT, as it was familiarly known, was formed to develop technologies for plants and animals to deal with the climate change. It was engineering alga that would eat toxic wastes, such as the oil and plastics, that were threatening our oceans. The company was developing crops that needed less water and could survive at high temperatures. There were no financial statements but their website indicated that they had a contract to assist NASA. NASA was going to Mars. ABT's work on crop research could be critical for supporting life on Mars. That explained her relationship with ABT, but he still didn't have an address.

Members had a list of other members, but Susan Carlton wasn't on it. She wasn't showing up in places where others in her field and those with her credentials should have. Ardale was right again.

He called the Institute back. "I'm still trying to breathe without pain and I want to find out if Doctor Carlton is doing okay. Do you have her telephone number or address?"

"Ordinarily I wouldn't give out that information but since it's you, Doctor Bryan, I think it's okay. And, by the way, that was a heroic thing you did in saving her."

The number was familiar. It was the same number he dialed to talk with the Colonel who informed him that Doctor Carlton was in Mars Mission Mode. The address was a total surprise.

Climate Fact:

Greta Thunberg was only 16 years old when she appeared before a gathering of the United Nations. In essence she said that Climate Change is short changing her generation.

What can you do about it? Every decision you make from here on will either feed the enemy or defeat the enemy.

As Danswirth waited for Marshall Hucklebee to call, he made his daily call to Evan Wycliff. Wycliff, in charge of product development, had been working on a new polymer, one that would open new markets for Danswirth Enterprises. Wycliff and he talked every day since the lab tests began on its application to cell phones as well as a substitute for a myriad of industrial and consumer products. In its finished form the new polymer would be as clear as Lucite, as light as balsa wood, as strong as steel and almost impenetrable.

"Let's get this into production," Danswirth said. Each prototype had five million dollars of research and development behind it, and he was eager to see a return on his investment.

"Angelina was working on the prototypes, and she's gone. No one knows where she is, and she's been gone for a couple of weeks" Wycliff said.

Danswirth had some experience with the prototype that he couldn't divulge. "No one else knows anything about this?"

"We work in teams. Each team on a different product. She led that team, but I could pull somebody over."

Danswirth thought he could make a screen for cell phones out of plastic. It would eliminate the breakage problem, and they were as adaptable to touch as glass. Anglina was the team leader on the cell phone screen.

"Only if it won't harm the other projects," Danswirth said.

"We need to replace her," Wycliff said.

"Do you have anyone in mind?" said Danswirth.

"We get applications all the time for researchers but she was special. PhD in molecular engineering. She knew her stuff and she was really easy to look at."

"I met her once or twice. She was a valuable asset. Check with HR. Tell them I gave you authorization to replace her."

"Sure. By the way, Mrs. Connelly, on the cleaning crew, said she saw you with Angelina in the lab a day or two before she disappeared. Did she say anything to you?"

"Nothing. I'll come to the lab in a couple of days to see how you're doing." Danswirth hanged up without saying another word.

Due to the Burning Man Festival, Black Rock City is the sixth largest city in Nevada for eight days each year. The combination art show and fantasy land migrated from the residential streets of San Francisco to the high desert in northwestern Nevada to accommodate the demand. For those eight days the festival transformed a bone dry, desert playa into an erotic and other worldly clime filled with peace, joy and imagination. And for those eight days it was one of the safest places you could be on Planet Earth. As one patron reported after a week in Black Rock, "*It's life the way it should be for, at least, one week of the year.*"

The rest of the time it is a treeless, wind driven and desolate piece of nature that was formed from a lake bottom four thousand feet above sea level. Upon this high desert mesa there is no electricity, no convenient store, no gas station and nothing of human convenience for seventy-eight miles. The temperature can incinerate you during the day and chill you to the bone at night. Just through inhalation the wind is filled with enough playa dust to add twenty pounds per year to your body weight. Except for eight days each year, if a Martian were kidnapped and dropped at Black Rock City, he would not know he had left home.

This was the address the Institute for Archaeology gave Derk when he asked where Doctor Susan Carlton lived.

"Very funny, Black Rock City. No one lives there," Derk said.

"It's on her application. Place of residence: Black Rock City."

"No shit!" Deark mumbled.

"What?"

After a lengthy pause he said, "Thank you," and hit End on his phone.

Climate Fact:

Public schools devote only 1-2 hours per year teaching about climate change. In 2023 the top news programs devote less than 1% of their air time to covering climate change. They cover the hurricanes, floods, fires and droughts but seldom discuss what makes them dangerous and more frequent.

What can you do about it? Get educated, get mad and get active.

22

Estee Sparks could have allowed her anger to consume her when her life's trajectory took a nosedive. She had lost a child and a husband. Her family's business was on life support. She was going to school long after she should have been settling into a career and nurturing a family. None of it was her fault. Her government failed to protect her and her family from the pollution in the Gulf. From the fertilizers, the pesticides and the serial oil spills. From the smokestacks of utility companies. From the toxins of the chemical companies, the exhaust of automobiles and the waste of the plastic producers. Her own government had failed to enforce the laws that should have prevented this.

Before he died her father convinced her that allowing resentment to dictate the road she chose to travel would result in a rocky path. "Hard work and perseverance have always been the tenets that drive our family," he said. "Focus your energy on the positive and you will rise again."

Although there were days when she was mad as hell—usually after hearing about the discovery of another toxic supersite or an animal on the verge of extinction—the anger had been supplanted by a numbness. She had read that the anger was common and often lasting among mothers who lost a child. Estee had lost everything. On some days it was as if her past was irrelevant—as if it belonged to someone else. If it had never occurred, she would probably be better for it. At least, she would have the prospect of different, kinder memories. The Gulf of Mexico was her living, her home and her playground. All of it had been taken from her.

A therapist told her, "Happiness is a choice." Sad, happy or somewhere in between, it was up to her. She tried to think happy and be happy, but where do you hang your hat when there are only hooks for sad hats? She feared that the life she once thought she would have was already past her. A fulltime job, law school and weekends running oyster lines had stretched her thin. She had no time for herself and, when she did, she was too tired. She had added three pounds to her trim physique and was sure the strand of hair she found in her sink last week was gray. When she looked in the mirror that cheerful, optimistic little girl that loved her life on the beach was nowhere in sight.

She joined the volunteers at Blue Skies/Clear Waters not just to clean up the mess but as a distraction, something to break her routine. She sometimes thought about Bobby, her ex. The oil spill and its aftermath left the oyster business in shambles. He begged her to move, especially after the death of their baby, "We have to leave this place, put these memories behind us," but she couldn't. Or she wouldn't. Her father's health began to fail as precipitously as his business. In an attempt to save each of them she spiraled into oblivion. Bobby relocated to Nevada and took a job as a croupier at a large resort. Eventually he stopped asking her to join him. When he filed for divorce, she was terrified and angry but not surprised. She had some formal training as a paralegal which helped her land a job with an attorney who represented the family's interests. It was a sheer gift but one that began to turn her life around. She wanted to study environmental law. He agreed to pay for her legal studies if she stayed with his firm for two years after she passed the bar exam.

At FSU law school she met Jones, Fendru and Teddy. They joined Blue Skies/Clear Waters after a representative visited one of their classes to talk about environmental law. The raid on the corporate office in Houston turned a distraction into a sensation, a thrill, a reason to get up each day. For the first time in several years, she was filled with purpose. Her new friends, especially Teddy, had aroused something else she hadn't felt in a long time. She was eager to put her plan into action with their help.

***

The success of their first raid had turned anonymity into camaraderie. Even though Estee was nearly as old as some of their mothers, she was a law student, a peer and a fellow interloper. She had a plan and was giddy that Teddy agreed to help.

The freezer that used to be filled with tubs of seafood processed by her family's business was now a collection point of maimed and deformed aquatic life. Estee had volunteered to allow the Blue Skies/Clear Waters organization to store dolphins with the plastic sixpack rings caught in their mouths, sharks trapped in discarded nets and an assortment of sailfish, tarpon and marlins that had died from the waste of cruise ships at her family's facility. Normally these items were kept in the freezer before being donated to university and governmental labs for study. There was so much dead seafood in cold storage she needed to get rid of some of it before Blue Skies/Clear Waters could organize another clean up event. After looking into the eye of the Ricei whale at the Coast Guard station she knew what to do with it.

Teddy called back to confirm that, "Fendru and Jones will join us, mostly because neither of them are in police custody." When he also confided that Jones told him, "She's hotter than any of our mothers," the extra pounds and the gray hair were forgotten.

She asked them to meet her in a supermarket parking lot in Panama City. Jones, Fendru and Teddy had come in the camper. Estee arrived in a white, unmarked refrigerated truck filled with the contents of the company's freezer.

With a grin and a wink that defied the nauseating reality of what she asking them do, she pointed to the refrigerated box. "When the stuff in there thaws, it's going to be an offal mess." She shook an imaginary cigar, Groucho Marx style.

Eager to see what Estee had in mind, each of them climbed out of the heat and into the back of the refrigerated cooler.

"Oh, my god!" said Fendru.

Jones shuddered. "How long have you been collecting this stuff?"

"This is a month or two of what comes in," she said.

"I had no idea it was this bad," said Jones, putting a handkerchief over his mouth.

"Brrrr. It's fucking cold in here," said Teddy before stepping out. The others followed.

"There are only two cars," she began.

"Actually, one car and one truck," Teddy corrected her.

"Yes," she said with half a smile and half a frown. "So, we'll have to divide the contents in two and make separate trips."

"No way. I'm not putting that stuff in my camper. All the way to Houston? No way," Jones said.

Estee raised her hands. "Calm down. I have coolers!"

"You have coolers that big?" Jones stretched out his arms. "Some of those fish are three or four feet long."

Fendru curled his top teeth over his lower gum and nodded. "He's right."

"You're not going to Houston. You're going to Mississippi," she said.

They were standing in the parking lot behind Estee's eighteen feet long refrigerated truck. The sun's angle in the western sky indicated it was mid-afternoon and that they were on time. She selected Friday because it was the end of the school week for her pals, and it was a weekday for their targets.

"Where in Mississippi and we're going to do what when we get there?" Jones said.

"You're going to drive right up to some fat ass CEO's home and dump this stuff on the fucker's doorsteps," Teddy said. His head bobbed up and down like a kid who had gotten a new bicycle for his birthday.

"Oh no. Are you serious?" Jones' and Fendru's faces contorted.

"It's a fantastic idea!" Teddy said and lifted Estee off the ground with a bear hug.

As he slowly lowered her, something danced inside her. His eyes never shied from hers. She was certain that Fendru and Jone noticed it, too.

"Whew!" she sighed as her feet came back to Earth, but she had to overcome her friends' reservations. "Wait a minute."

She ran to the cabin of the truck and returned with a stack of flyers containing pictures of extinct animals similar to the ones she left at Danswirth's office.

"Hand these out at each site. Hopefully, these—eco-ciders—will get the message."

"Is that too strong?" she said to Teddy.

"No. Eco-ciders, that's good," he said, awaiting confirmation from the others. They nodded. "Yea, that's what they are."

"Okay then, let's get going," Estee said.

Within fifteen minutes they had placed one half of the decaying remains of skewered fish, turtles and sea mammals into separate coolers and loaded them into Jones' camper. She gave Fendru and Jones the home addresses of the two CEOs in Mississippi whose companies manufactured plastic.

After Fendru and Jones left, Teddy held out his hands, as if inviting her to take them. When she reached for him, he backed away quickly, "No, yuk. Do you have anything to wash my hands?"

"In the truck," she said. Slightly embarrassed, she felt like a school girl with a crush.

As they climbed aboard Teddy tried not to touch anything. She handed him a container of Wash-n-Wipes. After washing his hands, Teddy held them out for her to smell.

"Okay," she nodded and held out hers.

He nodded his approval. "Ms. Sparks, you have very nice hands."

"Thank you, Mister _______?" she hesitated, realizing she didn't know his last name.

"Thromburton, Theodore Thromburton at your service."

"Named after Theodore Roosevelt I presume? How appropriate."

"Nope; Tom, Terry and Tony were already taken."

"So, you're a Teddy by default."

"It appears that way, Counselor," he said while she started the truck. "Estee?" he said and waved his hands in a questioning manner.

"Simone Teresa," she said.

"So very good to meet you, Simone Teresa Sparks." His face was gentle and his voice reassuring. "By the way Ms. Sparks, may I ask where we are going?"

Through a mischievous grin she said, "We're going to deliver some seafood to the personal residence of the CEO of Danswirth Enterprises."

23

Danswirth was meeting with Evan Wycliff in the company's research lab. Wycliff was ecstatic about one of prototypes of the material Danswirth used to suffocate Angelina.

"You can mold it into almost any shape," Wycliff said, holding up a sheet of plastic to the light, and offering it to Danswirth. "It's transparent, light weight and strong which makes it attractive to both the aerospace and auto industries as well as for cell phones."

Danswirth waved him off. He didn't need to hear this. He knew its capabilities. He couldn't erase the look in Angelina's eyes as he poured the molten liquid over her. He hadn't realized she had survived the blow to her head until that moment, but it was too late.

"Have you found her replacement yet?" Danswirth asked.

"Angelina? No, I'm still interviewing," Wycliff said.

"Is it money?" Danswirth had stolen Evan Wycliff from Chem Industries ten years ago with huge incentives to develop new products. He had never failed to surprise Danswirth with his ingenuity.

"She'll be hard to replace. It's a tight job market, especially for chemical engineers with her talent," said Wycliff, "but I'll find someone."

"Any idea where she went?"

Wycliff frowned and shook his head.

"Did she take anything with her?" Danswirth said.

Wham! Wycliff slammed a piece of the material against the marble countertop. "It's virtually indestructible. I don't know."

"Wasn't that her concern?" said Danswirth.

"Our children will have to live with the consequences of our actions for the rest of their lives," she told him, "and this stuff is virtually indestructible."

He thought her statement was made to provoke a reaction from him, actually a commitment. She made no secret of her intention. After Danswirth's wife died, Angelina expected him to marry her. He was sure that constituted the motivation behind her comments about *our children*. Maybe he had forgotten or overlooked that she had expressed her reservations a number of times.

His response was to placate her. "A lot things we use every day aren't good for us if we abuse them. That's why you're here --- to make them work better."

What he learned later was that she was an active member of the Union of Concerned Scientists. They had taken a highly publicized position on the need for a reduction in the use of fossil fuels due to their impact upon global warming and pollution. This position was a direct attack upon is business as far as Danswirth was concerned. Fossil fuels were the raw materials for ninety percent of his company's products.

That Angelina was movie star gorgeous made it easy to overlook her youthful idealism, and as Wycliff admitted, she was a talented chemist. He also assumed that Angelina relished their relationship more than their professional differences.

Their relationship began when Evan Wycliff suggested that Danswirth would benefit by being more involved in product development discussions. Danswirth went a step further upon meeting Angelina. He invited her to accompany him on what he called a business development trip. Then another. Then another. Their personal relationship was conducted as discretely as possible to avoid any internal conflicts. Of course, Danswirth also had to avoid the scrutiny of his wife until she slipped into a coma.

Eventually the business trips included fine wine, expensive jewelry and shopping for the latest fashions. Although almost twice her age, he was surprised to find that sharing the loss he was experiencing due to his wife's terminal illness, drew them closer.

Close enough that she shared her own dreams and aspirations. As the child of illegal immigrants and the first to go to college in her family, she wanted everything the American dream could offer. That included him. He was handsome, rich, confident and powerful. It didn't take long for him to succumb to her innocence and her lust. More than a couple of times she had enticed him into taking her on the cold marble of a lab table. To his dismay and pleasure, she reveled in the thrill of sex in public settings. Everything about her made Danswirth feel young and desirable.

As a result, he felt betrayed by the letter Wycliff discovered on her computer that she had written to the Union of Concerned Scientists. In the letter she listed her credentials, her current research and her knowledge of the dangers posed by the PFOs (perfluorooctanoic acid) and PFAs (perfluorooctanoic sulfonic acid).

She wrote,

"Since the 1940s these chemicals, with more than twelve thousand different compounds, have been used for everything from carpeting and non-stick cookware to firefighting foams and fast-food wrappers. Because they don't break down easily, they are forever chemicals and they have been shown to produce myriad of health risks that can lead to death including breast and kidney cancer, reduced fetal growth, thyroid disease, pregnancy induced hypertension and ulcerative colitis."

What angered Danswirth was the next line,

"How can we raise the alarm in regard to the introduction of this new product I've been developing without jeopardizing my position with the firm?"

She then described the exact product that she, along with Danswirth's engineers, had been developing.

Danswirth was livid after reading the letter. "Evan, I don't throw plastic bottles on the street and I don't toss trash into the ocean. In fact, we make those damn blue and yellow recycling bins. And I'm loyal to my people. This is fucking sabotage. Did she send this letter?"

"It was in her Sent file," Wycliff said.

"Damn, shit, fuck!" said Danswirth.

In the letter she hadn't mentioned his company or the product by name, but the UCS would know where she worked and exactly what she doing. Although he would have to prepare another expensive public relations campaign to counter the pressure he would feel from environmental zealots and governmental watchdogs, he worried about something more threatening. When someone eventually asked to speak with the author of the letter Danswirth and his business would come under a spotlight the size of the Moon.

Wycliff asked, "Do you want me to fire her?"

Danswirth's head bobbed up and down, but he wanted to do more than fire her. He wanted to punish her.

He changed his mind. "I'll take care of it," he said. And he did.

***

The day he was going to confront Angelina with the letter she called to tell him she had something very important to share with him.

"Can you meet me in the lab at seven?" She seemed both nervous and excited.

His ire was temporarily doused by her girlish giggle, a habit she deployed whenever she wanted to play—which usually involved sexual games.

Except for a few candles placed in a circle around a table, that had been cleared of everything except a greeting card, the lab was dark when Danswirth entered. It was on this same table she had ridden him like a cowgirl on a bucking bull on his fifty first birthday a couple of months earlier. He waited anxiously for her to emerge from the restroom.

In high heels she sashayed toward him wearing a white lab coat with her name on it. Under it he saw glimpses of the lavender dress he had bought for her in Palm Beach. Her cellphone played *"Let Me Entertain You"* while she removed the coat and swung it in the air around her head. Then she flung it across the room.

Danswirth was in no mood to be seduced, but she was giving him no choice. As the music played, she did a Gypsy Rose Lee rendition and slipped the dress over her head. Completely naked except for a necklace and red nails, her brown skin sparkled and her lips glistened in the candlelight. She laid the dress on her hip and tossed it to one side. She turned slightly to display her hip, the curve of her back and breasts that, to Danswirth, were as succulent as fruit.

His erection, although reflexive, beckoned her. The flicker of candle light danced in the room from the reflection off her silver necklace, the same one he had gotten her after their tryst in the Bahamas. She pushed him into a chair, loosened his trousers, kneeled and took him into her mouth.

When he was aroused almost to climax, she climbed onto the chair and took him deep within her. He thrust and, with each thrust, pulled her toward him. That's when she realized that something in his hand was irritating her back.

She tried to loosen his grip, but he held on more tightly, pushing himself deeper into her. Deeper and harder. He still wanted to punish her.

Sensing something wasn't right, she freed herself and his arm came loose. In his hand was a copy of the letter she had sent to the UCS. Her eyes tattled on her. In them he saw her composing each word and designing every paragraph to expose his secrets and betray him.

"I'm sorry," she said and reached for it.

He held it higher while he pushed into her, harder and harder. Each time she bounced away from him, the last time too quickly, forcing her backward. She slipped through his hands and her head ricocheted off the edge of the marble table. Her neck retorted and blood streamed from the back of her head. Danswirth vomited.

***

Pendleton Danswirth III may have been the only man in Texas who didn't listen to country music. If he had, he would have heard Slaid Cleaves' confession, "I'm not living like I should," enough times to question, at least, one thing about his own behavior. He didn't. As a result, things were going sideways faster than a snake in the grass.

As Evan Wycliff demonstrated the benefits of their new polycarbonate Danswirth relived the single most gruesome moment of his life. Wycliff had slammed the model onto the same lab table against which Angelina had fallen. The same lab table surrounded by candlelight that danced in her eyes on that evening. The betrayal, the anger, the arousal, the ecstasy and then the sound of her head against cold marble came rushing at him.

He stood in the same place where her naked body lay that night, the letter to the UCS clutched in his hand. He wiped his mouth again, thinking he was brushing off the taste of bile. He felt the shock, the disbelief and the paralysis again. At the time it seemed like a dream. Now it was the worst kind of nightmare. He shuddered and clutched his head in his hands, hoping the moment would pass. He closed his eyes and opened them, again and again, but each time her limp body lay at his feet, and the bile fouled his tongue.

"You okay?" Wycliff said.

"I don't know. Something just came over me," Danswirth said and looked for an office chair where he could sit down.

The real answer was, "Not really."

He should have called the police or, at least, an ambulance. It was an accident although a lurid one. He had an affair with an employee who betrayed his confidence. Then she is found dead in his own lab, naked and probably with his semen inside her. His marriage, his company, the vote he needed from the Believers' board and quite probably his freedom, were at stake.

No one knew he was there so he went into damage control mode. Everything he needed to dispose of her body was in the supply room. He would use the very product she claimed was so dangerous to dispose of her, and no one would ever know what happened. How ironic!

He stuck a note on the door, *No Cleaning Tonight.* In the supply room he found two Lucite boxes that, when placed end to end, were large enough to hold her body. With glue and heat he fused them together. Then he stripped off her clothes and jewelry and shaved off her beautiful hair, probably due to watching too many old detectives' shows before DNA analysis. After he placed her body into the Lucite mold, he poured the very product she had helped design over her remains. The liquid rose around her until she was completely encapsulated. Within a few minutes the contents hardened. He cleaned up the blood on the table and the floor, sloshed ammonia all over the place and wrapped her clothes, the jewelry and the bad memory into a black plastic trash bag. Then he put it into a paper grocery bag. As he was leaving, he noticed the greeting card that had fallen off the lab table and come to rest under a desk. As he opened it, he heard a noise in the hallway. He stuffed the card into the bag and waited for silence. No one came.

His would take the body to the marina, where he kept his boat, power out to the Gulf and drop the package into the water. All he needed to complete his get-away was a truck and some tools.

He drove home and parked on the street outside the gate to his estate. He punched in the code and entered without tripping the alarm. He stayed out of the light and away from the security cameras as he made his way to the side door of his garage. Inside the garage he threw a tool-kit and an extra roll of black plastic bags into the back of his dual cab Silverado. Before backing the truck out of the garage, he disabled the outdoor security cameras. Under an overcast sky the pickup crept out the driveway unnoticed. He left the truck running while he parked his car in the garage. At Home Depot he picked a roll of burlap, a sheet of plywood, a battery-operated skill saw and a flat dolly.

The next challenge was getting the plastic box that encased Angelina's body into the bed of his truck. Fortunately, a Danswirth family requisite for men was a degree in engineering. He had already estimated the dimensions of the ramp he would need to slide the clear plastic block onto the dolly. If that didn't work, he had purchased three broomsticks he could make into rollers. He hoped he could lift one end of the coffin onto one of the rollers without it falling off the ramp. Once he got all broomsticks under the box, he could roll it onto the bed of his truck. So that no one would hear the shrill of the skill saw, he stopped in an abandoned bank parking lot and cut the plywood and the broomsticks down to the width of the dolly.

When he returned to his plant, he parked away from the floodlamps at a corner of the building housing the lab. Inside, in spite of the gut-wrenching anxiety he was feeling, he was exhilarated to discover his company's new polymer was as light as advertised. It had all the properties of Lucite but was stronger and more resistant to heat as Wycliff had advertised. It would make him millions. He slid the box onto the dolly, covered it with a tarp and wheeled it outside. After loading it onto the bed of his truck he wrapped the box in burlap and covered it again with the trash bags which he held in place with rope.

It was a couple of hours before sunrise when he arrived at the marina on the Buffalo Bayou, forty-five minutes east of his Houston office. Fortunately, the dock where he kept his boat was not well lit, and the Moon hid behind overcast skies. The night air was humid but calm, and the only sound came from the waves slapping the pilons under the dock. If anyone was there, they were asleep on their boats.

He loaded the burlap covered box onto the dolly and wheeled it to the gangplank. After a couple of failed attempts, he realized he couldn't get the box from the dock onto his boat and then to the stern without help.

"Damn!" he cried out as his back gave way during one last attempt. The dolly was stuck half way across the gangplank. He looked around and was relieved to find that his cry appeared not to have waken anyone. Clouds now completely covered the moon.

He drove the short distance into Galena Park to an all-night diner. A couple of old men with unkept beards and bad breath were scrummaging through waste cans for table scraps at the back of the diner. With fifty dollars and a to-go order he coaxed the strongest one into helping him move a piece of furniture onto his boat.

He didn't ask the stranger's name nor did he provide one. As daylight broke, with the package now on board his boat, he returned his helper to the underpass of a bridge over the river near the diner. Then he left a message for Marshall Hucklebee to call him.

Returning to the present he shook his head and rubbed his forehead. "Yes, I'm okay, but "Shirley's not well, and I've got a lot on my plate. This is really good news, Evan. Keep up the good work, and let me know when you find a replacement for Angelina."

As perspiration formed on his brow Pendleton Danswirth III went back to his office.

Climate Fact:

Forests soak up more global warming gases than all of the oceans combined. Each year we cut down enough forests to cover twenty million football fields.

What can you do about it? Plant a tree. Grow a garden. Plant a tree.

24

Although he wasn't happy about it Derk knew there are only two reasons that flights are canceled: a problem with the airplane or a problem with the air. Under neither circumstance did he want to be traveling by airplane. The cancelation of the flight to Reno from Tampa was a minor setback. He made arrangements to fly into Salt Lake City.

It was three hundred miles further to Black Rock City from Salt Lake City than it was from Reno, but he was happy to get a flight until they were in the air. The turbulence was so rough he felt as if he'd been on Six Flags' roller coaster for three hours. Tired and wobbly he summoned enough energy to rent a car and drive to Winnemucca. It was the closest resemblance to a town east of Black Rock Desert. There he checked into a motel at the Inn and Casino and asked for a 7:30 a.m. wakeup call.

The call came early, stirring the arthritis in his left knee. He lazily dressed and went to the restaurant in the casino. While he waited for breakfast, he sipped black coffee and perused a stack of brochures he selected from a rack of local attractions. A Chamber of Commerce flyer put the population of Winnemucca, Nevada at eighty-six hundred and the elevation at about forty-three hundred feet. Winnemucca was a strategic location for the ranching and mining industries in the area. A small map situated the town just off Interstate 80 at the junction of U.S. Highways 93 and 40, about two hundred and twenty-four miles east of Black Rock City. The flyer also displayed a black and white photo of Chief Winnemucca from which the city drew its name. He looked regal in his headdress and deer skin trappings.

Although he would go unnoticed in jeans and boots, he didn't feel out of place in his oxford, button down, dress shirt and khakis or when he put his Tampa Bay Buccaneers hat on the table. He ordered dry wheat toast with jam and oatmeal with bananas and raisins. When the oatmeal came without the bananas the waitress said, "no one puts that in his oatmeal around here." At the same time three men in their thirties, at the table across from him, got up to leave. As they passed him, he noticed a NASA patch on the shirt of one of them.

After they left, he asked the woman behind the cash register, "Does NASA have a facility around here?"

"Not that I know, but I've only been here a few months. Ask Buddy. He's been here forever." The cashier was a squatty figure with a friendly demeanor in her mid-twenties. She turned and started to shout something into the kitchen.

Derk threw up his hand. "Oh, that's not necessary." He handed her his credit card.

"Are they in here often?"

"Sit anywhere," she said as a middle-aged couple in western wear entered. "The hostess is off today. Sorry, what did you say? Oh, yea, at least once a week. Always orders the Buffalo Hash, the short one does. Have you tried it?"

Derk shook his head. "Trying to cut down on red meat."

"Probably the fat," she said. She was distracted by folks at another table holding up their cups. "I'll be right with you."

"What?" she said to Derk.

"Nothing. Thank you. By the way, what is the fastest way to Black Rock City?"

"There isn't any," said a tall, wiry fellow with a panhandle mustache standing behind Derk.

"What do you mean?" Derk said.

"You've got to go down 80 and up 447. Takes three and a half to four hours on a good day." He left a twenty next to the register and left without further explanation.

"He's right," said the waitress. "I used to live in Reno."

Disappointed again, Derk thanked her. Why is nothing ever easy?

With his suitcase in hand, he checked out of the hotel. He loaded up on gas and bottled water before hitting the road. As he pulled away from the gas station the three men from the restaurant passed him in a four-wheel drive truck loaded with solar panels. Derk followed them. They headed north on eighty and, within a mile, turned west onto an unpaved road. Before long the four-wheeler disappeared ahead of him, but his rental car had to turn around. The road was too rough for anything but an armadillo or a four-wheeler.

He went back to the gas station where he approached a man, about his age, who was pumping gas into a weathered Jeep Wrangler.

"Excuse me, is there a place around here I can rent a Jeep?" Derk said.

The fellow pinched his lower lip as he was thinking. "There's a car rental place. No, that closed during the Pandemic. I'm not sure. Sorry."

He wanted to ask where the man bought his Jeep, but it could have been two decades ago in St. Louis. The heat was already ricocheting off the pavement and warming him like a sauna. He regretted not wearing shorts. He went inside the convenience store to cool off and ask the clerk for directions to a Jeep rental business. After the clerk confirmed what the customer at the gas pump had told him, Derk did a search on his cell phone for car rentals. Two were listed but neither had a Jeep or a four-wheeler on the lot. It was just a hunch about the guy with the NASA patch so he returned to his car, resolved to drive to Black Rock City. That's when he noticed a dirt-bike parked beside the store.

He Googled motorcycle shops. Within an hour he had rented a BMW 1200 with panniers. He bought a helmet, gloves and a pair of heavy boots. After a stop at a convenience store for a flash light, water and power bars, he hit the road—the same road the three men in the four-wheeler had taken a couple of hours earlier.

"Unless you're was an experienced rider," the salesman at the dealership advised after learning Derk wanted to take the shortcut to Black Rock City, "I wouldn't. It's seventy to eighty miles on that old mining road, and unless you want to become part of the landscape, I'd stay on the paved roads."

Less than thirty minutes from Winnemucca on the old mining road Derk discovered the wisdom of that advice.

A few blocks before arriving at the home of the owner of Danswirth Enterprises, Estee Sparks stopped on the side of a verdant, tree lined road on the outskirt of Houston.

Reaching behind the seat, she said, "Put this on your side of the truck."

She pulled out two magnetic signs. In every way, from the logo to the purple and orange lettering, they screamed FedEx, but they weren't. It wasn't until Teddy stood back and took a second look that he broke into laughter. "FedUp."

They high-fived and climbed into the truck. Teddy held out his hand again. When their hands met, he slid his fingers between hers, leaned over and kissed her gently on the back of her hand.

"Whew!" she felt it again, exhilarated as she drove away.

The gate at Danswirth's home was wide open. One was painting it. Another was checking the wiring on the security system. He said something had apparently turned off the security cameras a couple of nights ago. He waved them through the gate. Neither Teddy nor Estee said anything as they passed the bronzed lions at the entrance that served as sentries for Danswirth's sprawling estate. A kaleidoscope of colors filled their senses.

The road to the main house was adorned by impatiens and Bottlebrush trees in full bloom. An obligatory ten-foot high Barrell cactus was visible in the distance. A garden circumscribed a Century plant that had grown to the size of a small house.

"This is how the one-percenters live?" Teddy said.

In the middle of a circle that served as a driveway to the front door, was a Century plant as wide as Estee's living room and as tall as Estee's condo. Several old but glossy black hitching posts stood as a nod to Texas culture, and the Gargoyle at the beginning of the side walk to the main entrance was, indeed, gauche. They looked at each other and rolled their eyes. Estee parked as close to the front door as possible.

"Put these on," she said and tossed a pair of white rubber gloves to him. "Wait a minute." She held up one hand to stop his exit from the truck. She was surprised that no one had come to greet them. "Okay," she said and they went to work.

She opened the back of the truck and climbed in. Teddy, directly behind her, held a hand over his nose. "Why did you shut down the cooler?" he said.

Estee slid a large container toward the door where he was waiting.

"Wanted him to get the full affect," she said.

"This is really going to piss him off," said Teddy, squinting. The offal made his eyes water.

She pushed the containers toward Teddy and he dumped the contents upon Danswirth's doorstep and sidewalk. "Two hundred pounds of stinky fish usually gets everyone's attention," she said.

Slimy, putrid, rotting marlins, grouper, pompano and an assortment of fish Teddy had never seen covered the landing and each step leading to the entrance. There was so much it spilled onto the lawn.

"The grosser, the better," said Estee.

"Aw yuk!" said Teddy. A Tarpon, with a plastic six pack ring stuck in its gill, looked up with dismay from under Teddy's loafer.

"Told you to wear boots," Estee said.

With their baskets empty Estee said, "Put these in the truck." Then she rang the doorbell.

A voice on the intercom responded, "May I help you?"

"Delivery," Estee said.

As Teddy was throwing the last container into the truck she said, "Let's get out of here."

Teddy stepped on a rotting grouper with a plastic straw in its eye. "Damn it!" He said as he opened the door to the truck.

"What?" she said.

Teddy was looking at his shoes.

"Get in the truck!" she said. She was in a hurry.

If not for the positive memories, the aroma would have gotten to her too. For Teddy it had become unbearable. His shoes were a mess, he was breathing heavily and he was turning green. Any moment she was expecting him to puke, but they needed to escape. She hurried out the driveway, past the gate and turned right. A mile down the road she turned left onto a road where the homes sat back from the road on five acre lots. When there was no traffic visible from either direction, she veered off the road and stopped on the apron.

"Go, get out," she said and pushed Teddy, who was holding one hand over his mouth, toward the door.

Teddy jumped out, gulped, threw his head back and tried to release the nausea, but nothing came. Another vexing dry heave and then another. Estee climbed down from the cab of the truck and, as the heaves dissipated, put her arm around him. It was a motherly instinct that still surprised her.

"Deep breaths," she encouraged. He walked in a couple of circles, took a big gulp of air and wiped his hand across his mouth. His color was returning to normal.

She held out a scarf upon which he could to wipe his mouth. He took it, wiped his lips and buried his head in the silky material. When he looked up, he kissed her on the forehead. She held his gaze for an extended moment. Nothing was said her eyes couldn't hear.

They went to the back of the truck and climbed into the cooler, wreaking with aftermath of offal but now more tolerable. Estee stripped down to her tattoos. She tossed her smelly clothes into a large bag and tied it shut. She was pulling on shorts and a tank top when her eyes caught his again. Teddy stood, silently communicating his awe and his want. He rinsed off his shoes with a hose attached to the truck, threw the rain coat into the back of the truck and they took off again.

A couple of miles later Teddy broke into laughter.

"What?" Estee said, smiling. Teddy's laughter was infectious.

"How far were they going?"

"Jones and Fendru?" she said.

"They're not going to make it," he said, swiping his hand across his nose.

***

Six hundred and eighty miles away Jones and Fendru were making their final stop in Mississippi, home to some of the largest petrochemical and plastics producers in the country. That included Southern Extrusions, a manufacturer of extruded plastic parts and fibers, owned by Bartholomew J. Davis.

During a search of the targets on Estee's list Fendru reported, "We're probably sitting on something made by his company right now. These are vinyl. Right?" He was digging his fingernail into the seat fabric.

Jones was searching for the house numbers. "Was that four, one, two, five or four, five, two, one?"

"The latter," confirmed Fendru, glancing at the list Estee had typed for them.

"Don't rip my seat!" Jones said.

Fendru was looking closely at a piece of frayed fiber he had picked from the seat.

"Sorry, but this is plastic. We're sitting on plastic. It's everywhere."

"I know but that's my seat," Jones snapped.

"Sorry," Fendru said. "Didn't mean to, but it was already coming apart."

Jones' tolerance had been truncated by the all-day stench in his camper. "I just want to dump this shit and be done with it."

Each of them had tied bandanas over their noses as they strew rotting fish, the remains of a manatee lacerated by a propellor, and cruise ship waste onto some of the most ornate doorsteps in the southeast. The last of their rotting marine cargo had been placed in a large Styrofoam cooler and stored in the toilet of Jones' camper for delivery to Bartholomew Davis.

"That's it," said Fendru as they passed the address. It was past dusk and flood lights illuminated the entrance. A large concrete lion guarded each side of the closed gate.

"Oh shit. It's gated," said Jones. Up until now they did not have to deal with gates. "We're leaving it out here."

"Really? What about the signs?" Fendru said.

They had been securing the FedUp signs to Jones camper with duct tape because its sides were made of fiberglass, but Jones' patience with the routine had dwindled.

"It doesn't matter. We're not going inside."

"So, what's the plan?"

"Fuck it!" said Jones. "No one is going to mistake my camper for a FedEx truck."

They held their noses and scattered the dead fish onto the ornate pavers in front of the gate.

"I'll never order fish again in my life," said Jones, whose bandana had slid down to reveal his face, as he tossed the Styrofoam cooler onto the mess.

Fendru did a pirouette, ballet like, as he scattered the pictures of the extinct animals onto the pile, then pushed a button on the intercom.

When someone answered he said, "Delivery."

He ran to the open door of the waiting camper and they sped off.

***

The reason Catherine "Kitty" Dombrovsky didn't notice the camper stopped in front of her had nothing to do with the poor illumination of the intersection or that one of its break-lights was out. She was late for her night job, touching up her eye liner and talking on her cell phone with Lizzy "Lips" Davano, a fellow exotic dancer.

During the day Kitty was a private Home Health Aide but her husband, Dale, and she wanted another child so she danced on the weekends at Wildways. Exotic dancing had paid her way through nursing school. Now she wanted a bigger house, and jiggling her naked ass for two nights in front of a bunch of drooling, over-sexed reprobates brought in as much as taking care of frail old farts masturbating in their mansions.

"She said they should go to their own school. Can you believe that?" Kitty complained to Lizzy. She had attended a meeting at Alice Treadway's home because Alice had a four-year old son about to enter the same school district as Kitty's daughter.

Alice Treadway, a neighbor of Bartholomew J. Davis, was organizing a local chapter of Moms up for Freedom, a group that was in favor of traumatizing sexually confused kids at their most vulnerable time. MUFF was banning books and engaging in restroom wars all over the south.

"Is that bad?" Liz asked. "You don't want Gina having to compete with girls who are really boys, do you?"

"That's not the point. It's discrimination. They're banning books like the Christians did in Alexandria."

"Alexandria?"

161

"Her son is only four and she's already concerned that he might be tainted by reading The Catcher in the Rye."

"A baseball book?"

"Jesus, Lizzy. Sometimes I think you just came out from under a rock."

"You get all worked up sometimes for nothing," said Lizzy. "You'd better get in here. Al's in a bad mood tonight."

"Tell him I'm on my way. Mr. Garlin had an accident just as I was leaving. Oh shit!" she said as her mini-van bumped into the camper in front of her.

She tried to back away but her car pulled the truck with it.

"What the fuck!" Jones howled.

"How did they find us so soon?" Fendru said, looking in the side mirror and expecting to see flashing lights.

Instead, a mini-van was up their ass and a woman with makeup smeared across one cheek had her cell phone in one hand while she tried to back up. Each jerk of the mini-van to extricate itself from the camper resulted in whiplash.

"What's she doing?" Jones said. Jones jumped from the car and Fendru followed.

"At least, it's not the cops," said Fendru, massaging his neck.

"I'm sorry, so sorry. Are you okay?" said Kitty, who had also gotten out of her car. She was in nurse attire and still had her cell phone gripped in one hand.

"No, not at all," Jones said, shrugging his shoulders and cranking his neck.

Fendru jerked his head from side to side in an effort to free his occiput.

"You were on your cell phone?" said Jones. "What the hell were you thinking?"

Jones alternated glances between the nurse and his camper. The bumper of the nurse's mini-van had slid up and over the bumper of his camper less than a mile from an act of vandalism that could land him in jail and forever derail his career in law career.

"She was on her cell phone while driving. What's the penalty for that, Fendru?" Jones said.

Before Fendru could answer she apologized. "You're right. I shouldn't have. I had a long day and I'm late to my second job, but that's no excuse. Let me look at that. I'm a nurse," she said to Fendru, massaging his shoulders.

Fendru waved her off and wiggled between them to get a close look at the bumpers. "Her car's bumper is caught on your trailer hitch," he said to Jones.

Jones was too upset to look.

"Otherwise, there's was no damage," Fendru said.

Kitty shrugged, displaying impatience but seeking amends. "I'm sorry. What can we do about this? "I really am late for work and if there is no damage." She didn't finish her thought.

Jones took a look. "Let me try something," and he climbed onto the bumper of the camper. He jumped up and down on the bumper, trying to apply enough force to free the two vehicles from each other.

Kitty Dombrovsky was late for work but she wasn't worried that Al would fire her. She had a Hollywood body and an erotic demeanor that made her a top attraction. She didn't have to change clothes from her day job. She parlayed the nurse role with stethoscope to a climax that ended when men who stuffed twenties into her panties and would volunteer to have their pulse taken. She would display them onto a small screen she had rigged for the show as the crowd roared with delight. Ever the lady's man, even in the dim glare of her headlights, Jones couldn't help but notice there was something spicy about her.

"I'm sure this wasn't part of your evening plans," Jones said.

She acknowledged with a demure nod.

"Get up here." Jones motioned for Fendru to join him.

As they jumped up and down on the camper's bumper a black and white came to a stop behind them and turned on its Visibar. A heavy-set man in uniform, about fifty, with red curly hair and a mustache, got out of the car.

"Is there a problem?" asked the officer. Benson was printed on his lapel.

"Got our bumpers connected," Jones said as he stepped down from his camper.

"Everyone okay?" said the officer whose attention had been drawn to the woman with the hour glass figure in the white nurse's outfit.

"We're okay," Jones said.

"No problem, officer," said Kitty Dombrovsky.

"May I see your drivers' licenses?" He said, eyes glued to the woman.

When neither of the men complied, he added, "That's not a request."

After glancing at the nurse's identification, he handed it back, but looking at Jones, whose license was issued in Ohio, he said, "What brings you to Mississippi?"

"Going back to law school," Fendru said. "FSU." He nodded with nervous exuberance.

"Ohio," said the officer, alternating glances between their cars and the two men. "Seems a bit out of the way." He took pictures of Jones' and Fendru's driver licenses with his cell phone before returning them while Fendru fidgeted.

"Anything the matter?" said the officer.

"No, I'm okay," Fendru said, massaging his neck. "Tired, we've been driving all day."

Kitty said to Jones. "I really do have to get to work. "Can you get them apart?"

"Maybe. With Officer Benson's help."

Officer Benson frowned at the suggestion, but acquiesced when the nurse unbuttoned her blouse a notch and flashed her well coifed lashes.

"My goodness, it's hot. That would be so kind of you," she said with a syrupy Mississippi drawl.

Jones and Fendru climbed onto the bumper of the camper. Jones offered his hand to Officer Benson who was twenty-five pounds over the police requirement and one failed fitness test from a desk job. Kitty returned to her car.

"On three," Jones said. "One, two, three."

As Benson got a foot onto the bumper, Kitty backed up to free the camper's trailer hitch from the van's bumper. Simultaneously, the fetid aroma from the open window of the camper's back door came rushing out. Officer Benson, overwhelmed by the stench, slipped forward onto the van and fell onto the ground with a thud.

As deft as a manatee the officer tried to get to his feet. When he fell again his service revolver popped from its holster. He groped the ground in a frantic search for the gun while shielding his eyes from the glare of the van's headlamps.

"Turn off your lights," Benson shouted in absolute panic.

When Kitty turned off the lights Fendru held out his hand. "Looking for this?"

Officer Benson, now on all fours, took a reflexive lunge toward Fendru, then froze and held up his hands. Fendru, having grown up on reruns of NYPD, held the gun by its barrel and held it out for the officer to take.

"It fell out when you hit the ground. Are you okay?" Fendru said, offering to help the officer to his feet.

Benson took the gun and waved him off. As he climbed to his feet, he said, "What the fuck was that?" He fumbled to holster his gun while pointing to the back of the camper. "Smells like something's dead in there."

"Oh, yea. Fish," said Jones. "We didn't have a way to keep it cold."

"Fish? You boys don't look like fishermen."

"You're welcome to look inside," Jones was about to open the camper door.

"No, no. That's alright."

"Officer, may I go?" Kitty asked politely from her driver's seat.

"If it's okay with these gentlemen."

Jones nodded his approval. "Sorry we couldn't have met under different circumstances."

Officer Benson waved her on. "You guys can go, too."

Jones and Fendru said, "Thank you" and left.

By the time they reached Montgomery, Alabama an All-Points Bulletin had been issued for two men in a camper travelling through Mississippi. While they were dumping trash at the Bartholomew Davis home, a security camera was taking pictures of a camper with two men in it, one white and one dark skinned, as it exited the Davis driveway.

That was an hour after the landscaper reported to Mister Davis, who was on a gambling trip to Las Vegas, that someone had scattered stinky old fish in front of the entrance to his home. Bartholomew called the police and gave them access to security camera footage that had captured the license plate of a camper pulling away from his property.

Climate Fact:

Almost one gallon of oil is used to make a pound of beef which makes the cost of your burger as much about oil as it is about meat. Petroleum contributes 25% to the cost of a steak dinner. The space currently utilized for meat and dairy production takes up 1/3 of the habitable land on Earth.

What can you do about it? Buy local foods, eat local foods and eat less beef.

26

The BMW 1200 motorcycle Derk rented was designed to handle off-road trails. Rusting VW vans, abandoned by hippies taking the short route to Burning Man, skulls of coyotes, cattle and armadillos and an assortment of discarded camping equipment were scattered along the craggy route from Winnemucca to Black Rock. Washed out river beds, loose gravel and sharp stones reduced the trek to a crawl at times. Hot, dry, wind driven playa dust filled the air making it difficult to breathe. An occasional gust blinded him even though he wore goggles. The short cut from Winnemucca to Black Rock was as off road as Pluto.

Forty miles out he came upon a cross road. He stopped and wiped the dust from his face shield. It looked no different than the road he was on except for the ruts worn into the terrain. Something flashing in the distance caught his attention. It may only be light reflecting off the rocks or an abandoned vehicle, but he took a long swig from the canteen he had strapped onto his handlebar, checked his compass and headed north.

It was further than he expected, but when the objects came into view, they formed a semi-circle of one and a half story geodesic domes. The glass and white sided, Buckminster Fuller like structures stood out like Stonehenge in this desolate landscape. They were connected to each other by a series of enclosed passageways. In the center was an array of solar panels that moved with the sun's path.

On Mars there is nothing to eat, nothing to drink, the air is ninety-five percent carbon dioxide and the temperature reaches a teeth-clattering two hundred and thirty-five below zero on a sunny day. Life in such a climate is beyond the fringe of man's experience which is what made The Black Rock Desert an ideal location to prepare for the mission to Mars. Derk assumed he had found the NASA training facility.

He stopped at the entrance to the compound surrounded by a chain link fence. A small sign read Advanced Bio-Technology. "Bingo!" His hope of finding Susan Carlton had just received a shot of adrenaline.

He parked outside the gate and killed the engine. The truck he had seen in Winnemucca was being unloaded by two people wearing Space Suits. They were replacing solar panels from the array with the ones in the truck. A rover, like the one he saw in NASA footage of a past Lunar mission, was ferrying cargo from a low rise building to one of the domes.

No one noticed him until he slid open the gate. No one except for Danny DeVito, who popped up seemingly from nowhere. Under any other circumstances the sight of DaVito would have made him smile, even laugh, but this version of DaVito made his heart thump against his ribs. His body stiffened. Coming at him was Hollywood sci-fi technology. Think 3CPO or the Terminator, but it was as human as Ash in the first Alien movie. The only non-human identifier was the stiff, almost comical, nature of its movements, but, after all, it was Danny DaVito and he was singing.

"I am the Walrus, I am the Walrus," with a voice that resembled his former friend and his chiropractor, Doctor Jack. Followed by, "I hear you knocking but you can't come in." It was the Fats Domino's rendition, but with Doctor Jack's voice.

"What the fuck is going on?"

Doctor Jack died five years ago. Why would this robot use his old friend's voice? Dr. Jack was a swashbuckling adventurer that burned the candle at both ends. After folding up his practice due to an injury he studied with a Shaman in Peru and experimented endlessly with Ayahuasca. He spoke broken but passible Spanish, had blue eyes and a smile that always warmed the room. He could hold a tune well enough to be invited to sing with a rock band in Bolivia. As was destined, the drugs and alcohol were too much for his liver. How this package of wires, chips and bolts was able to make the connection between Derk's old friend and him both amused and frightened him. In fact, how did Danny DaVito know anything about Derk Bryan?

When Derk moved, the robot seemed to block his way, while it crooned "Strangers in the Night," in perfect Sinatra form this time. Derk moved the other direction and the bot moved with him. Was it dancing with him or was it about to pull out a ray gun and incinerate him.

"My God." Did DaVito just click his fingers to the music? Derk stopped and so did the bot.

"What is the nature of your visit?" it said, then added a soft shoe shuffle to its act.

"I'm here to see Doctor Susan Carlton."

The robot was unfazed by his answer, shook its head and broke into song with Ray Charles' voice. "Hit the road, Jack. Don't you come back no more, no more. Hit the road, Jack."

Befuddled and humored, Derk joined in, "What you say?"

The bot repeated, "Hit the road, Jack."

Derk followed with, "Old woman, old woman, don't treat me so mean. You're the meanest old woman that I've ever seen."

After the closest thing to a smile Derk had seen on a robot, it turned and shuffled away. After a few steps and a slight hitch in its gate the it changed tunes, "Ain't that a shame. My tears fell like rain." Then it danced his way along the perimeter of the compound until it and the music disappeared.

The founders of this camp apparently had a sense of humor, at least, enough to ease Derk's concern of being ray-gunned. He removed his motorcycle helmet and looped the chin strap over the handle bars. Hoping he had experienced the extent of the camp's security he went in search of Susan Carlton.

There must have been nine or ten domes along with a much larger flat roofed structure. He chose to begin with the last building on his left and work his way around the circle. The buildings were numbered and each had a short stairway leading up to a landing. No doors were visible but there was a lamp and a round box, located about where a door would be, attached to each geodesic structure.

Half way to the first building one of the men in the spacesuits noticed him and pointed to one of the buildings as he held up his hand. Only after he pointed to each finger, as if counting them, did Derk understand he was being directed to Building Five. He assumed that Building Five was for visitors.

On the other side of the circle a rover exited the flat roofed building carrying two people and some plastic boxes in its bed. In their oversized helmets and bulky suits, replete with oxygen backpacks, they looked the pictures on television he saw as a child when Americans walked on the Moon. Now human beings were preparing to go to Mars. Regardless of how foolhardy the idea was, in the face of global warming or maybe because of it, landing people on another planet would be an awesome accomplishment for mankind. He was simultaneously filled with angst and pride.

As the rover disappeared behind Building Three the sun reached its zenith. A steady breeze kicked playa dust into the air. He could not see into the domes and there appeared to be no windows, but he felt exposed, as if he were being watched.

He changed course and headed for Building Three where the rover had gone. He stood in front of what appeared to be a highly sanitary white structure. The outer shell was smooth and almost seamless. He climbed a short flight of stairs. Other than the lamp over his head and the big round button to his right, there was no door. Instinctively he pushed his palm against the button and a door opened. He stepped into a small compartment, half the size of a department store elevator. The door closed behind him. Moments later another door opened, releasing a gush of air. Either it was the sound of oxygen equalizing the pressure between the inner and outer chambers or he had watched too many sci-fi movies.

He stepped into a nursery. Every inch was crammed with containers, conventional and hydroponic, filled with sprouts and illuminated by overhead grow lights suspended upon a system of chains that automatically adjusted to the height of the plants. The roots of Mung beans, alfalfa, radish and wheat grass slowly and silently absorbed the nutrients from the medium. What he saw made sense. They were growing plant-based protein. Alfalfa sprouts contain all eight essential amino acids, the building blocks of protein. The one-way journey to Mars would take nine months, and you can't graze goats in a space capsule. A ready source of protein would be necessary for long distance travel as well as colonization.

Something didn't seem right. The air in most greenhouses was moist and refreshing. Not here.

He heard a movement at the other end of the greenhouse. It was somewhat mechanical but still human. Through the foliage he saw someone approaching.

"Hello!"

"Put that on," she said when she rounded a corner and faced him. She was pointing to a suit with a helmet and an oxygen pack in an open cabinet to his right. She passed him, with a dispassionate look on her face, and attached a tube to the oxygen tank.

"Susan. Doctor Carlton, it's Derk, Derk Bryan." He reached for her.

Boom!

***

"Where am I?" Derk asked himself as he gained consciousness.

It must have been morning, but he wasn't in his bedroom. At home he could tell the time by the slits of light on the floor from the sun sneaking through the blinds. Maybe he was in his hotel room. Another glance told him no. This room was all white and the TV was mounted on the wall.

"Oh no!" He sat up when he saw the handrails on his bed. He was in the hospital again. A middle-aged woman dressed in white entered the room.

He ran his hands up and down his arms, then thrust the sheets off his legs. Everything seemed to be intact. "Whew!" he let out a gigantic breath, but was still waiting for the pain that would signal that something was not normal.

"Well, Mr. Bryan, good to see you're up." The name on her coat was A. Collett, RN. She was a doting, heavy set, coffee complected woman with a long black ponytail. Possibly Pueblo or Navajo.

If he wasn't hurt, why was he here?

"Just a bump on the head," she said as she held a light stick up to his eyes. "Follow my hand across your face." Her nod he took as a positive sign. "As soon the doctor signs the release it looks like you can go home."

"A bump on the head?" he said and rubbed his head until he found what he thought was a sensitive spot. He pushed upon it, harder and harder, but still no discomfort.

"You're okay. We needed to be sure there was no concussion." She said as she drew back the blinds and opened the curtains.

Sunlight exploded into the room and ignited the memory of the blast. He felt something hit him, hence the blow to the head the nurse mentioned, and he rubbed his hand over his head again. No sign of damage.

"Whao!" He remembered seeing a piece of material impale a woman. "Is Doctor Carlton here? Is she okay?"

The nurse seemed puzzled. "Who? You're the only one they brought in."

"They?"

"A couple of guys. You were in a motorcycle accident."

"What?" He shook his head and was about to object but she stuck a thermometer in his mouth. Then she wrapped a blood pressure cuff around his arm.

As the cuff was deflating, she offered some advice, more motherly than medical. "I'm usually not one to get up in someone else's business but is it not kind of dangerous to ride one of those things without a helmet?"

He couldn't protest without spitting out the thermometer so he fidgeted.

"Mr. Bryan, are you always so hyper? You need to relax more," said the nurse.

He spit the thermometer onto the bed. "No one else was admitted with me?"

"Well," she said as she removed the blood pressure cuff, "I don't know every single person who was admitted around the time you came in but they brought you up here alone."

"So, how do you know it was two guys that brought me here?"

"That's what I was told."

He fidgeted with the bedrails. "Can you put these things down?"

"Do you have to use the bathroom?"

"Yes, ma'am."

As soon as she dropped one of the rails he slid out of bed, shielded his eyes from the sun and went to the window. From his second-floor room he could see the parking lot. Two men in blue smocks were removing someone from an ambulance that was backed up to the Emergency Entrance. In the distance was a high desert playa as far as he could see.

"Am I in Winnemucca?" He asked without turning to face her.

"Yes, you are, Mr. Bryan."

"And how do you know my name?" He faced her.

"It's on your chart, sir."

"Where are my belongings?"

"In the drawer." She pointed at a table next to the bed. He knew she was re-evaluating his condition. "Your clothes, what's left of them, are in the closet."

In the drawer he found his wallet, his cellphone and the keys to his rental car. There was no key for the motorcycle. He opened his cell phone but the battery was dead.

"You should get back in bed." Nurse Collette was freshening his bed covers and plumping up his pillow.

"What time is it?" Derk asked.

"Three thirty-five," she said, glancing at her watch.

He punched the ON button of the TV remote and scrolled to CNN. When nothing about the accident was reported, he turned to the other national news networks and then to the local ones. There was nothing about an explosion, and although a motorcycle accident wasn't national news, local television thrived on accident reports. There was nothing.

The nurse finished her perfunctory chores but didn't leave the room. He felt her observing him.

"Where can I get a local newspaper?"

"The gift shop," she said reluctantly.

"And a phone charger?" He asked, holding up his dead cell phone.

"There might be one at the nurse's station," Nurse Collett said as she emerged from the bathroom. "I'll check," she said as she left the room.

"Try this," she said when she returned, but her patient was gone. She craned her neck out the door and looked both ways. At the nurse's station she asked, "Has anyone seen Mr. Bryan in Room 215?"

Heads with nurse's caps shook NO without looking up from their stations. "Call the front desk," Nurse Collett urged.

As the duty nurse talked with security, Derk returned, thumbing through the pages of the Humboldt Sun. On the way to his room Nurse Collett's stern glare followed him. It was the same stern reproval that Mrs. Dunne, his first-grade teacher, used to put students in their places. She required everyone to wait in lines to use the bathroom. One day the call of nature was too great so he cut to the head of the line. When his transgression was reported to Mrs. Dunne she tried to drag him to principal's office. He stood his ground to avoid the principal who had an oft used wooden paddle mounted on the wall of his office. He didn't test Mrs. Dunne again and avoided eye contact with the principal until third grade. Today he folded the newspaper into a roll and passed nurse A. Collett with the best impression of contrition he could muster.

"There's nothing in here," he said, sitting on the edge of the bed.

"About what?" She had entered the room after him.

"A motorcycle accident. If someone gets hit on a motorcycle around her, it would be in the newspaper. Right?" Derk said.

"It's only a weekly," she said, "and you came in yesterday. It comes out on Friday, Mr. Bryan."

"It's Doctor Bryan," he corrected her.

"You a doctor? Then you should know you need to lie down. You took a nasty blow to the head," she said, hovering next to him.

"Excuse me." Derk gently waved her away with his hand. He plugged his cell phone into the new charger and waited for it to boot.

"What are you looking for?" she asked.

"The truth . . . and a woman," he said.

He hit the ON button and the screen on his cell phone lit up just as a television news report gripped their attention.

"There's something fishy about this next story," an attractive brunette in her thirties reported from behind a studio news desk. "Recently we reported that the corporate offices of several large companies had been vandalized by people who dumped trash all over their offices. They left behind pictures of animals, all of which are extinct. If that wasn't odd enough, today the homes of several corporate executives, whose companies manufacture plastic products, were attacked. Maybe not attacked, but unidentified groups left dead fish, including pieces of a Manatee and a shark, at the entrances to their homes."

Close up pictures of the dead fish emaciated by plastic waste appeared on the screen.

"These are pictures of some of the birds and animals that were left at the scene." As the television flashed images of Dodos, Mastodons and Aurochs the reporter continued, "We checked and all of these animals are extinct, and marine scientists tell us that we are losing more each and every day. It seems as if somebody is sending a message to these corporate leaders. In other news . . ."

Derk hit the pause button which froze a picture of a Baiji White Dolphin on the screen. He dialed the number for EPED, the EPA's investigation and enforcement division.

A familiar voice answered, "EPA."

"Joyce, it's Derk. I need you to make a couple of calls."

"I thought you were retired," she jested.

"Special assignment," he said.

"The S.T. Sparks case," she said. "I didn't know that was officially one of our cases."

"If anyone asks, I'm still working on it."

He told her what he needed and hit OFF.

***

Three nurses and a financial officer tried to detour him, but a half an hour later Derk was standing on the curb of the hospital's main entrance with his cell phone to his ear.

"Samson, I'm sorry," Derk said. He had forgotten to call his friend.

"You're going to miss the trip of a lifetime due to a hunch and an obsession?" Samson said.

Derk clenched his forehead in his hand before sliding it through his hair. "More or less," he said when he noticed a BMW 1200 motorcycle parked on the sidewalk.

"What the fuck! Samson, I have to call you back."

"Just tell me it's the woman. Am I right?" Samson said.

"Yes, it's the woman," Derk mumbled and hit OFF.

It was the same Beemer he had ridden to the Advanced Bio-Tech camp, and there wasn't a scratch on it. The key was in the ignition.

He looked in every direction. Was he being watched or was he paranoid? The stone logic of his scientist's head was spinning. He straddled the motorcycle. The shape and feel of the leather under him were pleasantly familiar. He tried to focus upon what else he knew for sure. There was a private camp in the desert that looked like it was on Mars. Doctor Carlton was there on behalf of NASA. And the place was patrolled by a singing robot that looked like Danny DaVito.

What was Doctor Carlton doing there that they didn't want her to talk about? Freak accident or not, someone lied about what happened to him and the injury to Doctor Carlton. He saw a piece of building material enter her body. That was no illusion. He wondered if she is working there under her own volition? Maybe NASA knows something about her and is coercing her? Now he was allowing his imagination or his empathy to creep into his normally rational routine. Samson was so right. It's the woman. Nevertheless, he wanted to know what the hell is going on out there and why are they covering it up?

He had a hunch about what to do next. He returned the rented bike, picked up his rental car and headed for the airport. The call from Joyce would tell him where he was going.

27

Danswirth, more anxious than a mouse in cat's house, was on hands and knees with a magnifying glass when Mrs. Connelly pushed her cleaning cart into the research lab. He was searching for a blood stain or a stray hair that could connect him to Angelina's disappearance. He had cleaned and disinfected every surface several times that fretful night, but his paranoia piqued with the suggestion that he may have been seen.

According to Evan Wycliff, Mrs. Connelly was the only one of the cleaning crew allowed in that lab. Someone in a crew before her had inadvertently thrown away something valuable, new polymers that had taken eleven months and a million dollars to produce. Mrs. Connelly, who was married with grown children, spent her days studying to become a dental lab assistant at the local community college. In the evenings she did the same job she'd done for eighteen years. She cleaned the offices of the Danswirth Enterprises corporate headquarters. She was recently assigned to handle cleaning in the lab because she knew what one should touch and what one should keep her hands off. With her credentials—she would complete her Associates Degree in two months—she commanded a raise with the new assignment. When it was denied until she completed her degree, Danswirth decided to intervene.

"Oh, sorry, Mr. Danswirth. Am I disturbing you?" she said. Her voice reminded him of his wife's sister. She was a full-figured, black woman in her late thirties donned with a white smock and plastic gloves.

"No, not at all. Come right in," he said.

"Did you lose something?" she said.

"Oh no. Dropped something, but I found it." He rose to his feet and hid the magnifying glass in his back pocket. "Don't mind me. Carry on."

He waited for her to empty the waste cans and begin her routine before approaching her.

"Mrs. Connelly, Mr. Wycliff said you saw Miss Rodriguez here a few a weeks ago, just before she disappeared. Have you seen her since then?"

"No, sir."

"Was she alone?"

"No sir. I think you were here."

"Yes, briefly. I was here to see Mr. Wycliff, but he had already left. She told me she was meeting someone later. Do you have any idea who that may have been?"

"No, sir."

"Well, if you remember anything, please let us know," he said. Half way to the door he turned to her. "Mrs. Connelly!" he shouted. She had turned on the floor polisher.

"Yes, sir?" Startled, she turned off the machine.

"I want to thank you. You were part of the crew that cleaned up my office after that big mess last week."

"Just doing my job, sir." She started to turn on the machine again.

"Mrs. Connelly," he said, holding up his hand for her to stop. "I was talking with the director of maintenance and we have an opening for a supervisor. It comes with a raise and a moving bonus."

"That's very kind, sir. What's a moving bonus?" she said.

"Too our Santiago location. We expect our employees to do more and we reward them when they do. We'll help you find a place to live and pay relocation expenses for you and your family," Danswirth said, heaping on the charm.

Her frown suggested she wasn't thrilled with his idea, but he had already considered that reaction. He mentioned Santiago because it would seem infinitely less attractive than Massachusetts which is where he was sending her.

"We'll make sure your husband has a job, too."

She fidgeted, searching for words to say what was written all over her. Her smile alternated between joy and dismay.

"If you don't mind, I'll talk with Mr. Stevenson about it. Thank you so much, Mrs. Connelly, and keep up the good work," he said.

He had already asked Stevenson, the director of maintenance, to arrange for her transfer to the Massachusetts facility. His phone rang as he left the lab.

"Where the fuck have you been?" Danswirth shouted at Marshall Hucklebee.

Climate Fact:

Solving the climate crisis is not a science problem. Nor does it involve complex science solutions. We have known that carbon dioxide (CO2) is a greenhouse gas since the early 1800s.

What can we do about it? Every person, business, institution and governmental entity must make reducing carbon emissions part of every decision.

28

"Samson," Derk said, "Sorry to call so late but I needed to reiterate how sorry I am about missing our trip."

"Derk, you wouldn't have done it unless something very important was taking place and at your age any woman that pays you more than passing attention is going to get priority over me," said Samson which prompted a hardy laugh from each of them.

"I appreciate your understanding. You are a good friend," Derk said.

"You have no idea!"

"Tell me."

"I got us another time slot. The director told me they would be honored to host our visit and said I could contact him as soon as your expedition into the Grand Canyon was completed. He wants to talk with you," said Samson.

"I never made it into the canyon."

"Details." Samson chuckled. "Are you with me or not?"

"You are one clever African!" Derk chuckled.

"So, how's it going?" Samson asked. They used to pal together on archaeological excursions. After a knee replacement Samson settled for vicarious thrills. His interest always piqued when one of Derk's cases involved a woman.

"Samson, how can a woman fall from an airplane, get cut in half by an explosion and brush it off like it was dandruff? Is that possible?"

"Is that what happened? You saw her?"

"I did, Samson, unless she has a double," Derk said.

"You mean a twin?"

"I don't know. I really don't know."

"But, she's okay? Did you talk with her?"

"I woke up in the hospital right after she said, *Put this on.*"

It was a couple of hours to the airport so Derk regurgitated the entire story as he drove. Occasionally he glanced at his watch and wondered why Joyce hadn't returned his call.

"I don't know what to tell you, but finding someone who does household chores, converses in polysyllables and is easy to look at . . . well, that's every man's dream," Samson jested.

"So, I'm not obsessed?" said Derk.

"No more than with that busty FBI agent who seduced you into being her partner at a gay billiards tournament?"

"I think you get off on my romantic misfortunes."

"Huh! The two Mensa queens who wanted to go tag team with you. That's not a misfortune. That's fodder for an over the hill college professor with a leaky prostrate. You're my hero."

"Oh, stop it!" Derk said. "Hold on. I'm getting another call." He fumbled with his phone to switch callers without losing Samson.

"Damn it. Hello."

"Es Eduardo. Is bad time to talk?"

"No. I was talking to a friend."

"Why you want rip up floor? Is perfectly good vinyl," said Eduardo in broken English. He had legally emigrated from Columbia years ago but retained a south of the border accent. He came recommended as one of the best tile installers on the beach.

"Eduardo, there's no such thing as good vinyl. It's an environmental catastrophe."

"But looks like new," Eduardo said.

"It's full of vinyl chloride, the same stuff that burned up in that train derailment in Ohio," Derk said. He knew Eduardo didn't call for a chemistry lesson, but he was a professor, always teaching.

"Es malo?"

"Bad? Not if you can live with cancer," Derk said. What he left out was that in the process of making vinyl flooring mercury is released into the air and falls upon us as acid rain. The principal ingredient in it is vinyl chloride which is toxic and carcinogenic. "It's only in the kitchen. Tile it like we discussed."

"No problemo, boss."

"Eduardo."

"Si."

"Don't let the cat out."

"Madre Santo!" There was panic in his voice. "I am sorry. You didn't tell me about cat."

Derk laughed aloud. "Lo siento, Eduardo. I'm just pulling your chain. I don't have a cat."

"Senior Derk. You bad hombre!"

"So, I've been told."

Derk toggled back to Samson but he was gone. He synced his cell phone to Pandora and turned to a Moody Blues station. Moments later, "Nights in white satin" fueled a memory of a warm summer night's ride on the beach in his old Mustang convertible with Jenny. A day hadn't passed that he didn't miss her, but at this moment he couldn't shake the image of Susan Carlton being impaled by a slice of building material.

29

The call from Joyce resulted in photos of two men in a camper, a name and telephone number in Cincinnati.

"Hello," said a male voice.

"May I speak with Palmer Jones?" Derk said.

"Who's calling?"

"This is Doctor Bryan from the EPA. Your car was seen in Mississippi a couple of days ago and may be involved in a case I'm investigating."

"That's not possible. My car hasn't left the state in months."

"There is a Roadstar RV registered in your name. Plate number . . ." Derk said.

"Oh, my camper. My son has it," Palmer Jones said.

"Is he there?"

"No, he's at school. What's this about?"

"Let me guess: Florida State." A few minutes later Derk had a name and an address in Tallahassee.

***

"Over here, Doctor Bryan," Ardale called out. He was parked outside Arrivals at the Tallahassee airport.

The air was palpable, hot and saturated. While walking from the gate to the baggage claim Derk heard a television announcer report that yesterday had been the hottest day ever recorded on Earth, and today would be no different. "The result," said the announcer, "Over one hundred forest fires are burning throughout the world. People on every continent but Antarctica have been advised not to go outside." As he took a seat next to Ardale the sweat rolling down his chest was a stark reminder that the chaos predicted from global warming had begun.

"Upgraded your ride," Derk said, nodding approvingly of the interior of the all-electric SUV.

"Hoped you'd like it since you paid for it," said Ardale. "Samantha said you were good for it."

Derk shook his head in disbelief but he didn't object. He adjusted the air vents in his direction.

"Do you mind rolling up the windows," Derk said.

"Oh, sorry. Just trying to save the battery," said Ardale.

"The range in this thing is three hundred plus. I think we'll be alright," Derk said. He knew the specs on most of the electric cars as a result of buying one a couple of years ago. After the windows were closed Derk asked, "Do you know anything about Baiji White Dolphins?"

"Baiji Dolphins?" said Ardale.

"You want a real story?" Derk challenged the reporter.

"About dolphins?" Ardale said as they merged into the exit traffic.

"Yes, about these dolphins and what happened to them," Derk said.

"What happened to them?"

"They're all gone. That's what happened to them." Derk was frustrated by the reporter's ignorance. He pointed to a traffic sign ahead of them. "Take two sixty-three south and head for downtown."

"Sorry, I don't know about dead dolphins. Is that really why you called me?"

"Dead as in extinct," Derk pushed his point. "Like saber tooth tigers, Dodos, and Wooly Mammals. Fucking gone, wiped out, and never to return."

Ardale was sitting next to a tenured professor and one of the EPA's top investigators, but as far as Derk could tell he wasn't grasping the significance of Derk's inference.

"I know you report the news, but do you ever read the news?" Derk said.

Ardale's only answer was a slight crook of his neck. As far as Derk could see Ardale was so focused upon his own agenda, so desperate for a story, he wasn't looking at the big picture.

"You're watching a ten-inch TV and everyone else has a big screen," Derk said.

"What are you saying?" Ardale scowled, apparently offended by that remark.

"You are aware that somebody has been dumping trash in the offices, and on the doorsteps, of the honchos of some of the largest companies in the country?" Derk said.

"Sort of. I've been busy."

"I can see that. You got a haircut. No, you shaved." Derk laid open his hands. Ardale had done neither. "Busy. You've been following me around. That's your story."

Ardale was as disheveled as ever. He made a turn that would take them straight to the campus of Florida State University.

"You are my story," Ardale retorted.

"No, I'm not. I'm going to ask you again. Do you want a real story?"

The tension between them was due to Derk's connection with the astronaut, Susan Carlton. Sure, he wanted to distract Ardale, and even though it was based upon a hunch, he invited Ardale to join him because he was sure the reporter would find a way to connect the dots involving Estee Sparks and her friends while Derk investigated the extent of the connection between Susan and NASA and ABT. Derk was also relying upon the notion that Estee would welcome the publicity.

Thus far he was puzzled by the apparent furtiveness of NASA. It was well known that, over the past two decades, its funding had fallen. There had been no urgency to go to the Moon or anywhere.

Going into space and sending up satellites had become commercialized. That was until going to Mars, and possibly establishing a colony on Mars, became fashionable. Now NASA was in full swing and back in the news. The spotlight of negative publicity, however, would be well received by its doubters. Those who were rankled by the enormous cost of such a venture, when there were other demands upon resources and increasing government deficits, would be buoyed by any NASA setback. He had no axe to grind with NASA, but something was going on; something was wrong. He wanted to find out without that bloodhound, Ardale, on his trail.

"Of course I do," Ardale relented.

"Then listen to me. They scattered pictures around of extinct animals, and I think I know who's doing it."

Ardale loosened his grip on the wheel and stroked his lower lip with two fingers, a sign that Ardale was giving it some thought.

"You think I should be asking why?" said Ardale.

Now, we're getting somewhere. It was the first time Derk had seen any joy on Ardale's face.

Climate Fact:

In 2023 the world reached $1.8 trillion in global investments to tackle the transition to clean energy. Unfortunately, $1.1 trillion went into oil and gas investments.

What can we do about it? Put our money in banks that do not loan to fossil fuel companies.

30

Derk Bryan and King Ardale Carver kept alternating glances between the photo and the students exiting the main entrance to the Florida State University law school. The sparsity of traffic suggested things hadn't changed much since Derk's image of law school from his college days. Law students seemed to be locked up in a huge brick dungeon and not allowed to come out until the end of each term. The milieux of archaeology majors may have been barren landscapes and dank, dark caves and sleeping on rocks, but he got to travel to interesting places.

Derk Bryan didn't carry a gun, and he couldn't arrest anyone. He was armed only with the photo of Jones and Fendru dumping dead fish at the front gate of the Bartholemew Davis home. Neither did he wear a uniform that would suggest any official capacity. He was comfortable in jeans, a button-down dress shirt and a ball cap. Ardale, in shorts and a Hawaiian shirt, was distracted by two female students passing on bicycles.

"Pay attention!" Derk elbowed Ardale in the side.

Jones' father told Derk he thought his son was studying environmental law so Derk and Ardale waited for the course on Waterway Rules and Regulations to be dismissed.

"What?"

"There he is," said Derk, making a head gesture in the direction of three young men submerged in conversation as they came from the building. Derk moved diagonally to block their path while motioning for Ardale to slip behind them.

"Excuse me, Kendrick Jones," Derk said, about six feet in front of them. "Derk Bryan, EPA."

Jones veered to his right, but was intercepted by the stranger wearing the Tampa Bay Rays' baseball cap.

"Who are you?" said Jones. The other students closed ranks.

Ardale was only slightly taller than the three future attorneys, but his arms were long enough to straddle a major highway. He herded the three men together.

Derk imprinted his authority upon Jones' buddies. "If none of you are Fendru Peterson Franklin, you can go."

Jones turned around, but Ardale blocked his escape, pinching him between Ardale and his classmates.

"NBA?" Derk acknowledged Ardale's wing span.

"G League." Ardale said proudly.

"Kendrick, we need to talk," Derk said. He motioned for Ardale to relax his grip. "Mr. Davis only wants you to pay for the cleanup, apologize and tell him why the fuck you think dumping dead fish on his lawn would change anything?"

Kendrick's friends back stepped. None of their expressions suggested they knew anything about the extracurricular activities of Fendru or Jones.

Whether it was fear or defiance that Derk saw in Kendrick Jones, the future attorney knew he had been caught. "How did you find me?"

"That was the plan, wasn't it? You were sending a message," Derk said.

"You guys should take off. I'm alright," Kendrick said.

Ardale held his ground until Derk assented. "They don't know anything."

Kendrick Jones feigned a smile and his friends departed. "I'll catch you later," he said.

Derk wasted no time. "Is there a place we can talk?"

Jones led them to a coffee shop inside one of the campus buildings. The walls were decorated with garnet and gold. Derk directed Jones to a table away from the other customers. As he sat down and wiped his forehead with a white hand-kerchief he introduced Jones to Ardale. He didn't mention that Ardale was a reporter. A server approached but Derk waved him off. Students and faculty wandered in, placed orders and wandered out. Of the ten tables, only two were occupied.

"I had a conversation with your father and he told me," Derk said before being interrupted by Jones.

He was nodding his head up and down. "I heard."

"He called you?" Derk said. Jones nodded again. He didn't seem frightened but he was worried. He should be. Criminal charges could derail his path toward a career in jurisprudence.

Derk got to the point. "If you pay for the cleanup, make up a believable story and beg for mercy, the charges will probably be dropped. I don't know what good it will do, but if you volunteer to do some environmental cleanup for one some philanthropic organization, that may help. I may even be able to get the dean to overlook the entire incident," Derk said.

Jones' relief was palpable until the weight of the other shoe fell upon him.

"Was this your or Estee Sparks idea?"

31

Ding. Ding. Ding.

Teddy and Estee were in bed when the doorbell rang. The tempo wasn't obnoxious, but its persistence suggested urgency.

Ding. Ding. Ding.

Reluctantly Estee uncoupled from Teddy. Like two planets drawn to each other by gravitational forces they spent the night at her condo in each other's arms. The last hurricane demolished her beach front cottage so she moved inland to avoid the storm surges. It was modest but the insurance settlement allowed her to pay cash. She couldn't have afforded a mortgage.

"Are you expecting someone?" Teddy said as she slithered through his grasp.

"No," she said.

A small heard of animals moved with her as she strolled into the living room naked. A peek through the blinds revealed two men on her porch. She repelled and almost tripped when she recognized one of them.

"It's the guy from the EPA," she said in a loud whisper as she tiptoed back to the bedroom. Before returning to the bedcovers and Teddy's embrace she pulled down the blinds down tightly.

Teddy sat upright. "We dumped dead fish on somebody's door step, but what does that have to do with the EPA?"

Estee stuttered, "I, I don't know." She paced back and forth.

Teddy held out his hand for her to take.

Knock. Knock. Knock.

She was trapped between Teddy's desire and the inevitability at her doorstep. She squeezed Teddy's hand before pulling away.

"I'll get rid of him," she said and donned a tee shirt and shorts.

On her way to the front door Teddy insisted, "You don't have to answer that you know."

Halfway there she turned around. "You are right," she said and returned to the bedroom.

"Does that thing ever get tired?" she said when she slid into bed.

His confidence was contagious. It felt good to be desired. She was all smiles on the outside, surprised she had been able to keep up with him, but on the inside, she forced a smile to camouflage her concern. As he pulled her close to him her cell phone rang.

"What now?" She reached for the phone on the bedside table and elbowed Teddy's nose.

"Ow!" His reaction almost dumped her out of the bed.

"Sorry," she said and upon recognizing the caller's name, entreated him, "You should probably go."

The urgency of her request didn't immediately impel him. Teddy was reshaping his nose to its original form.

"Seriously, you need to get out of here."

"Hello," she answered with caution.

"Ms. Sparks, this is Doctor Bryan. We need to talk. Please open your door."

"Go out the back," she whispered, waving at Teddy to hurry.

"Ms. Sparks?"

"Sorry, let me turn down the TV." She made a face at Teddy who was hopping on one leg while trying to get into his trousers.

"You can tell Mr. Thromburton to relax. That is his car parked next to yours?" Derk said.

"Who?" she said. When Derk didn't answer she added, "Please give me a moment. I'm dressing."

She closed her eyes and exhaled deeply as her chin drooped to her chest. She counted to five under her breath and readied herself for whatever was coming. She opened the front door as Teddy exited the back.

***

Estee lived in a condominium that was part of a complex of thirty units that partially surrounded the swimming pool. Given the heat-humidity index, Derk expected the pool to be full, but only two people were in the water. The index was so far into the danger zone that Derk's shirt was soaked and his perspiration evaporated upon hitting the concrete. Given the warnings of climate scientists he doubted there would ever be something called normal again.

He tapped his toes on the landing while he waited. The sand crunched under his feet. A gecko appeared on the stoop, sniffed the air and scurried into a pot of echeveria. The doormat spelled *Welcome,* but he doubted it was meant for Ardale and him. Ardale had gone to the rear of the building in case she decided to sneak out the back.

The previous day Kendrick Jones admitted that Kendru and he had dumped the fish at the Davis home. "If the people who know better don't do something, then we're all fucked," Jones confessed.

He claimed that the idea was his, not Estee's. Whether or not it was true Derk considered it an admirable display of chivalry. The law student said nothing about the attack upon the corporate offices, probably because Derk had no photos to confirm his involvement.

Ardale's interest was piqued upon learning that Kendrick Jones' father was a honcho at a corporation that manufactured many of the products that his son was protesting. Derk was now more hopeful that Ardale would follow the breadcrumbs Derk had placed in front of him.

"Wait until you meet Estee Sparks!" Derk said.

***

Estee greeted Derk with a worried glow. In short shorts and a tank tee Estee revealed herself to be leaner and tauter than Derk recalled. She had pulled her red hair into a pony tail and her face was flushed. He could smell the aftermath of sex.

"I didn't expect to see you again, Dr. Bryan. Are you going to be able to help us after all?" she said.

"I'm sorry, but it's about another matter," he said.

"The body I found?"

"No, may I come in?"

The Sparks' home was modestly furnished and featured family photos with boats and fish in them. Moments after entering Ardale escorted a man carrying his shirt and shoes into the living room. Estee's shoulders slumped so low Derk thought he could have skied off them.

Derk said calmly, "If only Kendrick and Fendru could join us."

Derk's experience in these situations told him that Kendrick had kept his word. He felt some remorse that he would be of little help to Kendrick if charges were filed against him. He had promised to put in a good word with the Dean if Kendrick didn't tell Estee Sparks or Theodore Thromburton about their conversation. In Florida, where the governor was banning books and climate change was considered part of a socialist conspiracy, no Florida college president would be allowed to let Kendrick's actions to go unfettered. At least, not based upon the word of an EPA official.

"Well then, I guess you're not here about the whale," Estee said.

"What whale?" Ardale said.

"This is Ardale. What whale?" Derk said.

"The Ricei whale. It was pregnant," she answered. "And who are you again?" She asked Ardale.

Ardale looked askance at Derk.

"An interested party," Derk said.

"A what?" said Teddy.

"This is King Ardale Carver and he's interested in what you have to say," Derk said. "Ardale, I'd like you to meet Simone Teresa Sparks."

Ardale held his out his hand in a polite gesture but couldn't divert his eyes from Estee's body-art. The result was a near miss as their hands skirted each other like two passing jets.

"And I gather this is Theodore Thromburton," said Derk.

Defiant resignation followed but they had been caught. "I'm Theodore Thromburton," said Teddy and held out his hand.

"About what?" Estee said.

"About the whale," Derk lied.

The rise of her brow hinted that she didn't believe him, but she played along.

"It's about time, and I have a lead," she said.

Teddy swallowed as his eyes dilated. He clearly knew nothing about the whale.

"I'm sure Mr. King is very interested in what you have to say," Derk hoped. Neither did he know anything about Estee's whale but Ardale had become mesmerized by her.

Estee took Ardale by the arm and offered him a seat on the couch. "Somebody ran over a Ricei whale with a propellor after it swallowed a beachball full of plastic. The plastic strangled her digestive organs so she and her calf starved to death," Estee said. "I found a piece of . . ." she stopped and feigned a slap to her forehead, "Where are my manners? Can I offer you something to drink."

Ardale allowed the couch to swallow him enough to relax. He stretched his arm over the back of the sofa.

"Yes, ma'am, that would be nice," said Ardale.

Teddy sat in a chair across from him. Derk rubbed a hand across his forehead. Estee Sparks' life was full of more drama than his.

She never stopped talking while she poured the drinks. "There's only fifty of them left; forty-nine now. Over three hundred thousand whales and dolphins are killed every year by stuff that's not supposed to be in the water. Now that's a story. What is the EPA doing about it? Nothing. Nor the Coast Guard." She scowled at Derk.

There was a childish optimism in her that she had retained in spite of suffering some grown up pain. He admired that.

As she offered Ardale a glass of water, she said, "Now who are you again?"

"Mr. Carver is a free-lance reporter. You have something to tell him and he wants to hear it," Derk said.

"About the whales?" Estee persisted.

"No, sweetheart," Teddy said. "We violated the space of some important people and they want to know why?"

Derk nodded and leaned in. These bright young folks, who were going to live the rest of their lives with the consequences of global warming had joined Blue Skies/Clear Waters in protest. He wondered what they would do next.

"Ms. Sparks," said Ardale. His voice resembled James Earl Jones although it wasn't as deep. "According to Doctor Bryan, oil spills and hurricanes have nearly put your family out of business. You think something in the water was responsible for your child's death and that same thing is killing the wildlife. For some reason you decided that dumping trash on the doorsteps of a few CEOs would make them come to their senses. Make them suddenly clean up their act and we could all sing Kumbaya. In case you hadn't noticed, to them and the rest of the Internet addicted world, you look like someone in a circus sideshow or, at least, an ad for a taxidermist. If you don't talk with me before someone from the National Enquirer gets hold of you, your credibility will be shot and your story will be as spoiled as the fish you threw on those lawns. I've been here for less than five minutes, and I don't know much about you, but I'm sure that's not what you want."

Wow, King Ardale Carver, where have you been? Derk tried to swallow his glee.

"By the way, Ms. Sparks and Mr. Thromburton, he can't arrest you. That's not even why we're here," Ardale said.

Estee tried to take a deep breath. "Mr.?"

"Carver, Ma'am, King Carver."

"May I get you anything stronger to drink?"

Climate Fact:

The richest 10% of the world's population is responsible for 50% of the global emissions while the poorest 50% accounts for only 12% of emissions. This imbalance is causing most of the world to be buried in the waste and pollution of a minority of people.

What can you do about it? We must motivate billionaires to invest in climate solutions.

32

Detective Louis Cordoza had been a Houston cop for over twenty-nine years. He had been shot at, stabbed and assaulted so many times he lost count. What he was able to keep track of was the next two hundred and forty-three days. He marked off each of them on his desk calendar. On that last day, before announcing his retirement, he would take his accumulated sick time to recover from a back injury he sustained while chasing a crack dealer down a dark alley behind the Galleria. Alleviating the pain in his sacroiliac would require surgery and six months of recovery.

Today, he was uber distraught. Not only were his back muscles tighter than a sailor's knot, his step-daughter asked him to take her to a clinic in Albuquerque for an abortion. He was bent over a chair to stretch his back when his daughter called. The call irritated him in two ways. First, that his daughter was pregnant with Carlos' seed. His opinion of Carlos was summed up in the nickname Cardoza had given him: Lax. When Carlos realized that the majority of the Texas legislature had decided to practice medicine without a license by prohibiting health care to needy women past six weeks of pregnancy, he was livid.

"And, you're just telling me this!" said Cardoza.

"I just found out," Rose told him, "I'm seven and a half weeks past my period."

Carlos shrugged. "Does Lax know?"

"I'm not going to drop out of college and give up on my dream so I can take care of two children, Carlos and the baby," she told Cordoza.

"Oh, really," Cardoza considered Carlos a slacker and found it a chore to hide his disdain, but this came as a relief. "Where is he now?"

"He's working and, of course, I'm going to make him pay for it," Rose said.

"Tell him if I have to do this, he has to get a vasectomy," Cardoza said.

"Oh, Lou-Dad," Rose's affectionate name for her stepfather. "You're too hard on him. Please take me to Albuquerque."

While oscillating between being a supportive parent and tough love his office phone rang.

"Missing Persons, Cardoza."

"It's my daughter, she's missing," said a frantic caller with a Spanish accent.

"And you are?" said Detective Cardoza.

"Por favor, I mean please. Her name is Angelina Rodriguez and I think someone killed her."

The voice was that of a middle-aged Hispanic woman from, Cardoza guessed, El Salvador. A large contingent of El Salvadorans moved to Houston in the 1980s to flee the war. The U.S. government's clandestine operation to supply arms to the Contras, paid for by cocaine sales, had become the grist of numerous books and movies. Many of these immigrants were illegal aliens and resisted communication with the police for fear of being repatriated.

"Lucinda Rodriguez?" he repeated the name on the caller ID, but the line went dead.

"Quien es?" Cardoza was surprised when the same voice answered when he called back. It was rife with trepidation.

"Mi nombre es Louis Cardoza. Soy de Departamento de Policia de Houston. You just called me. If your daughter is missing, I can help you find her, but I'm going to need a little more information."

He spoke to her in Spanish as calmly as his mood would allow. He had never gotten comfortable with his assignment to Missing Persons. It was a desk job, and he was used to the action. Most of the time lost kids showed up within a few hours at the home of a friend or a family member. There were times that a parent would call in a display of authority, sending a message to the child as to who was in control. Whichever this was he was in no mood to play games.

As soon as he confirmed the name, Angelina Rodriguez, he pulled up her photo and address from the DMV. He was able to massage her daughter's place of work from the mother and that she was dating a very wealthy and powerful man. That was over a month ago. He learned that the mother hadn't spoken with her daughter in over a month. They were used to speaking several times each week. That Lucinda Rodriguez waited an entire month to report her daughter as missing was a signal that Angelina Rodriguez's parents were here illegally. Another complication in his life. At the same time, someone gone for a month always aroused that ominous, hollowing feeling in the pit of his stomach. This time was no different.

Suddenly he recalled that Rose was waiting on his cell phone. By the time he said, "I'm sorry," she was gone.

"Damn, damn, damn!" he said.

Back to Lucinda Rodriguez; her line was dead. He really hated this job.

It wasn't department policy to look for missing children of illegal aliens, but Angelina was no child. She had a degree in engineering and worked for a major company. When he confirmed with Danswirth Enterprises that she had not reported to work in a month, he sent the Missing Persons' report to the National Crime Information Center. The next day he got a call from the Florida Department of Law Enforcement.

33

Danswirth hadn't allowed his disdain for Redding Hastings to become public so his donation to Hastings' "Family Values Council" could not be seen as a tit for tat. The one hundred thousand dollars tithe was more than enough to garner Hastings' support for *GodNet*. After that donation Hastings, with a smugly cheerful disposition, agreed to appear on Reverend Huck's radio program. Danswirth was in his office listening to the broadcast when his secretary notified him that a police detective was waiting to talk with him.

"I'm Detective Louis Cardoza," he said as he pulled his jacket back to reveal the badge on his belt. "According to Evan Wycliff, your own director of research, you were one of the last people to see Angelina Rodriguez alive."

Danswirth stood behind his office desk to greet him. He was aware that this day was inevitable, but he still wasn't prepared for it. Guilt ran up and down his spine.

"Has something happened to her?" Danswirth feigned surprise. He plopped into his seat and motioned for the detective to have a seat.

"When is the last time you saw her?" The detective slid onto the chair, gingerly.

"Angi," Danswirth began but corrected himself, "Ms. Rodriguez was a valuable part of our research team. She's been out for several weeks. We were hoping she would return. How did she die?"

"Does Corrine Connelly work for you?" said the detective.

Oh Shit! He knows about her? He tried not to display the fear that gripped him. "She

may. We have a lot of employees. Why do you ask?" He hoped the detective couldn't hear his heart thumping against his chest. He was suddenly perspiring.

"She's in maintenance," the detective interrupted him. "Mr. Wycliff said she saw you with Ms. Rodriguez outside the lab on," he checked his notes, "the last Thursday of the month."

Danswirth stroked his forehead with one hand and squinted, as if he were trying to recall something. "Possibly, but I don't recall. We're working on something new and I'm there often. How did she die?" He took a deep breath.

The detective didn't answer him. He had bent over to touch each foot with the opposite hand. When he sat upright, he said, "Bad back. Is she here now?"

"Who?" Danswirth said.

"Mrs. Connelly."

"Oh. I'll ask my secretary." Danswirth hit a button on his telephone and said, "Is Corrine Connelly here today?"

"Don't you remember? You sent her," his secretary said before Danswirth turned off the speaker function. "I'll wait."

Cardoza must have heard that, but he said nothing. The chatter on the radio filled the silence. Redding Hastings was twisting the idea of family values in ways that discriminated against gays, women and non-Christians in general.

"What do you think about that guy?" Danswirth said.

The detective was doing truck rotations in his chair. "Who?"

Danswirth wanted to say, "That pompous whack-job," but smiled and said, "Redding Hastings of the Family Values Council."

"Name sounds familiar but I can't place him," said Cardoza.

Danswirth's secretary entered and placed a note on his desk. Danswirth put down the telephone and lied. "She must have been mistaken about seeing me."

"Why's that?" said Cardoza, straightening up.

"Mrs. Connelly works in our Massachusetts office."

"Really," the detective said, as sober a church mouse. "Do you have her number?"

"That's personal, but I can give you the number to our plant manager." He reached for the telephone again. "I'll have my secretary give it to you. You never said what happened to Miss Rodriguez."

Cardoza stood and cranked his neck. His took a business card from the holder on Danswirth's desk.

"No, I didn't."

Danswirth stood up. "But something did happen to her? You said she was dead."

"No, I did not. Do you know anyone who would want to harm her?" The detective waited for an answer.

The pause was long enough that Danswirth fidgeted. "Why, no. For God sakes, no!"

"This the best number to reach you," asked Cardoza while pinching Danswirth's business card between his thumb and forefinger.

"Yes, sir, Detective," said Danswirth, deflated.

The Detective gave his card to the CEO, shrugged his shoulders and cranked his neck to one side. When he left the oxygen in the room left with him.

As soon as his door closed Danswirth called Roger McCadden, the manager of his Massachusetts location and had him assign Corrine Connelly to their Mumbai facility.

"Double her salary and fly her first class!" Danswirth said.

Climate Fact:

Most large corporations advertise their commitments to reducing greenhouse gases but few are actually doing it. This is called Greenwashing.

What can you do about it? Require that companies report their emissions. More important, you can require them to report their carbon reduction goals and their success in meeting them in their annual reports just like they report financial results.

34

"Do you believe her?" Derk tested Ardale on their way to the airport in Tallahassee. They had spent the past hour listening to Estee Sparks while Teddy sat, mouth agape, hearing a story that had him in tears.

"You're the expert. What about you?" said Ardale.

"In regard to the Ricei whale, I'm sure that's true. She's lived here all her life so she should know. The North Atlantic Right Whale is suffering the same fate."

"I mean about her child?"

"You're the reporter and it's your job to figure that one out."

"Come on, Professor. It's an impelling story, but only if it's true."

Ardale was hard to convince but that also made him a credible journalist. Derk respected anyone who followed the facts. He hoped that Estee Sparks trusted Ardale enough to continue their conversation.

"Plastic breaks down into miniscule particles. It's choking the ocean," Derk began to say as if he were facing a lecture hall full of students. He took a breath and resumed speaking in a less professorial tone, "It's polluting everything. Half the tap water in the country is contaminated. It's destroying the ocean's ability to absorb greenhouse gases. Did it kill her child? Maybe, probably, but it's hard to prove. Does it matter?"

Ardale shrugged. "What do you mean?"

"I read your piece comparing Christian Nationalists to the Taliban. It was a bold leap," Derk said.

Ardale swerved to pass a car. They were hurrying to make a flight back to Tampa. A late summer storm was in the Gulf, and flights into Tampa Bay would be delayed if the storm stayed on its present course.

"This is different," said Ardale. "The Taliban committed war crimes, abused women and bullied an entire society. It wasn't difficult to go from A to B to C."

"Religious zealots. You charted their path to theocracy and the dissolution of democracy. Your suggestion that the religious fanatics in this country were leading to the breakdown of democracy was impelling. You have an opportunity to put a face on the human tragedy caused by climate change." said Derk. "Too many people don't trust scientists. You're a reporter. You can make it happen."

Ardale laughed heartily. "What are you talking about? No one trusts reporters."

"I think she trusted you," Derk said.

"Maybe, but she sure isn't happy with the EPA." Ardale laughed.

"She agreed to talk with you again. Right?"

"I guess so. A lot of people do when I'm in their face. Then they don't answer the phone."

"Well, stay with it and please keep me in the loop," Derk said and handed Ardale a prepaid Visa card he had planned upon using in France.

"What's this?"

"Pay me back when you can," Derk said.

"No, I can't do that," Ardale said with a rise of one eyebrow but didn't complete his thought. He let out a deep breath and kept the card.

"Just follow her story and see where it goes," Derk said.

***

"Huh! I hope your friend takes a credit card," Derk quipped when Ardale asked for fifty dollars to reimburse a friend for paying his cab fare to the airport.

"Right!" said Ardale.

"What's wrong with your car?"

King Carver's aging convertible was parked in the driveway of an apartment building south of Kennedy in Tampa.

"It's old," Ardale retorted when he got out of Derk's car.

Derk dropped a hundred bucks into Ardale's hand. "Keep me posted."

"Will do."

"Hey, one more thing," Derk said as Ardale walked away. Ardale torqued his head to one side without turning around.

"Get a haircut."

On the ride home Derk was feeling satisfied with himself. He was sure he had pointed Ardale in the direction of a meaningful story. He was free to find out what was going on at Black Rock, what NASA was up to and who is Susan Carlton. And, he felt sorry Estee Sparks. To Estee Sparks and her friends, the EPA is the government. If the Environmental Protection Agency couldn't or wouldn't do anything to protect her from the abuse she has suffered, what should she do? If people like Simone Teresa Sparks lose hope and stop trying, what chance does the world have? She should know that she isn't alone. He knew what it felt like to be alone.

It was past midnight when Derk steered his quiet, electric car into his Pass-a-grille garage. Before carrying his bags upstairs, he walked to the street to breathe the night air. A thick breeze from the southwest was free of the distinctive daytime aroma with its hint of iodine, sunscreen and grilled fish. The sky was lit by a million tingling orbs so far away they resembled fireflies. He did a one-eighty and randomly picked one star. His physicist palls tell him they are virtually certain that circling around one of those stars is a planet that can sustain life. "Is this the one?" He hopes. He stares into the sky waiting for a twinkle as if someone out there was wishing him 'goodnight.' He wanted to believe that the quest for somethings is universal like knowledge, peace and love.

He faced his own house. It was one of four homes with common walls within a small community of condos that a college professor/parttime government employee could afford. Those who spent the summers here still had day jobs and were deep into REM sleep. The only light came from the street lamps and a half-moon passing between the only two clouds above him. He listened for the tide. Sometimes he could hear it in the dead of the night after the bars closed and the beach traffic slowed to a drizzle. Tonight, he couldn't tell whether he actually heard the waves gushing onto the shore or that he was imagining them. But it must be high tide because its *swish* lingered in the air longer than normally. Home had always been a refuge, so he never gave a second thought to climbing those stairs and entering his home at night . . . until Jenny died.

The darkness conjured a melancholia that, lately, had been creeping up on him. He sensed it was approaching time to move on, and he wondered where he would be going . . . and what he would do with all of the memories.

He dropped his bags in the bedroom and collected the mail. It included a package that surprised him because he hadn't ordered anything. He popped the cap off a new craft beer he had discovered at a local market and took a seat at the bar in his kitchen. He separated the mail into piles according to which were bills and what could be recycled. Then he took the brown paper off the package.

"Oh Samson, you didn't!" Derk said as if his friend were standing next to him.

"You can't go another day without reading this if you want to live long and leave a small carbon footprint," Samson told him.

Tired but intrigued he moved to the couch, took a sip of his beer and opened the book. The summary confirmed what he already knew. A diet with foods containing concentrated nutrients, the kind that comprise the diets of those in Blue Zones, can extend one's life. It wasn't an irony that a similar kind of diet would be essential for survival on Mars. Susan was going to Mars to plant gardens. For a brief moment he felt guilty for wanting her to stay.

He put the book on his lap and thought about what the nurse in the hospital had said, "You were the only one they brought up to my ward all night."

He took a long swig of the beer and replayed his encounter with the woman in the greenhouse. She looked like Susan but how could he be sure of that? Could it have been a sister or a twin? He recalled Samson's words, ". . . human but perfect in every way."

Like a robot. No way! The thought was repelling. His gut tightened. His head spun. He was on the verge of puking.

He held his head and breathed deeply. Then again and again and again. That's not possible. I would know. Any man would know.

The breathing helped to calm himself. He laid his head on the couch. After a few minutes, when the nausea had dissipated, he recreated the wont in her eyes, the hunger in her embrace and the moment he entered her. It was different in a way he could not describe, but it was beautiful. It was more real than anything he had ever experienced. But real? How could he be sure?

He returned to the images in his head. There was foreplay, but it was mostly a frenzied lust of life. They had saved each other. She took him into her slowly, at first, and then deeper and deeper. As he reached a rhythm, she synced her body with his. As he moved, she moved. It seemed as if she could go forever while he occasionally stopped to resuscitate himself. She urged him on. Their bodies became one; clinging to each other like magnets. Moments after his climax she followed. A euphoria, like none before, washed over him. This was new, a higher high. No machine could do that!

He savored the rest of his Belgium import and realized his larger fear—the one that would obliterate the possibility of love. Certainly, the kind of love that he knew. Shared by two warm, cogent, energetic and fallible people. He had slept with her. No machine could duplicate what he felt. Then again, he had seen Danny DaVito doing Ray Charels, Sinatra and Fats Domino followed by a soft shoe routine. A robot couldn't do that, but it did.

He did his normal pre-bed routine and tried to put his thoughts, any thoughts into hibernation before settling under 600 count Percale. It was a luxury Jenny and he were happy to indulge. He needed uninterrupted sleep.

That was not to happen. He replayed in slow-motion each frame of the encounter with the woman is the greenhouse. It began with the door. He pushed on it and it opened. Then the air hatch. Once inside the colors were vivid greens and purples. The air was pure. He retraced his movement. Wait! He heard something in the back of the greenhouse. Someone was approaching. He saw only parts of her clothing and a partially obstructed side of her face. Then, there she was. Susan Carlton was standing in front of him. Boom!

When the dream came back, he tried to resurrect her voice. He fast forwarded the tape in his head to the moment she spoke. He knew the voice. It was Susan's voice but something was missing. Then, Boom!

He focused upon the instant she looked at him. She recognized him. He was sure of that. She never paused or showed any doubt. "Put this on." It was the Susan's voice. He would never forget her voice. Boom!

As he was drifting into a profoundly needed sleep The William Tell Overture played on his cell phone. He had yet to replace it as he once promised Jenny. The Lone Ranger was the good guy. The number was familiar. He answered but said nothing.

"Doctor Bryan," said the caller. When Derk said nothing, the caller repeated, "Doctor Bryan."

"Do you know what time it is?" Derk said. Of course he did, but, if this was Ardale, his attempt to distract him had failed.

"Late, I guess," said Ardale, without a hint of guilt.

"Can it wait?"

"Jones and Fendru were arrested."

"What?"

"Not long after we left them."

Derk bristled just loud enough for Ardale to hear him. Then he said aloud, "I'm amazed we got there before the cops. How'd you find out?"

"Estee. She called me. She doesn't want to do the story. She's as tight as Nun's . . ." He didn't finish the sentence. "Sorry."

Derk knew what she feared. What led him to her were the pictures left at each scene. The cops were smart. They would piece it together if they hadn't already sweated it out of the two law students in custody.

"Maybe you can subtly convince her that talking with you is in her best interest."

"What do have in mind, Doctor?"

"It's Derk. Call me Derk."

"Yes, Doctor."

Surprised that he was now treating Ardale with renewed respect, he shared his idea with him.

"Ask her about the pictures left by Jones and Fendru? Tell her you noticed they were identical to those left at the corporate offices. Then," he hesitated, searching for the appropriate word, "somehow note the resemblance to her tats," Derk said.

"You think she was one of those who raided those corporate offices?" Ardale asked.

"Let's find out, and Ardale," Derk waited until Ardale assured him he was listening. "Be gentle with Estee."

"Of course, Doctor. I mean Derk. You like her?"

"She's been through a lot. Don't make it worse for her just to get a story."

"Understood. There's a soft heart under that diploma."

He couldn't arrest anyone. He didn't carry a gun. He didn't even have a badge. A man in his position could, however, be responsible for putting men behind bars. As far as he was concerned huge fines were not enough because the victims were seldom made whole. He felt an obligation to help them whenever he could.

"Goodnight, Ardale. I'm going back to sleep."

35

After a night of drinks, dinner and conversation with Lester, the loquacious bartender at the Longhorn Saloon, Derk Bryan waited in the parking lot of Advanced Bio-Technology.

This trip he flew into Reno and took a rental to Winnemucca. The next day he talked with people at the Chamber of Commerce and the library to get some sense of ABT's place in the community. Not a lot was known. Research, some said, but everything is secretive.

"My friend, they're training spacemen out there," Lester leaned over and said in a hushed tone.

The fiftyish man with a habit of referring to everyone as *my friend*, added, in a condescending manner, "ABT runs a research facility just outside of town, but those folks don't come in here." He went back to stacking beer mugs on the rack over his head.

"Why's that?" Derk asked.

Lester leaned over the bar and spoke just above a whisper, "They're so hush hush. Can't talk with you about anything, my friend. Can't get the time of day out of them. What do you think of that?"

"Tell me," Derk emulated the whispery tone.

"Frankenstein stuff."

"I thought they did crop research."

"Yea, that's what they say. On account of global warming . . . if you believe in that sort of thing." The barkeep dismissed the subject with a hand gesture and resumed his duties. Before Derk could respond the barkeep turned to him and said, "Been here all my life and haven't seen a flood or a hurricane. Can I get you a refill, my friend?"

"Not yet. What do you mean by Frankenstein?"

"Yea, what do they call it?" Lester pinched his lower lip with two fingers as he searched for the words. "Genitally modified seeds. That's it." He seemed proud of himself for remembering that. "They get loose and the whole food supply goes zombie. Then it's just a matter of time."

Lester probably meant to say *genetically* but what did that matter? Derk learned long ago not to get into a debate about zombies with a moron.

He decided to be polite. "Time for what?"

"Before we all turn into zombies," said Lester, baffled that Derk hadn't grasp such an obvious evolution.

"No shit! And it's happening out there at AB . . .?" Derk didn't finish the word." "Wow, how do you live with that every day." He leaned toward Lester.

When Lester came close enough for Derk to breath on him, Derk whispered, "It's probably already in the beer, but I won't tell anybody else. Bad for business. Could I have refill?"

Lester back pedaled with trepidation. He pulled a clean glass from his stash behind the bar and poured a fresh draft well short of the top. He placed it on the bar in front of Derk with the dexterity of a surgeon being careful not to allow a single drop to slosh out.

When Derk said, "Do you mind topping that off," Lester stared at him as if he were the devil incarnate and ran from the bar. Derk chugged half of it and laid a twenty on the counter.

✳✳✳

Derk watched as ABT's staff arrived in an assortment of Jeeps and four-wheel drives.

He had entered by the delivery road, one of two entrances, and circled the building before positioning his himself with a view of the entrance. The facility was modern, minimally landscaped as appropriate for its environs, and circumscribed by a paved parking lot. A blood orange sun was rising in the east and a fine dust swirled in the high desert air. It was already ninety-eight degrees so he had the air conditioning going full tilt. Unlike his electric car, he hoped the gas fired rental didn't overheat. To the uninitiated he would say, "Range anxiety is an emotion shared only by the inexperienced."

As Lester had said, the ABT plant was in the Black Rock Desert on the outskirts of Lovelock, about half way between Reno and Winnemucca. This facility had a different vibe from the one north of here where he had seen Susan Carlton. Security cameras were visible but he had seen neither people in spacesuits or singing robots.

To overcome the awkwardness of a cold call he asked Joyce to set up an appointment for him. "Call it *a get acquainted visit,*" he said.

"What if he asks for the real reason you're there?" Joyce said.

"Their plant is on property that abuts property under the auspices of the Bureau of Land Management. They're doing crop research next to BML managed land. That's like a national park, and BLM wants to dismiss any concerns about potential contamination from genetically engineered seeds."

"That's really creative, even for you, Derk Bryan," Joyce said. "And if that doesn't work?"

"Just tell them I'm the new guy," Derk said. "Figure out something."

"You know it's a private company, and they don't have to let you in without a court order," Joyce said. Joyce joined the EPA not long after Derk. She knew proper protocol.

"There are hundreds of cases of the havoc caused by the invasion of non-native species of animals and plants to an environment lacking the natural predators necessary to balance the impact. Kudzu and pythons are prime examples. Besides, they're working on a government contract," he said. "Do something. Please."

"Enough, but I still have to clear it with Sahith."

"No, you don't," Derk insisted.

"Okay," she said. "I'll take care of it. How are you feeling?"

"Every day vertical is a good day," he said, hit End and took a seat at the bar . . . and thus, his introduction to Lester.

As the sun creeped above the horizon, it revealed a few red rocky crags in the distance that put emphasis upon the severity of the barren landscape surrounding him. ABT is here in this exact location because this place mimics, however marginally, the challenges on Mars.

The reality of that fact was a gut punch to his optimistic side. He could not imagine living in a world without trees and grass and tulips and rabbits and Cocker Spaniels. What was becoming clearer to him was sobering. There are enough politically connected people in this country that think the ecological crisis is of sufficient threat that they're willing to finance the development of a fantastically hostile planet from the ground up—like Hollywood revealed in The Wrath of Khan, part of the Start Trek series.

The light, bouncing from a couple of Jeeps, aroused his attention as they entered the grounds. Son after, SUVs, jeeps and every type of four by four entered in a steady stream. It was approaching eight a.m. and he would enter with the work day crowd.

Fortunately, the dress at ABT was casual and his jeans and pin striped shirt fit with those beginning their day jobs. There was no one with two noses, an extra ear or any extra-human anomaly to ally Lester's impressions of the ABT staff, but he was still nervous. During his only two interactions with Susan Carlton, he had nearly drowned and been blown up. Someone with better self-preservation instincts would have given up, but a voice, like a tune that got into his head and wouldn't go away, kept telling him that ABT held the answers. Thus far, his stubborn determination had overcome the prospect of another "Boom," but he sensed trouble was lurching behind each door. That fear, however, was overcome by his determination to connect with Susan Carlton. Follow the money had always been a good rule of thumb, and ABT paid for her Susan's trip to the Grand Canyon. Why would they do that? No water has been discovered on the surface of Mars.

He stopped by the sign above the door read, *Employee Entrance.* People were entering with an I.D. Card or oral recognition. He had neither.

He turned in search of another entrance. Someone recognized his dilemma and pointed in the opposite direction. He feigned a tip of his hat in confirmation and offered a thankful smile as he passed the fortyish gentleman with premature graying.

So good, so far. No one had intercepted him. When he came to the door with the name, Advanced Bio-Technology, labeled above it, he hoped he had reached the main entrance. It was less than welcoming, being made of solid metal, with no glass, and locked, which he found, as he turned the knob.

To the right of the door was a glass screen about the size of a hand and an intercom with the message: *Push here to speak.* At the bottom of the glass screen were instructions: *Place right hand flat against the glass and wait for the beep.*

He placed his hand against the screen, but nothing happened. He spread his fingers and pressed his palm firmly against the glass. Nothing. A red alert appeared upon the screen and a voice declared: *Entry denied.* He hit the intercom button. In a nano-second, a female voice answered, "Welcome to Advanced Bio-tech, Doctor Bryan," and the door opened. Facial recognition. Joyce must have forwarded his mug shot.

Inside was a maze of glass cubicles and some offices but mostly a series of growing rooms: each one was its own little laboratory. They were of differing sizes, but each featured a different fauna. What was common to all: greens and root crops but no soil. Some had nutrient beds. They were growing every imaginable crop hydroponically without the earthy aroma of humous and, he imagined, without the use of pesticides.

Another revelation imprinted itself upon him. He had grown up among fertile farms, hiked Michigan pine forests and California sequoias. He had bathed in the mist of a Yosemite waterfall and taken evening walks on moonlit beaches. The people working here have accepted a fate that we either can't or won't adapt to our changing world in time to avoid the disaster.

He was perusing a plant layout posted on the wall when a bespectacled woman of fifty in a white lab coat approached him. He held out his hand.

"So nice to meet you, Doctor Bryan," she said but didn't extend her hand. He hoped it was because she was wearing latex gloves.

"Thank you for seeing me. I was afraid Joyce didn't get hold of you," he said.

The question mark on her face indicated she had no idea who Joyce was.

"Sahith Caldwell's office, EPA?" He said.

"Oh, yes," she said. "How can I help you?" His presence seemed to be an inconvenience to her.

"I've been assigned to your case."

"Case? Is there a problem?"

"None that I know. Mostly, this is an introduction."

"Introduction?"

"You know, you're doing food research, GMO stuff . . ."

She cut him off, "I thought that was the FDA's department."

He had no idea who she was or her level of authority, but she was the only one standing in front of him. "Your facility is next to a BLM tract and you have a government contract. With NASA. Am I correct?"

"I guess. You should know."

He did a one-eighty which gained him a quick view of the rooms in that part of the building. Grow rooms as far as he could determine. Down a long hall were connecting corridors. Another woman dressed in white emerged from one of them and walked in the opposite direction.

He put on a happy face. "How about a tour?"

At that moment a younger man of Asian descent appeared wearing a long white lab coat over a shirt and tie. A closely cropped goatee and a scar above his right eye were memorable features. His voice was condescending.

"That's okay, Helen. I'll take care of Mr. Bryan," he said.

"We weren't expecting you. Helen was wrong about that. What can I do for you?"

"Derk Bryan, EPA." He offered his hand again but was denied. Along with a memorable "Boom" he added arrogance and bad manners to his first impressions.

"Doctor Suzuki," was the terse retort. "Inside the building we discourage skin to skin contact. What brings the EPA way out here?"

"As I was explaining to," he began and pointed to Helen who was walking away from them, "I'm new and I came to introduce myself."

"Thank you, Mr. Bryan. Is there anything else?"

"Doctor," Derk said.

"Yes?" said Suzuki.

"It's Doctor Bryan."

"Of course, sorry," said Suzuki but he didn't sound sincere.

"Your associate was about to give me a tour. Will you be my guide?"

Suzuki glanced at his watch. "Is there anything specific I can show you that's not off limits?"

"Off limits?"

"Yes, we do proprietary research here. For clients' eyes only."

"You do that research adjacent to government managed land and under a government contract," Derk said.

"We were audited last month."

Audited, what's he talking about? "I'm with the EPA, not the treasury." He glanced up and down the hallway. "Is there a men's room I can use?"

With reluctance Suzuki pointed to a sign above the corridor to his left.

"Can you excuse me?" Derk said and headed down an antiseptically maintained hallway to the restroom.

He passed grow rooms on either side of the hallway. Each had a large glass window that allowed a view of the ongoing experiments. Beds of common vegetables and grains protruded from different growing media. Most of the crops looked familiar, but he knew they were probably strains designed to survive in the harsh conditions brought about by global warming or something that would grow on other worlds.

He turned the corner at the Restroom sign. There she was. Tending to some irrigation equipment in the first room on the left was Susan Carlton dressed in white from head to toe including cap and boots. He stood at the glass and waved long enough to distract her attention. She glanced at him and looked away.

"Susan, Susan!" he said but she couldn't hear him through the glass. He was sure she recognized him.

He went to the door but there was no handle. The pad on wall contained the same kind of screen as he saw at the entrance. Hand print or facial identification it appeared was necessary to gain entry.

He stood in front of the window and banged on it while he called out her name again. "Susan! Susan!"

After several knocks she looked up again, seemed to study him and then went on with her business. She carried no outward signs of injury.

He retraced his steps at a brisk pace. As he turned the corner, he collided with Doctor Suzuki, knocking his glasses cockeyed on his head.

"Sorry," said Derk.

"You can't just wander around here," Suzuki said while he rubbed his forehead and adjusted his glasses.

"I want to speak with Doctor Carlton. Now!"

He turned and retraced his steps. Suzuki hurried to stop him.

"Wait, Doctor Bryan. You can't . . ." Suzuki grabbed him by one arm.

Derk stood on his toes in front of the window where he had seen Susan Carlton. "Where is she?"

"Where is who?" said Suzuki, trying to place himself between Derk and the glass.

"Doctor Susan Carlton. I just saw her." Derk went to the door. "Let me in. Let me in."

Suzuki shook his head. "I don't know Susan Carlton. Doctor Felton runs this lab." He went to the intercom and pushed the button. "Wendy, come up front."

A dark-haired woman dressed in lab white acknowledged Doctor Suzuki and walked to the front of the room. She was holding a pair of stainless-steel tongs. Only a sheet of high-tensile strength glass separated them. The resemblance to Susan Carlton was stunning. Doctor Suzuki went to the intercom again.

"Wendy, say hello to Doctor Bryan."

"Good morning, Doctor Bryan."

The voice was recognizable. It sounded like Susan Carlton, but he was no longer sure.

"Hello, Wendy, I'm Derk Bryan. Have we met before?"

"I would remember that. I have 100% recall. No, we have not met, Doctor Derk Bryan."

Climate Fact:

The four largest banks in the United States loan over one trillion dollars per year for extraction of fossil fuels each year. If you have over one hundred thousand dollars on deposit with one of those banks, it is producing m ore carbon than the flying, cooking, heating, cooling and driving that the average American does in a year.

What you can do about it? This one's a no-brainer. Keep your money elsewhere.

36

"Where the hell are they?" Danswirth shouted to Dorothea, the maid, as he looked at his watch for the fourth time in the past five minutes. He was pacing back and forth in the atrium of his mansion southeast of Houston.

Danswirth was sure that Detective Cardoza, bad back and all, would be back. He was going to find the evidence that would link him to Angelina Rodriguez.

"I don't know. Maybe you should call them," said Dorothea in a huff as she descended the stairway carrying a travel bag.

"You are more territorial than a Siamese cat," Danswirth said. Tending to the Danswirth house was her domain, but he needed outside help for this task. He couldn't tell her why.

"But Mrs. Danswirth," she protested.

"Whatever Mrs. Danswirth said is not relevant now. Wouldn't you say?"

His wife had retreated into a coma not long after threatening him with the evidence that could put him away for a long time.

"She needs me now more than ever."

"She has help, and the time off will do you good. You've earned it. Do you have any idea what Mrs. Danswirth did with that bag of clothes you found?"

Dorothea had been taking care of their home for ten years. She practically lived there. She had no children, and her only family member was in Nicaragua. At least, she used to be. It had been three years since Dorothea last saw her niece. He paid for Dorothea's trip to Managua to attend her sister's funeral after she succumbed to cancer. After that her niece ran away with some suave gringo to wait tables at the beach in a Panamanian cantina.

"What am I going to do with a week all by myself?"

He didn't really care. He was desperate to find that blood-stained dress. But he put donned an empathetic attitude.

"You'll be fine," he empathized with a toothy grin and a pat on her shoulder. "Do you recall the bag of clothes?"

"You can't trust all those strangers in your home, Senior Danswirth. They will steal until you can't see anymore."

She made him laugh. "You mean they will steal me blind."

"Lo que," she mumbled and tossed up her hand.

Except for the nurse, who came during the day, he gave the rest of the housekeeping staff the week off, too. He wanted no one here when Acme Cleaning Service located the bag he sought. It was ten minutes after nine. Acme was only ten minutes late, but it was enough to curd the cream in his morning coffee.

"Es no necessito. Es no necessito," Dorothea kept saying.

It wasn't necessary. There was no indication from any of her doctors that anything in the home was causing her to remain in a coma, but Danswirth was insistent.

"We need to be sure that there is nothing in this house, be it a chemical, a toxin or a foul odor, that repels her to this state of unconsciousness," he told Dorothea. "It is the least we can do for Mrs. Danswirth. Don't you agree?"

His instructions to Melacai Hernandez, the Acme manager, had been simple, "I want every room in this house, every cabinet, every drawer, every nook and every cranny cleaned and disinfected. If you find anything out of the ordinary, wrap it up and bring it to my attention . . . el pronto." He met with her one hour after Cardoza left his office.

Dorothea was a proud woman. She dropped her suitcase in the middle of the Great Room with resignation. "Lo siento."

Danswirth usually became upset when any of the staff spoke Spanish in his house. This morning, he said nothing. He knew

Dorothea was sorry for his wife's condition and the toll it had taken upon the family.

"Let me help you with your bag." He picked up Dorothea's suitcase as the doorbell rang.

"I'll get it," Dorothea said.

"Es mi Uber," she said upon returning. "I sent the cleaners to the back door."

Ten minutes after Dorothea departed the house was filled with the sounds of vacuums and the chatter of Spanish speaking women.

When Melacai directed her crew to start on the second floor Danswirth interrupted her.

"Un momento," he said and took her by the hand to the kitchen. In a combination of English and Spanish he told her, "My wife is sleeping but you can't wake her."

"No, no!" She waved her hands and protested. "No can do."

"No muerta. Durmiente. Sleeping pills," he said. "It's okay." What is it with these fucking superstitions he thought, but Melacai was not convinced.

He took five freshly minted one-hundred-dollar bills from his wallet and held them in front of Melacai. "Mi esposa, she fell on her head and it knocked her out."

Melacai bristled, still shaking her head.

"Hear me," he said, waving the cash like a red flag in front of a bull. "She cut herself when she fell down. Her clothes were put in a bag along with a necklace. This happened at the hospital and we can't find them. The necklace was important, muy importante. If you find it, please bring it to me immediately. Por favor." He handed her the five hundred dollars. "Divide this among your staff as you see fit."

She stashed the bills in her bra and stomped away.

"Gracias," he said, warily.

37

Derk was seated at the bar in the Reno airport wondering why had he allowed Samson to convince him give up read meat. The guy next to him hadn't been swayed by the people in the Blue Zones or the United Nations guide to a, "Diet for a Sustainable Planet." He was about to clamp down on a Montana sized Bison burger with so much Roquefort on it the cheese melted over the edge of the sandwich. The Bison burger, Derk knew, is leaner and lower in cholesterol than beef and takes much less energy to produce, but he moved over a couple of seats to reduce the temptation. He opened the menu to salads and opted for a piece of fresh water trout over chopped greens. As he waited for his order to arrive, he called Samson.

"Professor, I'm sitting in front of bowl of farrow, olives and prawns. This better be good," said Samson.

Derk glanced at his watch. It was dinner time in Nigeria.

"I saw her again," said Derk.

"The astronaut?"

"Yes."

"You talked with her? She's okay? I mean she's not split in half?"

"She looked directly at me and said she didn't know me," Derk said.

"Really!" Samson asked.

"I was at a crop research facility for ABT, Advanced Bio-Technology. Ever heard of them?"

After a pause, Samson answered, "Sounds familiar, but I don't know why."

"Something's not right, but I don't know what it is," Derk said.

"I told you that from the start."

"They're covering up something."

"Who's covering and what are they hiding?"

"ABT, NASA or both. I asked Joyce. Remember her, the EPA secretary who tried to hook me up with her niece?"

There was silence.

"If you're nodding, I can't hear you," said Derk.

"Sorry, these prawns are, excuse my Nigerian, fucking delicious! What about her?" said Samson.

"I asked her to set up an appointment for me so I could get inside, but her boss told her not to do it. So, I went in cold. Didn't matter. They knew who I was. Said they were expecting me. Even had my photo and hand print ID."

"High security," Samson said.

"Everywhere. But I saw her. Or her double. She looked me in the eyes and said she didn't know me. Then they escorted me out like they didn't want me to see anything."

"Very interesting," Samson mimicked Dr. Watson addressing Sherlock Holmes.

"I know it was her, but something was different. Her eyes, maybe, a little colder. It was Susan's voice," he paused while he replayed that moment in the greenhouse, "but it had a different tonal quality, somewhat metallic. You know the way digital recordings sounded when they first came out."

"What are you going to do?" said Samson through a mouth full of food.

"I'm sorry. I'm interrupting your dinner. I don't know. When are you coming back?"

"At the end of the semester, but we're going to Lascaux first. Can I call you later?"

"Sure. Enjoy your dinner. Be well, my friend," Derk said and hit off.

Climate Fact:

It is estimated that it will take twelve trillion dollars of investment to get to net zero emissions.

What can you do about it? Wow! There will be so many great jobs requiring all kinds of skills. Choose a career in a field that will reward you and the environment at the same time.

38

Estee Sparks should have been studying courtroom procedures. She had taken a couple of days off her para-legal job for that purpose. Instead, Jones had asked her to meet him on the patio at Bowden's near the FSU campus. She expected Fendru to join them and tell her they had ratted her out so she hadn't been this anxious since her period was late after Bobbie Humphreys broke her cherry in high school. Her cell phone rang. It was King Carver.

"I told you I can't do it," she said, maybe too abruptly.

"I know you left those pictures in Danswirth's office," Ardale said. "I know you dumped the seafood potpourri on his lawn, and I guarantee you that making your story public is the best way and maybe the only way to keep you out of trouble."

"No, Mr. Carver, telling my story is the surest way to get me into trouble."

There was no one on the patio but she lowered her voice anyway. She was hyper-suspicious.

"I can't talk right now," she whispered as Jones and Fendru approached her table.

"May I call you later?"

"I guess so," she relented, but she didn't mean it. She hit Off.

"Hello," she greeted them with forced delight.

Jones made a hand gesture in place of hello and took a seat.

Fendru sheepishly said, "Hello," and sat across from her, placing his Notepad on the table. His eyes were flooded with apprehension.

Estee alternated her attention between the two of them and the entrance to the patio.

"He's not coming," Jones said.

"Why not?" She knew he was referring to Teddy.

Jones rubbed one hand across his face and around his neck. Fendru started to say something as a young gal wearing an apron approached them.

"Coffee," Jones said to the waitress. Fendru nodded yes.

"Anything for you?" She looked at Estee.

She waved the waitress away.

"You guys got arrested. How did that happen?" she said.

"Video cameras. They got our license plate," Jones said.

"They have pictures of you?" she said.

Their heads bobbed in unison. Jones shut his eyes and fidgeted.

"What?" she said.

"They want us to give up some names, tell them who was behind it," Jones confessed.

"Behind what?" she said.

"They know we dumped the trash in those offices," Fendru said.

"Know or think? It's not important what they think. It's what they can prove," she said.

"They have us at the scene," Fendru said. "We have to give them something or . . ."

"Or what?" she said, mustering a combination of defiance and legal knowledge.

"They said they would elevate the charges," Fendru said. He was so nervous he rose and paced.

She had never seen Fendru so unsure of himself. She reached for his hand and he took the seat across from her.

"Listen to me. It's only a misdemeanor. You can't be kicked out of school over a misdemeanor," she said.

Fendru and Jones traded glances, then avoided eye contact with her. She wondered if they had already agreed to something that was not being communicated.

"Listen to me, you guys." This time her voice was that of an angry mother in the process of disciplining her kids. "You want to be lawyers, then start thinking like lawyers. They have nothing linking you or any of us to those offices. This will go away if you let it."

"How's that?" Jones retorted. "Teddy said you were approached by a guy from the EPA and he knows everything."

"Yea, and a reporter," Fendru added.

"I'm not giving them a story," she said.

"What did you tell them?" Jones asked.

"They have presumptions. They've connected some dots but they can't prove anything either," she said. "And another thing. If you didn't transport a minor over State lines or a banned substance or something like that, the charges against you, if any, cannot be elevated. What you did occurred in another State. You won't even be extradited. Do you understand what I'm telling you?"

The tension was interrupted by the waitress delivering their drinks.

"Anything else?" she asked as she held out the guest check.

Jones handed the gal thirty bucks and said, "Not now. What time do you get off?"

She stepped back, seemingly dismayed, surveyed him from head to toe and quipped, "The better question is how?" She turned and walked away with a flirty bounce in her step.

Estee was dismayed but didn't want to show it. Fendru was frozen with astonishment and, probably, envy. Jones had just hooked up with a complete stranger in the middle of a career bending crisis.

Estee had been a mother only briefly, but the paternal instincts that accompanied motherhood had become part of her. She smiled, a gesture designed to disarm her younger friends, opened her arms and invited them to get closer. She leaned in, close enough that the guys could inhale the scent of Clairol.

"Boys, it's time to grow up and start using your heads. You know the stuff they've been drilling into us since we got here? It's time to start using it," she said. "You're going to be lawyers."

She smiled again, the patronizing kind, the stern kind that was usually followed a parental command. She leaned back, cradled her nape in her hands and took a deep breath.

"What is that thing everyone learned in grade school?" she said.

Fendru and Jones were in full attention, as if Estee was their Sergeant barking orders. Neither one answered.

"Keep your mouths shut. Isn't that what a good attorney tells his client?" Estee said.

Jones relaxed with a sigh and sat back in his chair. "I think it's *Don't hire a fool for your lawyer.*"

When Estee laughed Fendru followed. With the tension released they agreed to remain quiet. Estee would inform Teddy of their decision.

39

Detective Louis Cardoza was cantilevered over his office chair canting *"Auummmmm!"* With one hand he touched his toes. In the other hand was his phone.

Manny Ortega, a fireman who did foot massage on the side, recommended the stretch. The *Auuuummmm* came from a yoga instructor he met at a Batchelor party.

Unfortunately the *Auuummmms* and the stretches provided only temporary relief, but he would have tried snake oil if it promised to alleviate the twinge in his lower back. He stood up, Ouch! He sat down, Ouch! It was a constant nuisance.

He raised up, one vertebrate at a time, shrugged his shoulders, not once but twice, arched his back and leaned over again. His confidence replenished, he raised up again at a normal pace.

"Ouch!" He cried out. "Sorry. Hello. Sorry." The caller had excused herself to look for information that Cardoza requested.

"Cardoza!" shouted Bremmer, a detective on the other side of the room. "Did you see the autopsy report on that missing girl?"

Cardoza shared an office with twenty other cops. The shouting was annoying but normal. Having a telephone converse with a potential vic over this constant din was a chore. Lucky Bremmer. He was retiring a month before Cardoza, if his prostate held up that long.

"Where?" Cardoza shuffled through papers on his desk. "Is that the last known address?" he said to the caller.

As he held up a report Bremmer said, "She was alive when someone stuffed her into that box."

"No shit!" Cardoza said. "Sorry Ma'am. "Can I call you right back?" He put down the receiver before she could answer and looked for Cause of Death.

"**Cause of Death:** Affixiation. Victim suffered severe blow to the back of the head, but it was not the immediate cause of death. A form of plastic was poured over her. Her lungs filled with plastic that suffocated her."

He was still reading when Bremmer announced, "Vic was pregnant, too."

Cardoza slumped into his chair. He dreaded telling a woman that her daughter was murdered and it under some gruesome fucking circumstances. It was the worst part of working in Missing Persons, but only one of the reasons he hated this job.

Another thing irritated him like a wool sweater on a hot day. Depending upon the State in which she was killed this case could be declared a double homicide, get flipped to Homicide, and turned into a political football. That would not stop the grieving of Angelina's mother or guarantee her justice.

This much he knew. Mrs. Rodriguez said her daughter was seeing some rich guy and had hinted about a big announcement. She's pregnant. That's big news.

Danswirth, president of Danswirth Enterprises, initially referred to the vic familiarly, by her first name - - - as if he was familiar with her. Cardoza couldn't forget the glint of joy in Danswirth's eyes at the mention of her and the sadness that followed. Cardoza's job depended upon his ability to read people. Danswirth may have been more than familiar with the woman.

After his visit with Danswirth, Cardoza called Massachusetts to find that his only lead to the victim's disappearance had been transferred to Mumbai. How convenient, he mused.

If he could link the two of them together romantically or, even better, get a DNA match, he might be able to lock someone up even if he couldn't promise justice. Until he is otherwise informed, this is still his case.

He did this to pump himself up for a case and to bring out the dedicated and optimistic cop within him. That side of him could get his picture in the paper. The down side of pursuing Danswirth was that he would get his picture in the paper. In his experience, there are only two times that a cop gets his picture in the newspaper; when he saves somebody's life or when he dies trying.

He sat up in his chair and pondered how he could get a sample of Pendleton Danswirth's DNA.

Climate Fact:

Ninety nine percent of the species that have ever lived on Earth are extinct. The average age of a species on Earth is estimated to be 2.5 million years. Humans have been on Earth about 2.5 million years.

What can you do about it? We know what we need to do to keep from becoming extinct. The Earth is still a marvelous bounty of plants and animals and hopes and dreams. Rise each day with a commitment to keep it that way.

40

As Derk awakened he scissored his legs across the cool percale. Luscious! He stretched his injured arm without discomfort and took a couple of deep breaths. Satisfied that Humpty-Dumpty was back together again he sat on the edge of the bed and stretched, albeit gingerly. Some body parts were in no hurry to welcome the new day.

For the first time in a week, he felt rested. His dreams had been free of falls, drowning and explosions, and he was among familiar trappings. He took another deep breath, ran his hands through his hair, and slipped into his Birkenstocks, the kind that massaged his feet while making little impressions on his soles. He was eager to begin the daily routine.

He wasn't a slave to routines but he had gotten into a habit of taking a glass of orange juice to his balcony patio and reading The Times. He found the morning newspaper, wrapped in a plastic bag, in its usual place on the driveway. The sun had begun its ascent over the Gulf and a slight breeze from the southwest contained a hint of eggs and bacon. A couple of joggers in shorts and tank tees passed him on their way to the beach.

It was past nine and the absence of reporters, workmen and power tools was a refreshing. He was climbing the stairway in the garage when he heard his cell phone play the familiar Rosini tune.

"Are you calling to apologize?" Derk said, half winded after bounding up the remaining set of stairs.

"That wasn't my call, Doctor." The only time Joyce referred to him by his degree was when someone of rank was within earshot of her desk.

"Is it Sahith?"

"Uh huh," she said.

"He doesn't seem to like me."

"You could be a little warmer to him."

"I was resuscitating an Astronaut when he called."

"Mouth to mouth as I recall."

While talking with the EPED secretary he was standing in his kitchen and getting his first look at the newly installed vinyl floor. His flight had arrived so late he had gone straight to bed without thinking about it.

More than pleased, his first glance suggested that a fresh coat of paint and some new handles on the drawers would turn his kitchen into a photo op for one of those home design magazines. Jenny would have been proud of him. The color of tile blended with those in the countertop and the backsplash. The grout tone mimicked the wall color, and the pattern was ornate but not too busy. He had been anxious about those choices, because Jenny usually selected the colors and passed them by him for his confirmation. What augured his enthusiasm was that replacing the vinyl floor was not a necessity, and it fit the décor quite well. After learning that the manufacturing of vinyl flooring creates toxic chemicals that end up in the water he opted for a more sustainable material. As he regularly lectured his students, "You're either part of the solution or you are part of the problem." He couldn't suppress the idea that his days here were numbered. He could only hope that the next owner would share his enthusiasm for making this home more environmentally friendly.

"You know that first impressions are only eight seconds long," Joyce said. She was a long-time colleague and his part-time mother. "Anyway, did you get the list?"

"List?" he said.

"Of the plastics manufacturers?"

After his initial meeting with Estee Sparks, he had asked Joyce to comprise a list of plastics manufacturers in the Gulf States.

"Sorry, I've been busy."

"I know . . . resuscitating."

"So, what did you find out?"

"What are you looking for?"

"I'm not sure but thank you," he said and hit End.

He poured a glass of orange juice and booted up his PC. As always, Joyce was thorough. There were, at least, thirty names on a list that included makers of Plexiglas, extrusions, packing materials, industrial products and consumer goods. The Hopalong Cassidy theme on his phone played again.

"Doctor Bryan, this is Simone Sparks and I need to talk with you."

He sensed trouble. Her tone was urgent and she used her first name.

"I have a lead that might help us," she said.

"A lead?"

"Yes, I got a call—"

"About the dead girl? Have you called the police?" he interrupted her.

"No. She could have been killed anywhere in the Gulf. The only reason the Sunshine State has taken any interest is because the body turned up on Florida shores. As far as they're concerned it's the Coast Guard's problem."

"You're talking about the woman in the box?" he said.

"No, I talking the Ricei whale. I need you to help me get the guy who ran over her."

"Hold on. What's this have to do with the dead girl or anything else?" He had put Estee and Ardale together so she could tell her story. Now she was talking about a dead whale.

"Doctor Bryan, I read your file. I thought you were someone who cared."

"My file?"

"I mean I checked you out. They call you the Indiana Jones of the EPA."

"Nonsense and I'm mostly retired now."

"You were retired when you showed up at my doorstep?"

"On a sabbatical really," he mumbled, "but that's not important. Ms. Sparks, I have no idea what you are talking about and a dead whale is the Coast Guard's bailiwick."

"I got a call from a marine repair shop about the broken propellor. If we follow the propellor we'll find the boat," she said, completely ignoring his attempt to dismiss what had become an obsession with her.

"I'm sorry, but . . ."

"Find the boat and it will lead us to its owner. Will you help me?"

"Estee, is that really why you called me?" he said. His attempt to connect her to Ardale was not going as planned.

"You dropped a reporter on my doorstep instead of a cop. This is as personal to you as it is to me."

"Have you talked with Ardale, I mean Mr. King, about this?"

"No," she said emphatically. "The only story I have for him is about the Ricei whale."

"You should. He's a good man. You should trust him."

"It's complicated."

"He knows that, and he's very good at protecting his sources," Derk said although he had nothing to support that claim.

"If I think about it, will you help me? Quid pro quo?" she said.

"Find someone who ran over a whale?"

"Yes, sir, I mean, Doctor."

His hope for a relaxing day on the beach was in jeopardy. After a giant sigh he asked, "How can I help you?"

41

"Pendleton Danswirth the Third, I think we have some unfinished business," said Princess Duval.

There was something about her voice that fueled his libido. "So what are we going to do about it?" said Danswirth.

"Why don't you meet me in Flagstaff?" she said.

He bit his lip and grimaced. He was running a multinational corporation while dealing with a dead lover, a missing boat, a rogue radio host, a nosey detective and someone with a grudge big enough to trash his home and his office.

"Princess, my bunny rabbit, I'm not sure this is the best time."

"Why not, Penny dear?" she said, allowing the dear to drift in his thoughts.

He needed her like the fog needed the morning air. Her confidence, her pheromones, her lust and even her power enticed him. He was used to being in control, but she could take him or leave him on a whim. He didn't care. He was ready to be swept into her realm for however long she would have him. They were rich and influential. There was nothing they couldn't do together.

"There's a cleaning crew in my house. I can't leave," he said. He was searching for something in his basement.

"Pendleton, sweety, you are a multimillionaire. You don't clean. That's why you have maids." Her voice was affectionate but not unlike his aunt's when reminding him of his sinful ways.

"I'm sorry. The maids are gone and the nurse has the weekend off. I really can't." He opened and closed cabinets as he spoke. He sorted through piles of books, old clothes and knickknacks on the shelves, occasionally tossing something aside for a latter inspection.

"What's that noise? What are you doing?" she said.

His home was now more sanitary than a hospital burn ward. Still, the cleaning crew had found nothing. No bloody clothes, no jewelry, no bag. Somehow in his highly disciplined executive mindset, the next move was to douse his house with gasoline and light a match. Where is that damn gas can?

"Nothing, Bunny," he said, shaking a half empty can of laundry detergent. "Can I get a raincheck?"

"I guess, Dear," she relented. "But don't wait too long."

"I promise we'll be together soon. By the way, I've heard nothing from the BOA?" He stopped and looked around for anyplace he hadn't searched. "Oh fuck! It's in the garage," he realized, loud enough for her to hear.

"What's in the garage, dear?"

"Nothing. What's taking them so long?"

"I think they're going to announce it next month. They're busy with elections. Where are you? Pendleton, can you tell me what's really going on?"

Alas, some good news. Their influence upon elections is precisely why he created *GodNet*. Religious organizations couldn't promote or support particular candidates for office or they could lose their tax-exempt status, but they could influence decisions.

"Nothing, Bunny, but I've got to go," he said.

She ended with a reminder. "Penny, dear, they organize people around issues important to them and they spread the message. It's their duty to God. As far as they're concerned *GodNet* is a gift from God, and you are nothing short of an angel."

Princess Duval had no boundaries.

"And you are my Princess," he said. He heard a kiss and then she was gone.

Climate Fact:

Nutrients in some vegetables today are substantially lower than they were 70 years ago

due to depleted soil while our food system is spewing out one third of greenhouse gases.

What you can do about it? It's is difficult to entirely avoid foods from mega-industrial farms buying mostly organic products is a huge step forward. Besides, pesticides don't taste very good!

42

Derk agreed to meet Estee Sparks at the George Bush International Airport in Houston. It was late afternoon when he arrived and the runway was hot enough to grill an Armadillo. She collected him at the curb in an old van with a fading sign on its side: Sparks Seafood.

To his surprise she was dressed in a skirt and blouse. As he settled into his seat and placed his bag under his feet a faint musk drifted in the air. He couldn't tell whether it emanated from her perfume or the fresh ink on her wrist.

"Javan Rhino?" he said.

"Precisely, Doctor Bryan, such a pleasant surprise," she said with a twinkle that grew into a full throttled grin.

"That I showed up?"

"No, that you know about the Javan."

"From what I've read their days are numbered," he said.

"The only ones left are in Ujung Kulon National Park."

"In Indonesia," he said. "Otherwise, it wouldn't show up on you. May I ask where we're going?"

"Not much for idle chit chat, are we?" she said as she merged into exit traffic.

"It's your party. I'm just along for the ride." His attention oscillated between Estee and her new tattoo.

"What?" she said with an arched eye.

"You're running out of room."

"We'll all be gone soon if you guys don't—"

"Do something about it. I know," he said. He had heard it all before. Why was it always the responsibility of the EPA to solve the climate crisis? The EPA wasn't throwing its trash into the water.

A cloud shadowed her cheerful mood. "I'm sorry. I know you're trying," she said.

He shrugged. "So, where are we going?" He wanted to be more positive but he had other pressing things to do and this trip was on his own dime.

"To see a man about a propellor," she said.

***

"I gather we're in a hurry," Derk said, tightening his seatbelt. Estee seemed anxious, like a game bird in a dog kennel, as she weaved back and forth in traffic.

"I want to get there before closing," she said.

"And where is?"

"Bud's Marina."

He held out both hands, palms up, and frowned.

"Lynchburg," she said. "It's on the coast, about thirty miles from Houston."

He Googled Bud's Marina. It had no website and the Better Business Bureau reported no complaints. A reference reported that Lynchburg, originally known as Lynch's Ferry, is famous for its landmark, the Point of Honor, and for being the home of Doctor George Campbell, Patrick Henry's physician.

"Give me liberty or give me death," Derk murmured.

"What?" Estee darted between a semi and a Dodge Ram hauling a boat and trailer.

Derk answered with a head shake. "Do we have a plan?"

She rolled her eyes and exhaled deeply. "Yes."

"Not really?" Derk said.

"Sort of. A guy I know who runs a marina called me. He got a call about repairing the kind of propellor that was on the boat that . . ."

Derk interrupted her, "It was like the kind or it was actually the one that was on the boat?"

"Okay, it's a long shot and Al isn't always all there," she said, "but I trust Al."

He restrained an eye roll and forced a smile. What the hell, he was spending the day with an attractive woman and he was on the way to the beach.

They arrived at five thirty. According to the sign on the door Bud's was open until six. As marinas go it was nothing special. Outside appearances suggested it had a show room, repair shop and a storage yard where boats were stacked upon racks two to three high. Behind the building was a dock that jutted into an offshoot of Galveston Bay. The storage yard was surrounded by a chain link fence meant to constrain intruders from rummaging through the arthritic racks that strained to support a myriad of crafts that had seen better days. Derk guessed that this marina was on its last days or earned its keep from a sideline.

Estee parked next to two trucks in front of a variegated steel building that was in need of a fresh coat of paint. She got out and stood at the entrance to the front gate.

"Is this part of the plan?" Derk said after joining her.

"I'm looking for a boat with a broken propellor."

"Your only lead is a broken propellor?" Derk said.

"Right now, it is." She appeared to spot something and headed for the entrance.

"Hold up," he said, hurrying to catch her. He grabbed her by one arm. "Are you going in there and ask them if they have a boat with a broken propellor that ran over a whale?"

She turned to face him. "Yea, that's the plan."

"How do you know he'll tell you the truth?"

"Why would he lie?" She tossed her hands into the air.

"Money, sex, religion . . ." Derk counted on his fingers.

"Are you always so cynical?" she said.

"Haven't you ever watched Suits?" Derk said.

Again, she tossed up her hands. Her hair wafted above her sinewy and tan shoulders. In addition to being stunningly alluring she was fabulously naive.

"You asked for my help," he said.

"So, what would you do, Doc?"

"We need irrefutable evidence," he said. "The kind they can't lie about."

"Okay," she said and pointed toward the storage yard. "There's a boat over there with a broken propellor. It looks like the kind of boat that would use the kind of propellor that killed the whale. Does that qualify as irrefutable evidence?"

After a quick scan of the boats on the racks he nodded. "It could."

"Okay, so that's where I'm going," she said, proud that she was a step ahead of one of the EPA's crack investigators.

As she was opening the door, "Whoa. Not so fast," he said.

"What is it with you?"

"It's just a suggestion, but why don't you walk in, ask what time he opens tomorrow and look around for a dog."

"A dog?"

"Yes, a dog."

"And then?"

"Say thank you and leave."

"A dog?" she protested.

"Yes. Just leave, and I'll buy you a nice dinner," said Derk, sprouting a mischievous grin.

***

From Bud's Marina a ten-minute drive took them to Channelview, a port city settled largely by oil refinery workers. A quick Google search led them to a used clothing store.

"You're going to need a change of clothes," Derk told her. "I suggest something dark, lightweight and comfortable. I'm going across the street to the pharmacy."

After a brief protest he promised to reveal the rest of his plan to her over dinner.

Twenty minutes later Estee climbed into the van with a pair of white sneakers, red shorts and a yellow tee shirt. Derk was on the telephone.

"Call me as soon as you get it," Derk said while fumbling a box of pills in his lap.

"What was that about?" Estee said.

"Nothing," he said with a disdainful smirk.

"Secret agent life?"

"If you must know I'm trying to locate someone," he said. "What did I tell you to get?

"Black's not my color."

Another eyeroll, but to her defense he hadn't told her he wanted to return to Bud's after dark.

"Do you have his cell number?" Estee said, dismissing his objection.

"It's a she."

"A Mrs. Bryan?"

"No, my wife died awhile back."

"I'm so sorry," Estee said. "It's none of my business."

"I don't have a clue why I'm telling you this, but I am trying to locate a woman." Just saying it he found was somewhat cathartic.

"Does she want to be found?" said Estee while removing her blouse in the van.

"I've actually found her, but—"

"I'm listening," she said as she pulled the yellow tee shirt over her shoulders.

Looking away he said, "She disappears."

"Disappears? Doctor," she said and held his arm. "I want to hear this story, but you promised me dinner."

"Of course," he said. The shirt left exposed part of a furry creature that clung to her chest. He was momentarily jealous. After a nervous glance at his watch he added, "It'll be dark in a couple of hours so we need to get going."

"I saw a diner a couple of blocks back," she said.

"Sounds good." He stuffed the box of Doxylamine into his pocket.

"You okay, Doc?" she asked, nodding at the pills.

"Dog food," Derk said.

"You have a dog?" she said as she removed her skirt.

He didn't look away this time. She had a runner's legs, long and smooth as a naked willow tree.

"No," he said. The mischievous grin returned. Whether she deduced it was lust or his plan for the dogfood didn't matter to him. "Secret agent stuff."

For a moment she was speechless although her new outfit was louder than a police siren.

***

After they ordered Derk told her about the missing woman.

"Relationship! Sounds like something in a James Bond movie," she said.

254

Her verve reminded him of Susan Carlton.

"This woman is a shark attack. Move on, Doctor," she said.

"Maybe so. I know almost nothing about her but I can't stop thinking about her," he said.

It was a confession that resulted in some immediate introspection. What have I done? He forked the baked flounder in front of him as his phone played a familiar tune.

"Hi ho, hi ho, Silver," Estee lip synced as he answered.

"This is Bryan. What did you find out?" He listened to FBI Special Agent Kitteridge.

"Really? Do you have an address?" He scrambled for a piece of paper, but none was nearby. "Text it to me?"

He hit Off and sat still for a moment, assessing what he had been told.

"More secret agent stuff?" Estee said.

He wanted to tell her but changed the subject. "It's all good. So, tell me about Teddy. How long have you known each other?"

"We're law students," she said.

"Ms. Sparks, Estee, you're clearly more than that. Isn't that why I'm here? You want to know what I'm going to do," Derk said.

"It had crossed my mind," she said. The worry in her eyes returned.

"I don't know. What are you going to do next? Put plastic cups in some exec's gas tank? Strangle his dog with six pack rings?" He immediately regretted saying it.

"What are you doing?" she retorted.

"I'm sorry," he said, "I'm here helping you."

He held up a hand to summon the waitress. "I'd like two hamburgers to go, preferably uncooked, and bring us the check."

***

Bud's Marina was located on a heavily industrial street where a westerly wind kept the whiff of detritus to an almost tolerable level. The marina didn't look any more appealing in the glow of moonlight and neon than it did during the day. The light from two large stanchions illuminated the boatyard which was enclosed by a ten-foot chain link fence. A U-Haul truck was backed up to a padlocked gate.

They parked Estee's van a couple of blocks from Bud's and walked to the marina. Only one car passed on their way. The "d" was faded, but the neon sign over the door read *Closed*.

"Up there," Estee said, standing on the street side of the fence. She was pointing to the same boat she had seen earlier. "It looks like part of the prop is missing. What do you think?"

"Not sure." Derk said and maneuvered for a better vantage point. A rack of aging trawlers obstructed his sight.

"I've got to get in there," she said and began climbing the fence.

"No, Estee!" Derk shouted, more loudly than he preferred. "Come here."

His voice aroused the attention of the Rottweiler Estee had encountered during her brief visit to Bud's a few hours earlier. They hurried to the other side of the U-Haul truck. He held out the paper bag containing the to-go order.

"Is that part of the plan?' she said.

"Sort of," he said, but it was before the gun fire.

***

To build a nest egg in anticipation of his retirement Detective Louis Cardoza had volunteered to be part of an interjurisdictional task force on human smuggling. He wanted the overtime pay. Unfortunately, he had to be available at some highly inconvenient times.

"Holy mother of fucking Virginia!" he said after receiving the call about gun fire at Bud's Marina.

He had just washed down a Viagra with a shot of sake and shared some mind-blowing sativa with his wife. As part of their ritual, which was to include the first sex his back had allowed in weeks, they had dialed up Enya on Pandora—some of the passages aroused his most primitive instincts—and set up a full array of sushi that they would eat afterward. Now, he had to dress, high tail it to the bay and hope the buzz disappeared before he had to draw his gun.

By the time Cardoza arrived at the marina a bevy of police cruisers, with lights flashing, were parked in front of Bud's. An officer was interviewing a woman with a zoo of body art and a man in wet clothes. The gate was locked and the business was closed. Cardoza stayed long enough to say hello to Doctor Derk Bryan and Simone Teresa Sparks. He left knowing that he would receive a full report the next day. On the way home he popped another blue pill and lit a joint.

***

There were two accounts of that evening's adventure at Bud's Marina. The one Estee and Derk shared with the officer in charge and what actually took place.

As far as the cops were concerned Estee and Derk had gone to Bud's because she was looking to buy an old boat she could restore. A friend told her that Bud's had an assortment and, quite likely, the exact one she sought. Her friend had even told her the name of the boat.

"We got here too late," Estee said. "It was after closing hours and we saw some people by the dock."

"At first," Derk picked up on the story. "We thought they had come back from fishing, but then a couple of them started running."

"That's when you heard shots," the officer said.

"Yes," Estee and Derk said in chorus.

"You saw someone get hit?" the Sergeant said.

"Not sure," Derk and Estee shook their heads. "Too dark," Estee added.

"So, we called the police," Derk said, nodding in an exaggerated fashion.

"How did you know they were illegals?" the Sergeant asked.

"Running and guns. Duh!" Estee said.

The sergeant nodded. "From this number?" He held out his report pad with her cell phone number.

"Yes, I mean no," she said. "From his phone." She tilted her head toward Derk. "It was from your phone, wasn't it, sweetie?" She leaned her shoulder against Derk's.

When the Sergeant raised an eye brow, Derk interjected, "When the shooting started, we took off, and I dropped my phone." He waved his hands over his head. "I thought we were goners."

"There were bullets all over the place," Estee said. She took Derk's hand and pulled him close to her. "But I picked it up, his phone, and we called you," said Estee and she hugged him.

Neither the sergeant nor Detective Louis Cardoza, who was fighting the boner in his trousers, had any idea that they were questioning an EPA investigator and a future lawyer.

"Tell me again. How did your clothes get wet?" said the officer.

"Well, you're not going to believe this, but I have overactive sweat glands," Derk confessed with an embarrassing grin.

"He does. Especially when he's under a lot of stress," Estee said. "He sweats more than a . . ."

"Sweetheart," Derk tugged on her to stop. He lowered his chin and averted his eyes from the officer. "I hope this isn't in your report but I peed my pants," Derk said with a self-deprecating scowl. Estee offered a sympathetic smile and kissed his cheek.

That drew another raised eye brow from the officer, but nothing more.

With a wounded grin she said. "You gotta love him."

"Could you identify any of them?" said the Sergeant.

Derk shook his head, "I'm sorry, but it was too dark."

"Do you think we should come back tomorrow?" Estee said to Derk. "Will it be okay?" she asked the officer.

The Sergeant didn't respond. His attention was focused upon a point beyond the fence at the back of the marina. By the look on the sergeant's face Derk seemed confident that Estee and he were of no further use to him.

"Can we go now?" Estee asked. "He needs to get out of these wet clothes."

"Sign your statements," said the sergeant, "and you can go."

As they were leaving, the sergeant said, "What's the name of the boat you were looking for?"

"The Salty Glider," she said and they departed.

Derk was quite sure they had wandered into was a human trafficking operation, but he didn't want to involve Estee in another investigation. Why was he always trying to protect the women in his life? He'd leave that question for another day. He was still processing what really occurred at Bud's.

After Estee climbed down from the fence, Derk laced the burgers with enough sleep aides to quiet an NFL lineman before tossing them over the fence. Within thirty minutes Fido was snoozing on the gravel a few feet from them. Derk climbed the fence and dropped to the other side.

"Start over there," Estee directed him.

In the dark they lost sight of each other so he used his cell phone to communicate with her while he rummaged through the racks.

"Look for a broken propellor on a long, fast boat," she said.

"How do I know it's fast?' he said.

"The fast ones have a shallower hull," she said.

"You mean the bottom?"

"Oh, stop it!" she said. "You live on the beach. Don't you own a boat?'

"A motorcycle. Nineteen forty-nine Panhead. Okay, I'm standing in front of it."

"Take a picture and send it to me," she said. "What's a Panhead?"

"A Harley-Davidson." He snapped the photo and texted it to her.

"So, you're a Harley man. Sort of makes sense," she said.

"What does that mean?"

"Independent, rugged individual type," she said. "Sorry, that's not it."

He kept looking. When he came across anything similar to her description, he took a picture and texted it to her. The yard was full of broken-down old boats with motors dissected for parts. Most hadn't seen duty in years. The boats were stacked three high. He moved from rack to rack, climbed up and down while he searched for a motor with a piece missing from its propellor.

"Are you sure you saw it?" he said.

A light came on at the back of the marina.

"Derk, there's a boat coming in," Estee said with urgency.

"I see it."

His view was blocked, but he had seen the light flicker in the racks. He put the phone in his pocket, and climbed onto the last rack. At the top he found the kind of long speedy boat Estee had described. A ratty tarp partially covered the motors, three huge Mercruisers. He needed to maneuver to the other side to get a view of the propellors.

"Get out of there now!" Estee's voice rose above the sound of the boat's motor shifting into reverse.

"They're docking, Derk. Get out!" Estee shouted.

He couldn't see them, but he heard the voices on the dock. If he could hear Estee shout, they probably heard her, too. He had to hurry.

He could barely make out two people in dark clothes as he scratched the frayed tarp away from the three pack. One of them jumped from the boat onto the dock while the other moored the boat to the dock with a large rope. Derk climbed up to the peak of the metal structure to get a clearer view. One of the men had drawn a weapon and was signaling to the other.

"Estee, get out of there! Run!"

He snapped a picture of the Mercruiser with the broken propellor, climbed down and ran to the port side of craft. He had made enough noise that the gunman was now aware of him.

"Hey you, come over here." The man with the gun stepped off the entrance to the dock.

With a rack of boats blocking his view, Derk couldn't see the gunman but he knew he was coming. Derk took a chance on the water. He began to run, but stopped when he passed the boat with a broken propellor. The name on stern was the Salty Glider. He snapped a picture and ran. When he cleared the boat racks, he was only twenty feet from the dock where the second man was hustling people out of the boat.

"Bang, bang!" Bullets whirred by Derk and smashed into the metal siding of the marina.

The other man turned and pulled a gun from behind his back. As he did two Hispanics jumped from the boat onto the dock. Derk wasn't sure of their status until they ran head long into the gunman and shoved him into the water.

With that, two women jumped from the boat onto the dock, and the four of them started running. Another shot collided with the

Galvanized sheeting which stopped the migrants in their tracks. They held up their hands.

Certain he could not outrun the trafficker's bullets, Derk turned toward Estee. He saw only flittering images of her running back and forth on the other side of the fence.

The gunman splashing around in the water and shouted to his partner. "Help me, Raoul. I can't swim."

As the gunman ran to help his partner floundering in the bay water, some of the illegal immigrants ran for the exit. Others dived into the water.

Derk changed his mind and sprinted for the fence. Twenty feet from Estee the Rottweiler came to life with a growl and a grille that meant Fido was done napping. Derk tossed his cell phone high into the air and over the fence. "Get out of here!" He shouted to her.

Estee cupped her hands, snagged the phone and ran toward the van. With Fido in full pursuit, Derk zigzagged through the storage racks until he was within a few yards of the dock. As the man climbed the steps of the dock with the help of his buddy, he pulled his gun from his soggy pants. Derk lowered his shoulder. The collision bowled each of them over backwards onto the deck of the boat. The gun dislodged from the gunman's hand and discharged. Derk bounced up, not knowing if he was shot or not, took a huge leap and dived into the water. Moments later, bullets streaked by him as he churned for deeper water. He had never kicked so hard in his life.

When he could no longer hold his breath, he surfaced, took another breath, went under again and swam toward the tail of the bay. The moon had drifted behind a cloud making vision difficult. The water was heavy with an industrial flavor. He used every stroke he knew to keep going. When he could kick no more, he dog paddled to a dock several hundred yards from Bud's and waited. He listened for the sound of an approaching motor or voices, anything that tattled upon those whom wanted him dead. He waited until only the wash of waves against the dock's pylons and the engine of a tanker pushing its cargo toward the Gulf of Mexico were the only audible sounds.

When it seemed safe, he swam until he found a ramp that promised purchase to the street. From there he made his way back toward Bud's, on the same street where Estee had parked the van. After a couple of blocks, he realized the van was gone.

"Oh no!" Could they have gotten to Estee. Panic! He rushed to the other side of the street, hoping for a better view of the marina. Red and blue flashing lights ricocheted off the Bud's storefront. Police. Then relief. Estee was talking with one of them.

He let out a deep breath, shook off the water, and ran his hands through his wet scalp as he cooked up a good story for the cops.

43

Derk and Estee were sitting in the parking lot of the Doo-Drop Inn surrounded by utility trucks. Every motel room on the bay was occupied by Texas Power crews restoring electricity after last week's storm. The desk clerk said they could use his room since he was going into the city to check upon his mother.

Derk paid the guy an extra twenty bucks to use the office computer. A public records search for the owner of the Salty Glider turned up Shirley Maxwell Danswirth along with her address and telephone number. He didn't mention the name to Estee, but asked for an early wake-up call.

An awkward moment was avoided when they found the room had two beds. While Estee showered Derk called Shirley Danswirth. Estee emerged from the shower with only a towel to corral her wild animals. Her crimson hair had been tied into bun exposing her sinewy neck and the terrycloth was insufficient to cover all of her more exotic real estate.

Upon first glance Estee Sparks might appear to be a circus oddity, but Derk was beyond initial impressions. Simone Teresa Sparks was a remarkable woman, beautiful and intelligent, which aroused thoughts of his deceased wife and Susan Carlton. He was still processing what Special Agent Kittridge had told him, "Calls to Doctor Carlton's number responded only to electronic beats."

When a man answered Derk asked to speak with Shirley Danswirth.

"Mrs. Danswirth is not available and may never be," said a male voice. "Who's calling?"

"Do you know if she is the owner of the Salty Glider?"

"Who is asking?"

"Is this Mr. Danswirth?"

"Yes, Pendleton Danswirth."

"You own a boat called the Salty Glider?" Derk said.

"Actually, my wife does. Who is this?"

"Derk Bryan with the EPA."

"Have you found it? I reported it stolen a couple of weeks ago."

"Your boat appears to be the one that ran over a Ricei whale," Derk said.

"A what?"

"A whale, an endangered one. There's no more than fifty left, and this one was pregnant. We're investigating—"

Danswirth interrupted him, "So, you did find my boat?"

"Sort of. It's parked in the storage yard at Bud's Marina. Are you familiar with Bud's Marina?"

"No, we keep the boat at Galena Park on the bayou. EPA?"

"Yes, EPA."

"I thought this sort of thing was the Coast Guard's job."

"We work with them all the time," Derk lied. He never had a case that involved the Coast Guard.

Estee waved her hand, trying to get Derk's attention when the towel slipped off her breasts. Derk nodded his approval.

"Ask him when the boat was stolen?" she said.

"Mr. Danswirth, do you know the day the Salty Glider was stolen?" Derk said. He could not pretend he didn't see and he didn't want to. They were real.

"I'm not sure. We drove out to use it one morning and it was gone. When can I get it back?"

"You'll need to talk with the police about that. By the way, does anyone else use your boat? A friend, relative, someone you work with," Derk said.

"That's a five hundred thousand Baja speedboat. It never leaves the dock unless I'm on it," Danswirth said.

"What about your wife? Any of her friends?"

"Unlikely."

"How's that?"

"She's not well," Danswirth said in a suspicious tone. "Was there anything unusual about the Salty Glider when you found it?"

"Not that I could tell. Sorry to hear that."

"What's that?"

"About your wife. Thank you for your time," Derk said and hit Off.

"So, what do you think?" Estee said, coquettishly. She was drying her hair.

He wasn't going there. With nod and a smirk, he answered, "If someone stole your car, your boat or broke into your home what's the first thing you would want to know?" he said.

She turned off the hair dryer.

"Who did it and was there any damage?" she said.

"He didn't ask either."

"Who?"

"Pendleton Danswirth."

His name made her shudder. She repelled to the bathroom.

"We have to go back to Bud's Marina," Derk said as she closed the door.

"Are you crazy?" Her words were muffled by the bathroom door.

Derk was changing into drier clothes when she emerged from the bathroom.

"Look. They're the same," he pointed to their cell phones on the bed. The photos he took of the Salty Glider matched the ones she had taken of the broken propellor. "We found the boat. Now we need to find out who was driving it."

"Piloting," she said, still fidgeting.

"Of course, sorry," he said. "What's wrong?"

She took her clothes back to the bathroom but left the door ajar. "You were chased by a dog, shot at and nearly drowned. Why do you want to go back there?"

"I thought you wanted my help," he said.

She laughed but not in a funny way. "It's too dangerous. We've got the pictures. That's all we need."

He went to the bathroom and opened the door halfway. "As soon as that boat leaves the yard, we've got nothing."

"Then we call the cops and tell them what we know."

She slid by him and sat in front of the mirror with the hair dryer.

"Estee," he said. "Estee," he repeated when she didn't respond.

"What?"

"You already did that."

She put down the hair dryer and turned to face him, as if she wanted to tell him something. The absence of make-up and lip stick revealed her age. She wasn't as young as he first guessed which put her closer to his age. For an instant he wondered if she liked sushi, what was her favorite color and did she like Blue Oyster Cult. Simultaneously he realized she was correct. They couldn't waltz into Bud's Marina like nothing happened.

"You're right," he said. "Here's what we're going to do."

Climate Fact:

Sir Francis Bacon, the father of modern philosophy, laid the groundwork for Christianity's relationship of man to the Earth with this portrayal: "For man to gain knowledge of the world, build his empire of knowledge and wealth, and propel himself out of poverty, man must conquer nature."

What you can do about it? In man's attempts at conquering nature, we have created for ingredients for the Anthropocene --- a human cause extinction. We must re-learn old concepts and practices in which man respected the rights of other creatures and lived in concert with the land its wildlife.

44

"Welcome to *Don't Back Talk God*," said Reverend Huck. "My guests today are, well, let's say it like it is. They don't agree with each other. In fact, I don't think I've ever had on the show two people who are so diametrically different in their points of view --- especially in regard to today's topic. Today we're going to talk about those miracles described in the bible --- that stuff about parting seas, walking upon water and blind folks whose vision was restored. Did those things really happen or not?"

On his right was the Pastor of the Seventy Ninth Street Baptist Church. He arrived wearing a black cassock and a silver chain with a cross the size of blender paddle dangling from it. To his left was a representative of Atheists in Action. His tee white shirt read, *Not afraid of burning in Hell,* in large red letters.

Huck loved this part of the show. Characters like these drew huge audiences, and he never knew what was going to transpire.

"Okay, let's get to it. Were they really miracles or things that the science of the times could not yet explain?" Huck said.

Without hesitation the Pastor went on offense. "Only God could do these things. That's why they're called miracles."

The Atheist countered with a condescending chuckle. "A God might be able to walk on water, but Jesus was a man and men sink in water. Most guys can't even float." Still laughing, he faced the rotund Pastor and said, "Pastor, have you ever tried to walk on water? You'd sink like a ball bearing. Reverend Hucklebee, ask your callers if any of them have ever walked on water?"

The phone rang immediately.

"You'll have to walk on water after I dump your ass into the bay!" said the voice.

Reverend Huck disconnected the call from Pendleton Danswirth III. "Sorry, gentlemen, there's a lot of crazy people out there."

"Blasphemy!" said the Pastor. "You can't talk about the Lord's work like that." He was so animated his cross banged against the microphone and left a metallic screech in the studio.

"He thinks there's an old man in the sky with a magic wand," said the Atheist, shaking his head and mocking the Pastor with his laughter.

The Pastor leaned forward and crossed himself before doing the same for the Atheist.

"Get out of here," said the Atheist, brushing back the Pastor's gesture.

"You are going straight to hell and I can't stop it," said the Pastor.

"Get him away from me," said the Atheist to Reverend Huck.

"For those of you listening I think the Pastor just administered last rites to my guest," said Huck.

"I don't need him to save my soul," said the Atheist. "And, by the way, think about this. A guy falls six floors at a construction site, gets up and goes back to work. People say it was a miracle. It wasn't. It was a stroke of good fortune. That's all."

"Heathen!" said the Pastor.

"Charlatan," said the Atheist. "Lies, fabrications and fantasies. I couldn't get through one of your sermons without two No-Doze."

"There is a devil and I have met him," said the Pastor, bounding from his seat and waving his cross shaped pendant at the other guest.

"Get away from me!" shouted the Atheist.

"It is my duty to exorcise the devil from you," the Pastor retorted.

The Atheist repelled in his chair as he slapped the cross from the Pastor's hands. The Pastor reached across Huck, grabbed the Atheist by both arms and shook him as hard as he could.

"In the name of the Almighty, I command you to leave."

The Atheist's chair rolled backward. "Get off me! Get off me!"

With the Pastor sprawled across Huck's desk, the microphone fell to the floor producing a thud and boom in the studio.

"Hey, hey! Enough," said Huck. He reached into the desk drawer, took out a small pistol and fired two rounds into the air.

His guests froze in fear as he waved the gun back and forth, entreating them to separate.

"Fuck me," lip-synced the Atheist, back-pedaling while holding his hands in the air.

The Pastor rolled off the desk onto the floor at Huck's feet. He got to his feet and backed against one wall. Neither guest said anything.

"That's better. Okay, now for the prayer of the day," Huck said and punched a key on his control board.

Up came a prerecorded statement by a Buddhist monk. "There is no beginning. There is no end. We are all part of the cycle of life, death and renewal . . ."

Huck was in a feisty mood. No Eric Burden and the Animals today.

45

Derk Bryan was well aware that in the field of law enforcement he worked for an agency whose authority was being whittled down by multiple unsympathetic, climate change denying State Attorney Generals one law suit at a time. He never understood that, given their lives and the lives of their constituents were as much at stake as anyone's. It was okay with Derk that people had differences of opinion about things, but a society that doesn't value science more than this one is destined for misery. He wasn't about to suggest that there is a quick scientific fix for global warming. The science about carbon dioxide as a greenhouse gas had been determined in the 1800s. No one debates it like no one debates what keeps us from flying off the planet, gravity. He wished he could get the science in front of more people. That is one of the reasons he still taught classes at the university. It was in that capacity he could elucidate the need for electric cars and solar panels. It was expected of him. This job was to go after the really bad actors, the ones who had no reservations about endangering others and would kill to protect themselves and their interests. Too often these miscreants represented entire industries. They were rich, powerful and so connected they had manipulated our institutions and governments into assisting them. Despite insistent protests his own university's pension funds were rife with fossil fuel assets. This job had always been demanding and it challenged his creative side. Although some cases consumed him Jenny never complained. Her reason being, "She would never interfere with someone's passion." She knew him well. Climate justice is human justice. That notion kept in the game. Recently, things were changing. He found himself wondering how much longer he was willing to be blown up, shot at and drowned—twice since he met Susan Carlton and Estee Sparks. He wasn't sure about that but one thing had to stop—this stuff was seeping into his dreams and keeping him awake at night.

It was two a.m. when he woke the first time in a cold sweat. In the dream he had ducked the bullets but frantic paddling was getting him no closer to the surface. He was sure his breath would run out before he reached the surface. He sat up in bed, gasping for air. Estee was as quiet as a church mouse in the bed next to him. He tried to sleep, but images of Susan Carlton, unscathed and smiling, returned, always followed by some catastrophe. He was exhausted when the wakeup call came but he made a mental note to call Doctor William Schulter, a colleague who knew about dream interpretation, before sitting on the edge of the bed.

Scant light filtered through the calico curtains of the motel room. In the bed next to him he watched the sheets over Estee Sparks rise and fall in gentle rhythm with her breathing. It had been a long time since he slept in the same room with another woman. He missed the intimacy of a lover's breathe on his neck, a hand nestling into his and the promise of another day. He got up to make coffee, a habit he had developed for Jenny to make up for the days he was away.

There was no coffee. He threw on a shirt and went to the office. When he came back with the two cups of coffee Estee was seated in front of the mirror with her back to him while she teased her hair. She had yet to dress. She was either beyond worrying about her modesty or she considered him too old to be interested in her.

"The call from the FBI, was it about Doctor Carlton?" she said.

As he passed behind her, he sucked in his tummy. "He said her phone responds to electronic signals." Her breasts, reflected in the mirror, were like sculptures, the kind that lingered with you long after first impressions.

"That's odd," she said as he sat the coffee on the dresser in front of her. When their eyes met, he offered an approving nod.

"Apparently, she doesn't respond to voices," he said. He inhaled her while he waited for her to take the cup in her hand.

"She or her phone?" She cupped her hand over his.

It was a flippant response but he hadn't separated the two. "Oh my god!" He backed away and plopped onto the edge of the bed. "That can't be," he said in a hushed tone.

"What?" Estee said while forming her hair into a pony tail.

"I was thinking about something Samson said."

"Who's that?"

"A colleague," was all he wanted to say at the moment. He had slept with Susan Carlton, held her so close they had become one. He waved off the thought.

"After breakfast we need to go back to the second-hand store," he said.

***

It was late morning when Derk and Estee returned to Bud's Marina. Donned in coveralls, long sleeve work shirts and ball caps rummaged from a Goodwill location, they hoped to elude anyone's attention.

"Yucky fucky!" said Estee.

"Yucky fucky?" Derk repeated, surprised by her expansive vocabulary.

She offered a coy smirk and tilted her head in the direction of the cops milling around Bud's parking lot.

"Ah," Derk sighed. Among them was the same detective who took their statements the previous evening. Derk lowered his hat to hide his brow. Estee followed his lead.

"Here, take this." Derk handed her a clipboard that had been stuffed into the door panel. "Got a pen?"

She produced a pen from the console between them.

"Go to the back and get a couple of coolers," Estee said. She seemed to understand the need for subterfuge.

A cock of the head signified he understood. "I'll go first. Wait 'til I pass the van. Then get out and stay behind me."

In an instant her anxiety of the past twenty-four hours ebbed like the tide. On her face was an expression he could only describe as pride. He couldn't tell whether that emotion was in response to him or a rise in her self-confidence but it boosted his own morale.

"Ready?" he said.

They each took a deep breath before Derk got out. No one paid attention to him as he walked casually to the back of the van. When he opened the double doors the impact of dead fish and ammonia melted his sinuses and repelled him so quickly, he lost his balance. As he was returning to his feet the detective came to help. Derk pulled the hat over his eyes as the officer lifted him up with one arm.

"Thank you, thank you, Laddie. It's my bum knee," Derk said in the voice of a Scottish Highlander while massaging his leg. "Motorcycle accident."

The doors at the back of the van were ajar which seemed to attract the officer's interest. As he reached to open them Derk said, "You might want this," and handed him a handkerchief.

The detective, a stocky symbol of masculinity, brushed his offer aside and parted the doors. One whiff sent him reeling.

"Holy shit, what's in there?"

"Seafood," Derk said proudly while maintaining the brogue. He held his breath, reached into the back of the van and selected two white plastic bins from an assortment. The officer stepped back to avoid the pungent aroma of decayed seafood and cleaning fluids. Derk closed the door and headed for the entrance to Bud's. Estee joined him.

"Do you think he recognized me?" Estee said, once inside Bud's showroom. "He didn't take his eye off me on our way in."

A shrug was Derk's response. He sat the boxes on the floor away from traffic. The showroom was longer than wide, replete with minimally supplied aisles of marine products and an extended sales counter. Behind the counter a heavy-set woman, with eyeglasses too large for her face, chomped on a wad of gum while she rearranged parts on the pegboard wall behind her.

"We're here to clean the Salty Water," Derk said when she turned to face him. His accent could not be mistaken for anything other than that of an Appalachian hillfolk.

The clerk's chomping turned to dismay.

"Glider," said Estee, who had drifted toward the window that provided her with a view of the boat yard.

"Oh yea, Salty Glider," said Derk. "Mr. Danswirth sent us." Derk loosened the red bandana from his neck he had offered the officer and blew into it with a bellowing honk.

"Bud," called out the befuddled gum chewing clerk to the swinging door at the end of the counter.

Bold script letters above the door read, *"Employees only."*

A well-dressed but nervous looking, middle-aged man entered the marina, nodded to Derk and walked to a window with a view of the boat yard. He stood close enough to Estee that she could smell his cologne. Moments later a tall man with a goatee and a scowl parted the swinging doors at the end of the sales counter. A Rottweiler trailed him.

"I just told you guys," Bud began saying as he waved his hand in the direction of the front door, until the sight of a man and a woman dressed in coveralls and ballcaps, not police uniforms, truncated his thought.

"They're here about a boat," said his plus sized helper whose jaw churned like a washing machine out of balance.

The dog eyed Derk, offered a perfunctory growl and slumped its chin on the floor. Its eyes were cloudy.

Bud sneered at the dog. "I don't know what happened to him. Used to be a good watch dog."

"The Salty Water, I mean Glider," said Derk, maintaining the accent.

As the words Salty Glider came from his mouth, Derk noticed the well-dressed man move closer until there was only one full aisle between them.

The name also seemed to perk Bud's ears. His attention darted back and forth between the two folks in work clothes. Estee pulled a sleeve over her tattoo and made a couple pecks on the clipboard with her pen as she scoured the yard for the boat with the broken propellor.

"What about it? Bud snarled.

"Do you know Pendleton Danswirth?" Derk said, dispensing with the charade.

"Who?" The voices were both Bud's and Estee's.

Estee's face turned pale while the man shuffling between the aisles headed for the exit. Danswirth's name was on the list of manufacturers that Joyce had sent him, and Estee recognized the name. He had seen the same reaction the night before after his talk with Danswirth.

"The owner of the Salty Glider," Derk said, having dropped the accent.

"Never heard of him," Bud said.

"If you don't know Pendleton Danswirth III, how did his boat get into your yard?"

Derk held up his cell phone with the pictures of the Salty Glider and the neon sign in front of Bud's Marina.

"Who are you guys?" Bud snarled. The Rottweiler lifted his chin long enough to expose a row of canines and offer a wimpish growl before dropping into a puddle of drool.

"EPA." Derk pocketed his phone and held out his official business card. "You can talk with us or those gentlemen that just left. I doubt your little side line needs that kind of attention."

"What are you talking about?" Bud said.

"You may not be part of their operation, but those human traffickers aren't docking at your marina without paying rent," Derk said.

"Derk," Estee said, waving her hand. She pointed to the boatyard and shook her head.

"Gone?" Derk lip synced. Estee nodded.

"Where is it?' Derk said to Bud.

"What?" said Bud.

"So, you want to play dumb. Estee, would you ask that detective who just left to join us."

"Somebody took it out this morning," Bud mumbled. "Have we met before?" He was looking at Estee.

"That boat killed a Ricei whale," she said, scuffing off all pretense.

"We need a name," Derk said.

Bud shuffled his feet. "This is about a dead whale?"

"For now," said Derk.

The watch dog rose, took one step and collapsed.

"I think you're right. He's useless. Maybe two boxes of Diphenhydramine are too much for a dog his size," said Derk. "What do you think?"

"You son-of-a-bitch!" Bud said as if a vice were tightening around his head.

"That's right, Bud. Sleeping pills."

Bud clinched his fists. Fire filled his eyes. He oscillated glances between Derk and something under the counter.

"All we need to know right now is who took the Salty Glider?" Derk lowered his voice, aware that Bud may have a gun stowed under the counter.

The gum chewing clerk stood in front of the monitor at the sales counter. She looked to Bud for confirmation. When he said nothing, she hit a couple of keys on the computer to begin a records search. Nothing came up. She hit more keys.

"Nothing," she said.

Estee walked behind the counter and nudged the clerk away from the PC. She punched a few keys and turned the computer screen toward Derk.

"Why is there no record of the Salty Glider?" Derk said.

"Excuse me," said Bud to Estee and clicked a couple more keys on the PC. He turned the screen toward Derk.

"Marshall Hucklebee?" said Derk, surprised.

"Yes, Reverend Marshall Hucklebee," repeated Bud.

Climate Fact:

The outcome is not pre-determined. It is dependent upon what action we take.

What can you do about it? Do what you can. Do what makes you happy. And you will become a model for others.

<h1 style="text-align:center">46</h1>

Rarely is a single individual liable for the extinction of an entire species, but within the past month Reverend Marshall Hucklebee had become responsible for accelerating the demise of two marine mammals. He was only fifty but both the Ricei whale and the Manatee would probably be gone before he was.

Hucklebee may have been less oblivious to this evolutionary tragedy if he had not been in a hurry to destroy evidence used in the commission of a felony. While he had never seen a Manatee and wouldn't intentionally harm one, while racing through Galveston Bay in violation of the No Wake signs, he left a yawning gash above the dorsal fin of a pregnant cow. Either offense would send him back into lockup. He had to sink Danswirth's cigarette boat. Things weren't going as planned.

"Fuck, fuck, fuck!" said Hucklebee, chastising himself for violating his first rule of crime: never take on a partner.

Twice he had broken his primary rule. He had paid the marina operator a grand to get rid of the Salty Glider. "Chop it up, burn it or bury it. I don't care. Just get rid of it!" he told Bud.

He assumed he wasn't the first to dock at Bud's after transporting illegals through the Gulf. It seemed safe. Bud was low profile and didn't ask a lot of questions. And he was regretting that he had gotten involved with Pendleton Danswirth III. Now he was in the custody of the U.S. Coast Guard in Galveston.

After shutting down the radio broadcast and hustling his guests out the door of his studio with the barrel of a toy cap-gun, he fishtailed his way to Bud's Marina. He had called ahead and asked Bud to put the boat in the water. It didn't matter to him that the propellor was broken. He wasn't going far, just fast.

After someone reported the incident involving the manatee to the Coast Guard, the Guard began stopping boats in the Bay. When they came upon the Salty Glider, Reverend Huck had already chopped a hole in its hull and was treading water on his way to shore.

"Call Pendleton Danswirth," Reverend Huck kept saying. "He is the CEO of Danswirth Enterprises, a very important man around here, and he can clear this up."

"We'll do that but someone saw your boat hit a Manatee at high speed," said the Coast Guard officer.

Hucklebee had felt something at the moment of impact but dismissed it.

"This whole thing started because Mister Danswirth implored me to bury his dog at sea. That's not a crime," Huck said, applying the tone he had successfully used to con people for years.

The room in which he waited was full of pictures of Coast Guard vessels. He had no idea there were so many different types, and none of them looked anything like the Salty Glider.

"Officer, have you been on any of those boats?" Huck asked, changing the subject. "They're huge and probably very complicated to operate."

"No sir. We've tried to reach Mister Danswirth but he's not in his office," said the officer, dressed in crisp, clean whites and shoes that gleamed. "And there's still the matter of the Manatee."

"There are things much bigger than dogs in the ocean and they die all the time," said Huck, assuming his most reverend role. "Although they are among God's creatures, no one grieves for them. The death of a Manatee is unfortunate, and I would be most displeased to discover I had anything to do with that, but I didn't hit a Manatee. I would have known that, wouldn't I, sir?"

When the officer did not respond Huck added, "I didn't do anything wrong. Just call Mister Danswirth. He'll tell you."

Danswirth was rich, loaded with connections and had plenty to lose if Huck ratted him out, but he didn't know if he could count upon him. Huck waited, still in damp clothes, with a blanket to keep him warm. Thinking back, it was too damned easy. There were always risks, but he should have known better. Getting out of that hell hole by faking a religious conversion seemed like such a good idea, and even the prison chaplain had encouraged him.

"Call him again. I am sure you can clear up this entire thing with one call," Reverend Huck repeated.

The officer wasn't paying attention. He was perusing a document someone has placed upon his desk.

"He is the president of Danswirth Enterprises and the founder of the radio station where I work. I'm sure you've heard of *Don't Back Talk God*. That's my show. I'm Reverend Huck, God's voice on Earth."

"I'm sorry, Mr. Hucklebee, but Mr. Danswirth reported the boat stolen several weeks ago." said the officer, "Besides, you violated the No Wake zone and ran over an endangered animal."

"Did you tell him I was here?"

The officer punched in a number on his desk phone. "Tell the security officer to get in here," he said and hanged up. "I couldn't reach him." The officer rose and took out a pair of handcuffs.

"What?" protested Huck.

As the security officer, a young man in Coast Guard whites with a sidearm, entered the room, Huck was handcuffed.

"Lieutenant," the security officer addressed his superior. The Lieutenant nodded.

"Put this guy in lockup."

The security officer took Huck by the arm. "Are you really Reverend Huck?"

"Yes, my son, I am," said Huck.

The security officer lit up like holiday lights.

"You know this guy?" said the Lieutenant.

"Yes. I mean yes, Sir!"

"Seaman," said the Lieutenant, "Go see this Danswirth guy and clear this up. Take him with you."

<h1 style="text-align:center">47</h1>

Detective Louis Cardoza now regretted volunteering for the Interjurisdictional Task Force on human smuggling. The trip to Lynchburg had interrupted a good buzz and an erotic evening with his wife. Sleep deprived, but no longer stoned, he should have been basking in the glow of the best sex he had had in six months, but the bumping and grinding had served only to spur a spasm in his lower back. He was in no mood for serious police business.

Before skimming the new missing persons reports he poured a cup of coffee and suffered a few humorless jokes from Officer Greavy, fresh out of Boot Camp. Greavy was filling in for Detective Bremmer who was out on sick leave. It was mid-morning when Cardoza got to the footnote about the Salty Glider reported to be at Bud's Marina.

"Que cono!" *(What the fuck!)* Pendleton Danswirth's boat was at Bud's Marina.

Two minutes later Cardoza and Greavy were in an unmarked car in route to Lynchburg.

Climate Fact:

Less than 8% of materials on Earth are recycled.

What can you do about it? Recycle, re-use and re-purpose.

48

Feed your brain what you want it to believe. That was a lesson Pendleton Danswirth learned from a management guru his company sponsored a few years ago.

"I didn't kill her. It was an accident. I didn't kill her. It was an accident," he kept repeating on the way to Bud's Marina. He wasn't making that up. It was the truth, but he hadn't convinced himself that the cops would see it that way. "I didn't kill her. It was an accident . . ."

It wasn't working. Walls were closing around him. Like the time he got locked in a closet during a children's game. In threatening situations, the claustrophobia would emerge.

It was one of the reasons everything in his life was so large. Big cars. Big boats. His estate was one of the largest in the county. His office was three times the size of everyone else's.

When the mantra failed, he resorted to deep breathing. When that didn't work, he would pop a couple of Xanax his wife kept in her medicine cabinet. She said she took them to tolerate him, but he assumed she was joking. He was a normally mellow guy with an envious lifestyle. He couldn't comprehend anyone being unable to tolerate being rich.

The sight of two police cruisers and a crime lab truck in the parking lot did nothing to ease his concern. He popped the Xanax as he passed the marina, craned his neck toward the passenger side, and looked for a glimpse of the Salty Glider. When the guy behind him laid on the horn he sped past the marina and found a place to park. He walked a block back to Bud's. It was too hot for his custom made, blended three-piece wool suit, but Danswirth's dress was a symbol of his power and authority. People in charge of anything important don't wear anything off the rack. He was dripping like a sponge when he stopped to peer through the chain link fence at Bud's. There was no sign of the Salty Glider.

A man and a woman in coveralls and ball caps entered Bud's as two men in street clothes came out. They were followed by a third man wearing a jacket with the words Evidence Tech on the back. He was sure the police had confiscated his boat and scoured every inch in their search for anything that could send him to Texas State Prison for the rest of his life. He held back, stayed on the sidewalk and tried to look casual—as casual as a guy in a two-thousand-dollar suit driving a red Land Rover could be in this neighborhood.

He sensed tension in the air when he entered the marina. He nodded politely to the man in coveralls at the sale counter and headed down an aisle to the side of the store that offered a view of the boatyard. A woman in coveralls, holding a clipboard, alternated her attention between something in the boatyard and her counterpart at the sales counter. He avoided eye contact with her. A tall man with a goatee and a sneer was eyeing the woman with the clipboard with suspicion. When someone mentioned the Salty Glider, he moved closer to the conversation. When his name came up, he turned around and abruptly walked out. It sounded like the guy from the EPA who called him the previous night. What the hell is going on?

Back in the Land Rover he called Marshall Hucklebee. The call went straight to voice mail. He called two more times on his way to Hucklebee's mobile home. The last time he left a four-letter word filled invective.

The closer he got to Hucklebee's home the more he regretted getting involved with an ex-con. Why did he think he could trust him, even though he had supposedly gone over to God? While he pondered what to do with his rogue preacher his phone rang.

"Pendleton, dear, are you home?" said Princess Duval.

"No, I'm a little busy."

"They're on their way," she said.

"Who? What are you talking about?"

He imagined the worst. The cops were coming. A creature clawed at his insides and the pounding in his head returned. He popped another Xanax.

"Pendleton, sweetie, they want you to run for the Senate," Princess said. "They're on their way to your house now."

49

"You're sure this is the right place?" Derk said as Estee maneuvered the van through the gate to the Little Dogies Mobile Home Park.

"This is the address you gave me," Estee said.

Derk obtained the address from a Google search for Reverend Marshall Hucklebee.

"This guy hosts the *Don't Back Talk God* radio program," Derk said. He had been watching a YouTube video of Reverend Marshall Hucklebee behind his mobile home pulpit interviewing a Senator.

"How can that be? This is a trailer park," Estee said.

"Can you believe this guy?" said Derk without looking up. "He changed his name from Thurgood to Reverend."

"So now we're looking for a fake reverend?" Estee said.

She parked in front of a scantily landscaped double wide. There was room for two cars but none were there. The plastic cross above the door was lit even though it was close to noon and the sun was at full strength. When she removed her shirt and rolled the coveralls up to her knees sweat trickled from one of the ancient animals that had become her billboard. Derk took a deep breath, shook his head and smiled inside.

"What a scam, and they're raking in millions," said Derk.

"What's so funny? He's also a killer," said Estee.

"I wouldn't go that far."

"He is if he killed that whale," she said.

They got out of the truck and Derk rang the doorbell. "I'm going around back," Derk said when no one answered. "He's not here," Derk said after circling the home.

"I'm trying the number we got from Bud. No answer," she said with the cell phone pressed to one ear.

Back in the truck Derk called Joyce, "Find out what you can about Thurgood Marshall Hucklebee aka Reverend Marshall Hucklebee. He has a radio program called *Don't Back Talk God*. Affiliations, backers, anything you can find. I need it now."

"Any news about Doctor Carlton?" Joyce asked, always nosy about Derk's extracurricular life.

"No, nothing. It's a dead end," he said and hit End. He was placating her, but it was also true.

"Now what!" Estee said.

"Have you ever had real Texas chili?" Derk said.

"Doctor Bryan, you really do know how to show a girl a good time."

Climate Fact:

Global warming is occurring ten times faster today than it did at the end of the last glaciation and at the end of all those that preceded it. To keep up with this change all organisms, plants, trees and animals will have to adapt ten times quicker than in the past. We are about to find out if we are one of the many species that will not survive.

What you can do about it? This is the greatest challenge mankind has faced, but it is not greater than us. We invented the telephone, the computer chip and sent men into space. We created social security, Medicare and unemployment compensation to share the risks and rewards of humanity. Preventing the worst outcome will require all hands on-deck. Everyone must play a part because we are all in this together.

50

"What do you mean, it's gone?" Detective Louis Cardoza held out his credentials as he asked to see the Salty Glider.

A heavy-set woman on the other side of the Bud's Marina sales counter labored on some chewing gum. "Somebody took it out this morning."

Cardoza followed her eyes across the room. A man on a lift-truck was moving a boat into storage. From her position behind the counter, she had a clear view of the boatyard through a large window on the opposite side of the room. Cardoza couldn't imagine anything leaving Bud's yard without her knowledge.

He pulled back his jacket to reveal a pair of handcuffs and asked Officer Greavy, "Melvin, do you know what the penalty is now for withholding evidence?"

"In a murder case?" Officer Greavy said. He wasn't as green as Cardoza thought.

Moments later Cardoza was on his phone to dispatch. "Have a black and white meet us at the home of Reverend Marshall Hucklebee."

51

"Do you know what distinguishes Texas chili from all other chili?" Derk said. He was perusing the options posted on a large wall menu behind the counter at Texas Pete's Chili Dilli.

"Not really," Estee said with less than enthusiastic interest.

"Will you look at that?" Derk said, pointing at the menu. "That's Cincinnati chili."

"Cincinnati or Texas, what's the difference?" she asked.

"Meat, beans, spaghetti and sauce, onions and cheese. That's a five-way. Anything less is a four-way or three-way. Cincinnati," he said.

She rolled her eyes, a gesture he couldn't allow to go without a retort.

"He's a copycat or this cowboy is from Ohio," Derk said.

She smirked. "Chili is chili."

Derk held up a forefinger. "To the unsophisticated palate."

"I'm a vegetarian," she said.

"What! No one doesn't eat chili," said Derk.

"I don't." Her mouth curled in one corner.

"TVP."

"TV what," she said.

"Textured vegetable protein," he said. She pierced her lips and gritted as if she had swallowed pickle juice. "It's what you eat when you give up meat completely. Right?" he said.

She shook her head. "Sounds processed, unnatural."

"It's soy beans. What do you mean, unnatural?"

She began to say something as the William Tell overture interrupted them.

"Have you checked your email," Joyce said.

“I’ve been busy,” he said.

“Where are you?”

“In Texas tracking a fake pastor who we think ran over a Ricei whale,” he said.

“We? Never mind; check your email,” she said.

***

“Why did you target Danswirth Enterprises?” Derk said.

He was reading a report on the Reverend Marshall Hucklebee that Joyce had pulled together. Estee sat across from him and nibbled on a Vegie sub she ordered from a gas station deli.

“He killed my baby!” she said. Her defiance was accompanied by a tear.

This was as personal as it got. He moved into the booth beside her and put an arm around her. She stiffened.

“I know how it feels to lose somebody,” he said. In his arm was a strong but vulnerable woman. “Well finish these on the way.”

He wrapped their orders in a to go bag. When he said, “I’ll drive,” she didn’t object. He sat in the van without the engine on. “Tell me what happened.”

“I had to do something. I owed it to Lincoln,” she said.

He took a napkin from her lap and wiped a tear from her face.

“I want you to know that I’m doing everything I can to help,” he said.

She slid up against his shoulder. “What now?’ she said. Before he could answer she took his arm. “By the way, thank you.”

“You’re welcome,” he said. “Maybe we can bring some justice to your life.”

“I hope so,” she said and forced a happy face. “You’re a good man, Doctor Bryan.”

295

"It's Derk. Call me Derk."

"Okay, Derk Bryan. So, what now?"

"I'm wondering if the dots connect Danswirth to anything we can prove?"

"You're thinking he's at the bottom of all this?" she said.

Derk pierced his lips and nodded. Then he cranked the engine.

"You're not thinking of paying him a visit?" she said with obvious angst.

"Well, you think his boat ran over a whale."

Her nod was clouded with reservation.

"They're each involved, and I don't think his boat was stolen," said Derk.

Climate Fact:

Human beings have succeeded at the expense of other species.

What can you do about it? This is each individual's challenge. We know what to do. Pick something and do it.

<h1 style="text-align:center">52</h1>

Before the accident King Ardale Carver's batting average on hunches was Hall of Fame material. After the accident the meds interfered with that and everything else. They numbed his senses and misplaced his priorities. At the low point in his recovery, he could identify with a zombie. He felt as close to dead as one could get while still walking. When the meds wore off, he turned to Fentanyl, his drug of choice, but anything worked in a pinch. He lost his job and his home. Until Samantha Card offered to help, he had no prospects. He probably should have been more appreciative of Derk Bryan.

Doctor Bryan's credit card enabled him to rent a room that didn't have a wad of Code Violations stuck to the door. It even had a place he could check his email and log into the Internet. His pledge to Bryan, a public official, was conditioned, at least in his mind, upon the evolution of a meaningful story. Since Estee Sparks put an end to that, his loyalty was being stretched like bedsheets blowing in the wind. He spent a couple of days lamenting his predicament until Samantha called.

"Connect the dots between Estee Sparks and the people whose homes and offices she despoiled. Then you'll have your story," Samantha Card told him. "I know you want to do a story on Doctor Bryan—he's an interesting character—but you can get back to that."

With the help of protein bars and heavily caffeinated soft drinks he decided to follow the veteran journalist's advice. Where to begin? The way he always did. He took out a legal pad and began a list of what he knew for sure.

Estee and her cronies had targeted the leaders of some very high-profile companies. An Internet search revealed each of them manufactured some kind of plastic. To his surprise the concern about plastic pollution wasn't unique to Estee Sparks. The problem was ubiquitous. Almost every organism on the planet had ingested plastic. The ultimate blame, scientists said, laid with fossil fuels, and the fossil fuels were taking us to a tipping point—a point beyond which there is no return. Ardale had only a rudimentary knowledge of chemistry, but this wasn't all that complicated. Scientists have known since the early 1800s that carbon dioxide is a greenhouse gas. What shocked him was their conclusion. On the current course global warming would change the planet's ecosystems forever.

Where had he been? This had been occurring for many years and he hadn't paid the slightest attention to it. Estee Sparks is neither an exhibitionist nor a tree hugging environmentalist. She is a heroine, a warrior on the front line of unprecedented global chaos, and he had to help her tell her story.

Since she feared exposure and wouldn't talk with him his next best option was to talk with the leaders of the companies that she targeted. He made a list of the CEOs and called them one by one for their reaction to what had occurred. He didn't represent any particular publication so most of the time he was put off or referred to the company's website for a statement of their commitment to environmental safety. Occasionally he was directed to public relations where he received the standard spin about the benefits of plastic. He was getting nowhere until he told the secretary for the Chairman of Danswirth Enterprises that he knew who was responsible for trashing Pendleton Danswirth's office. She put him on Danswirth's appointment schedule.

Upon his arrival in Houston, he discovered that the CEO had neither come into the office nor called him to reschedule the appointment. Desperate and unable to afford the wait for another appointment, he searched the Texas corporate records for the home address of the Danswirth chairman of the board. He was going to speak with Pendleton Danswirth III if he had to wait on his front porch.

53

"Mr. Danswirth, sir, there are peoples waiting for you. Should I tell them to call and make an appointment?" said Dorothea. She had been Pendleton Danswirth's maid for years and he had yet to break her of her annoying habit of making words plural that weren't.

"It's people, Dorothea," he reminded her for the umpteenth time. "And what do you mean by people waiting? Where are you? I need you to come back." With important people headed to his house he was willing to gravel to get her to come back from the vacation he imposed upon her.

"I never really left, sir."

"Never left."

"I put my things in the guest house, sir," she admitted sheepishly.

"I should never have sent you away. I'm sorry. Tell them I'll be there in five minutes," he said. He was brimming with so much pride, he couldn't resist telling Dorothea, "They're going to ask me to run for the Senate."

A sort of giddiness had replaced the angst caused by his radio reverend's fuckups. So much he dismissed Dorothea's admonition, "I'm not sure you be expecting these folks."

It was another error in diction he had swallow. What did he expect. Dorothea was his maid, not his in-house poet laureate.

"Get them refreshments and . . . I'm sorry. You know what to do," he said. Dorothea had catered to CEOs, senators and presidents. She knew exactly what was required in these situations.

The eclectic mix of cars in his driveway—two Land Rovers, a Coast Guard jeep, a seafood delivery van and an aging ragtop convertible—he interpreted as the diverse appeal of his candidacy. He had been peddling influence for years, but nothing could be better for his business and his legacy than holding the very office he had been subsidizing for years. The announcement of Senator Angus

Yarntwriller's retirement was only days old, but the political machinery was already at work generating his replacement.

His mood had turned from despair to euphoria in less time than it took to punch out a gross of single use, plastic drinking cups, one of his company's most prolific products. After the election his first action would be to squash the efforts to ban single use plastic. He already a campaign in mind: *Freedom good, bans bad. Plastic good, bans bad.*

"Mr. Danswirth, sir, one more thing," Dorothea added.

"What is it, Dorothea?"

"Mrs. Danswirth turned over."

"She's awake!"

"She turned onto one side. It's a good sign. Si, Senior?"

Probably not. The last time she emerged from hibernation, she was as hostile as a grizzly bear.

"What did the nurse say?" he said.

"She's not here today."

"Please shut her door and make sure she's not disturbed. I'll check on her when I get home."

Climate Fact:

A majority of Americans believe that combatting the danger of our changing climate should be a top priority for elected officials.

What can you do about it? Make reduction of global warming and greenhouse gas emissions a priority for every elected official.

54

One reporter, two nattily dressed men in their sixties, a Coast Guard officer escorting a middle-aged man dressed in soggy clerical attire, and the Executive Director of the Believers of America, referred to as Deacon, were waiting in Pendleton Danswirth's atrium when Derk and Estee arrived.

"Thank you, Ma'am," said Spade Christenson to Dorothea. He was sporting a belt buckle in the shape of an oil rig the size of Rhode Island.

Accompanying him was, "Colonel Conrad Oglethorpe, Ma'am," whose distinctive feature was an unruly tuft of white hair, and Deacon. Their focus was upon the armed Coast Guard official and the man in handcuffs until Derk and Estee entered the room and introduced themselves. In rolled up coveralls and tee shirt, to the uninitiated, Estee was a living, breathing Barnum and Bailey side show.

The maid, used only to people in suits entering the front door, was thoroughly confused. Repairmen and deliveries were always greeted at the back door.

"Derk Bryan, Ma'am, EPA," Derk said which only added to her consternation. Dorothea eyed Estee with a scrutiny she likely reserved for homeless beggars. "We're here to see Mr. Danswirth about his boat."

"You can have a seat in the Grand Room. He'll be here soon," she said and walked away.

"What are you doing here?" Derk said upon seeing Ardale.

"Following the story," Ardale retorted just above a whisper, "and I know you and Danswirth have a connection."

King Ardale Carver had shaved, gotten a haircut and upgraded his wardrobe, judging by the long pants that had replaced his standard attire, shorts and a shirt that appeared as if it had been wadded-up in a duffel bag.

"I see you're giving my credit card a workout," Derk said. Ardale acknowledged Derk's quip with a cock of his head and a grin.

Dorothea invited Danswirth's guests into a much larger waiting room which featured paintings of Danswirth family members and a glittering chandelier. She offered refreshments and announced, "Mr. Danswirth will be here soon." As the guests separated into three groups the doorbell rang again.

"I'm here to see Pendleton Danswirth" said Detective Louis Cardoza, pulling his coat back to display his badge. "This is Officer Greavy."

"Join the crowd." Dorothea rolled her eyes. "He'll be here soon."

"How soon?" said Cardoza.

"Minutos," she said.

The detective made a gesture with his hand to Greavy. "What else do we have to do?"

Greavy shrugged, "It's your party, Detective," and they entered.

Dorothea led the policemen into the atrium and asked if they would like a beverage. One look at the opulent surroundings and Cardoza asked for a mineral water.

After a stern raise of the eyebrow by Dorothea he said, "A glass of water will do." Greavy took a seat while Cardoza did some trunk rotations and bent over to touch his toes.

"The doc says I need to stretch more," Cardoza said.

The Coast Guard officer was the only man in uniform which meant that Derk didn't know there were four people in the room with guns. Two cops, a Coast Guard officer and Spade Christensen. He kept a derringer in his boot.

"So, why are you here?" Ardale whispered as he sipped on a ginger ale.

"Danswirth's boat killed a Ricei whale," Estee said. Her voice echoed throughout the room.

Cardoza arose from a stretch so quickly Greavy had to catch him before he lost his balance.

"Excuse me, Ma'am," said the Seaman to Estee. He escorted Huck across the room. "This man says Mr. Danswirth allowed him to use his boat. Do you know him?"

"You're Marshall Hucklebee!" Derk said.

"Reverend Huck," responded Huck, gleeful that someone recognized him. He held out his cuffed hands for Derk to shake.

The Deacon choked on one-hundred and twenty-five dollar Burbon. The voice of *GodNet* was in handcuffs, being accused of killing a whale by a woman with multiple tattoos.

"Whatever he calls himself, he's no preacher," Estee answered the Seaman.

"Do you have any idea what you've done?" she said to Huck.

The accusation by a complete stranger, circus animals and all, that Huck was a fraud was a blow to his pseudo-celebrity status. He slumped into a state of dismay.

Cardoza moved in and held up his badge. "Hucklebee, we need to talk."

The Seaman blocked Cardoza's advance as Pendleton Danswirth III entered the room.

"Gentlemen," Danswirth said with a Texas-sized grin, "and lady, thanks for coming."

He motioned to the sitting room, "Please, come with me."

When no one moved, Danswirth, now puzzled, scanned the faces of his guests.

"Detective, um, I . . . I didn't expect to see you," said Danswirth as if he had seen a ghost. "Um, uh . . . heard you found my boat."

The only movement or sound came from Dorothea who was wheeling a beverage tray into the sitting room. Everyone awaited a response from Cardoza as if he were about to provide the answer to a double Jeopardy question.

The atrium was a ballroom sized area with a two and one-half story high, domed ceiling. The largest chandelier Derk had ever seen was suspended above them. Pictures of three generations of Danswirth men were displayed on the walls. A staircase with gold embroidered, red carpet, spiraled up to a landing opposite the entryway. It reminded him of an old Hollywood movie setting in which royalty descended from the throne to mingle with the masses. He recalled, as he entered the estate, not seeing a single solar panel on any roof. This place was an energy hog. If the government couldn't impose a tax on size, it ought to tax the carbon necessary to produce and maintain this type of monstrosity. He had written his congressman about legislation mandating that all elected officials be housed in flood plains. He wondered if six feet of water in the congressman's living room would get his attention.

The Detective and the Seaman were still in a standoff, so Derk took the initiative.

"Mr. Danswirth, I'm Doctor Bryan from the EPA. We spoke on the phone. You told me your boat was stolen, but Mr. Hucklebee works for you. Is that correct?"

"Well, um. It appears—" Danswirth mumbled.

Reverend Huck maneuvered around the Coast Guard officer and Cardoza. "You told me I could take it. Tell them, Mr. Danswirth. I didn't steal it."

Danswirth, mouth agape and eyes the size of walnuts, put his hand over his mouth. "Oh my God, he's right. I completely forgot." His head sank into hands. "I'm so sorry. It's my wife. She's been ill."

Derk noticed a collective sigh on the faces of Oglethorpe and Christensen. Deacon took another sip of Bourbon. Greavy, unable to hide his disinterest, groaned and made a gesture toward the door for Cardoza. The Detective stood his ground.

"Where is it?" Danswirth said to Cardoza.

"At the bottom of the bay, sir," said the Seaman. "This man says he hit something and it capsized. What he hit was a manatee, sir, and I'm sure it was in a No Wake zone, but we can't prove he was speeding. Your boat is at the bottom of a bay and you'll have to get it out. If you don't, the Coast Guard will salvage it and you'll be responsible for the cost," the Seaman hesitated before saying, "Sir."

"Of course. I'll take care of everything," Danswirth said. He made an odious face at Huck.

Cardoza shrugged but made no effort to leave, and Danswirth's guests seemed satisfied by the explanation.

"We'll wait for you in here," said Oglethorpe. He guided Spade and Deacon toward to the sitting room.

Cardoza motioned for Greavy to guard the exit.

Reverend Hucklebee held open his hands for the Coast Guard officer to remove the cuffs. An air of satisfaction enveloped him. As the Seaman moved to unlock the cuffs on Hucklebee, Estee slipped between them.

"No way. He ran over a mother Ricei. Killed it and its calf," she said.

"Excuse me, Ma'am, but that is the wildest accusation I've ever heard," said Reverend Huck.

Oglethorpe held the door for Dorothea who was returning from the sitting room, this time empty handed. She stopped and waited for Mr. Danswirth's orders.

"Will there be anything else, sir?"

Danswirth lip synced, "No," and she disappeared into the hallway.

Oglethorpe, Christensen and Deacon turned to hear Estee's explanation.

"Show him," Estee said to Derk.

Derk held up his cell phone for the Coast Guard officer to see. Cardoza and the Seaman moved closer.

"This is a picture I took of the Salty Glider and its broken propellor. Show him yours," he said to Estee.

"Officer," Danswirth interjected, "I told you I forgot that he took my boat and now it's in the Bay. I'll get it out."

Cardoza said. "I'd like to hear what the young lady has to say."

Estee held her phone next to Derk's. Everyone edged closer for a better view. On the screen was a photo she had taken of the propellor at the Coast Guard station.

The heads of Spade, Conrad and Deacon bobbed up and down.

"So, what!" Hucklebee protested. Cardoza, Greavy and the Seaman moved to corral Hucklebee, who was wrangling for an opening.

"That doesn't prove anything and if it did, so what? It was an accident," said Huck, squirming.

"Maybe, but it doesn't matter," said Derk.

"Tell him why," said Detective Cardoza.

"Mr. Hucklebee, you left the boat at Bud's Marina, a known smuggling destination," Derk began.

Cardoza smiled as if he knew what Derk was going to say.

Hucklebee squirmed. "No, that's not true. I left it there for a repair."

"My guess is you came through the Gulf at night so you wouldn't be detected. It's also the time that the whales surface. You probably even noticed the thud when a piece of the propellor lodged into the Ricei's spinal cord, killing it instantly, but you needed to be in port before dawn so you kept going. The calf's death was less immediate but just as violent. With its smother dead it suffocated after its oxygen supply was severed. You probably didn't know that but you're still responsible."

Hucklebee, shaking his head, "No, no, no," tried to get free, but Greavy and the Seaman sandwiched him.

Cardoza seemed content to have the EPA official build a case for him. He crossed his arms while Derk continued.

"I'm sure you cut some deal with Bud. He stayed out of sight so he can deny culpability and everything was done with cash so the Detective here," Derk pointed to Cardoza, "can't chase it. But—" he paused as he noticed the three men, there to discuss the formation of a PAC to determine the feasibility of a Danswirth run for the Senate, seemed caught off guard by this revelation.

"The Coast Guard says you killed a manatee," Derk said. The Seaman nodded. "Probably while speeding in a no wake zone." The Seaman nodded again. "And you're on parole. Are you with me so far?"

Everyone but the fake reverend nodded.

Cardoza picked up the story from there. "Killing an endangered mammal is a third-degree felony and if doing so during the commission of another crime --- well, I'd expect an immediate visit by your parole officer. Am I correct, Officer Greavy?"

"Yes, sir. That's the law," Greavy said.

"Cuff him," said Cardoza, forgetting that he was already in handcuffs.

"Dear God, how can this be?" Deacon interjected. "This is Reverend Hucklebee, a man of God, the voice of *Don't Back Talk God*. There must be a mistake." He looked to Danswirth for confirmation. "You loaned him your boat. Right, Pendleton?"

Confirmation came in the form of a contorted grin.

"Where did you go with the boat?" The Deacon asked Reverend Hucklebee.

"He asked me to bury Farnsworth at sea. That's all I did," Hucklebee said, trying to shake Officer Greavy's grip on his arm.

"His dog," added Hucklebee to the question on everyone's faces.

"Pendleton, that's all this is about, your dog?" said Colonel Oglethorpe to Danswirth.

A humble shrug was Danswirth's response.

The maid returned with a tray of dates and sweet tarts. Danswirth gritted his teeth and shewed her away with a wave on one hand.

Estee was squirming to say something but Derk squeezed her hand and addressed Cardoza, "Detective, what brought you here?"

"I was hoping to see Danswirth's boat, but I gather it's at the bottom of the bay," said Cardoza. He sighed as he massaged his sacrum.

"Bad back?" said Derk.

Cardoza nodded. Derk rubbed his hands. "Arthritis. Have you given up red meat?"

"Will it help?" said Cardoza.

Derk's expression suggested, "Maybe," but he said, "Now that you know his boat was not stolen, why is it of interest to you?"

"I'm investigating the disappearance of a woman who used to work for Mr. Danswirth," Cardoza said. "One Angelina Rodriguez."

"Missing persons?" said Derk.

"Not anymore," said Cardoza. "She turned up in a plastic box. The only thing she had on was red nail polish."

***

"It was you," said Estee, pointing at Danswirth. "You killed her."

Derk was inclined to agree with her. His hunch told him the radio reverend had made a U-turn and was headed back to the pen. There was proof he killed the Ricei and probably the Manatee, each

310

of which is on the endangered list. Most likely he dumped the body of Angelina Rodriguez into sea, even though, he thought it was a dog. He was also sure that Cardoza had Hucklebee's parole officer's number on speed dial, but the detective was after bigger fish. He had linked Pendleton Danswirth III to the death of Angelina Rodriguez and would have him in cuffs already if he had the evidence linking him to her. That didn't matter to Estee Sparks who was so emotionally invested there was no holding her fury.

Her wrath stunned everyone. She grabbed the handcuffs Greavy was going to put on Hucklebee and rushed at Danswirth. "You murdered her. Arrest him!"

Danswirth back pedaled but not fast enough. Estee pounded his chest with the cuffs until fell backwards into Oglethorpe and lost his balance. Estee followed him down, formed a handcuff into a set of knuckles and pummeled the rich executive. There was no objective way to link Danswirth to the death of her son, but it didn't matter. He died from the collective waste of plastic that permeated the water and Danswirth's company was partly responsible. She was letting him feel the full force of her anger and her conviction.

Greavy tried to stop her but she kept swinging her arms at Danswirth whose face would soon become shades of charcoal and blue, Derk knelt over and pulled her into his arms.

"You got. You got him," Derk said softly. She squirmed and rustled in his grasp. "It's over. Let the Detective do his job."

The room became quiet, pin drop still, as Derk pulled Estee from the shaken CEO. "Let's sit down over there," Derk said. Greavy followed them.

By the look on their faces Oglethorpe, Christensen and the Deacon were stunned. They just discovered that their host had hired an ex-con to become a fake preacher, and both were implicated in a murder investigation. They were looking for a way to excuse themselves.

"No, no," said Danswirth, still on the floor, "Gentlemen, this is all a mistake."

"Excuse me, officer," Derk said to Greavy whose intent was aimed at taking Estee into custody.

When Derk stood between Estee and the officer, Greavy said, "Just want to get my cuffs back."

With a cock of his head, he assured her she would be okay, and she handed the wrist bands to Greavy.

"Thank you," he said and backed away.

Standing over her Derk put his hands upon her shoulders. "I believe you. I think the Detective believes you," and he gestured to Cardoza, "but you know better than I do that it's not what you know, it's what you can prove. Right?"

He waited, along with everyone else, for her response. Animosity morphed into disappointment and then resignation. She took a deep breath and acknowledged him.

"Can either of you," Derk turned to face Cardoza and the Coast Guard officer, "place either of these men at the scene of any of these events?" He pointed to Danswirth and Hucklebee.

The Coast Guard officer, teetering between his options, relented. "All I've got is a sunken boat and a dead Manatee."

"That's a start," said Derk.

Cardoza said, "That's not my job. That's the prosecutor's job. But, hell, I'll be retired by the time this case goes to trial. Like you, I've got nothing but hunches."

With that resolved the real preacher helped Danswirth to his feet. He opened his arms to invite Spade, Conrad and Danswirth to join him in the other room.

"Gentlemen and lady, we have important business with Mr. Danswirth. If there is nothing else, would you please excuse us," Deacon said to the others.

Estee began to protest. Derk held her back, and whispered, "Another time, another place."

Reverend Huck seemed relieved but disgruntled when Danswirth offered him a smug, "Not now." Clearly, Huck needed something more from his boss.

It was an odd but revealing combination, the smugness that over-shadowed the fresh marks on Danswirth's face. Derk had seen this face before. It wasn't just the satisfaction that he had gotten away with murder. It wasn't Danswirth's money, his friends or his influence that Derk despised. It was Danswirth's arrogance. Derk had dealt with those whose greed and myopia led to oil spills, contaminated water, toxic runoffs and marine kills. The worst would kill to cover their sins. The common denominator: all of them thought their lives were more important than others. Danswirth was surely one of them. His products, all derived from fossil fuels, are feeding an addiction that is warming the planet to an unsustainable level and rushing us to a climatic tipping point from which we may not recover. He was not one of the good guys, and Derk hated to walk away. All he could do now was promise Estee that the good guys would prevail and that he doubted Cardoza would let it go. He had been around enough cops to sense that this guy was a bloodhound. Derk excused himself, took Estee's arm and started to leave.

"Hold up," said Cardoza. "I take it you're not going to press charges against Ms. …" He was asking Danswirth while he waved his hand at Estee.

Danswirth stopped, turned around and thought about it. "Not right now, Detective, but I might change my mind."

"You'll pay for this," Estee snarled at him.

Derk could no longer bare Danswirth's impudence.

"Excuse me, may I ask why you are here to see Mr. Danswirth?"

Deacon tunned to face Derk, "It's a private matter …"

Danswirth, unable to quiet his ambition, interrupted Deacon, "They're here to discuss the Senate seat being vacated by Senator Yarntwriller."

"And I suppose they want to know if you'd be their candidate?" Derk said.

Danswirth looked to his three comrades for confirmation. Their smiles were not revealing.

With a cocky grin Danswirth added, "Senator Danswirth, it has a nice ring to it. Don't you think?"

At that exact moment Dorothea was assisting a frail woman, in a white bathrobe and frenzied hair, onto the landing at the top of the stairway. All eyes turned in her direction when Dorothea said, "Be careful, Mrs. Danswirth. Let me take that."

Shirley Maxwell Danswirth rose from her wheelchair appearing so weak that if she fell she would never rise again. She reached for the railing to brace herself. From a pillow she had clutched in one hand she removed a small bag. From the bag she removed a blood-stained evening gown and a necklace. Upon tossing them over the railing, in a low, raspy voice and barely discernible voice, she uttered, "Where you're going, Pendleton Danswirth the third, you won't be able to run for fly catcher."

55

Derk slept in his own bed and awakened an hour later than usual. Relieved, relaxed and refreshed he took an OJ and the newspaper to the patio.

As he read the Times' account of the threat that the Ricei and Right whales are facing he gazed over the great blue plains in front of him and imagined a mother Ricei frolicking in the waves with her newborn calf. The Ricei can weigh thirty tons and grow to forty feet, but it breeds only once every nine years. Its numbers are so few, if a child dies before birth, it is likely the entire species will perish with it. The grimmest challenge any species will ever confront, survival or demise, was taking place in Derk's front yard. Beyond the restaurants, the boutiques and the tee-shirt shops that lined the beach a mother whale was pregnant and expecting to live long enough to give birth to another generation and more. While couples strolled the beach, hand in hand on once a year vacations, the whales were unaware that the folly of these people, the human species, was a greater threat than any predator they would ever encounter.

For Derk the fate of the Ricei would forever be linked to Estee Sparks. She was one of the most courageous people he had ever met. He had no doubt she would keep up the fight.

"We caught the bad guys, but the damage had already been done," she said. "Although these whales live, work and play in the sea, they are our neighbors and our kin. They have the same ambitions as those of us on land --- to raise their children and take care of their families. Like us, they need an uncontaminated supply of food, air and water. Unlike us, they bring balance to their environment. Doing better for them will be better for us."

"We need them more than they need us, and you are their hero," he said.

"Thank you," she said and kissed him on the cheek.

They hugged and she said goodbye.

No charges were brought against her or her friends after they agreed to pay for the cleanup at the homes they raided. The assaults upon the corporate offices are still open cases.

Pendleton Danswirth III was out on bail, awaiting trial for manslaughter, and *GodNet* had been dismantled. Marshall Hucklebee's parole had been revoked, but his attempt to reprise the *Don't Back Talk God* program turned into a successful prison comedy show. For a while rumors had Jon Stewart turning it into reality show.

Joyce retired from the EPA. When past and present staff members chipped in to rent a condo for her on the beach in St. Kitts, she revealed that she didn't swim and she hated hot weather. Derk bought her an assortment of coffees and a multi-colored comforter. She hugged him and whispered into his ear, "I'd like to introduce you to my friend, Alyss. Her husband died last year and she's a knockout." As always, he thanked her and said he would think about it.

He didn't like all the "Good-byes" that retirement brought. He had suffered too many lately. Life is subject to changes and with aging the challenge of change, some have said, is greater. He had no idea if that were true or not, but he couldn't deny the emotional drain caused by the deaths of his wife and his mother in such a short time. At Joyce's retirement party he decided to defer the announcement that his sabbatical would become permanent. He never really stopped working. He needed time to reflect and adapt. There was much to be done.

The story of greed, sex, religion and murder, involving one of the country's richest families, revived Ardale's career. He would turn it into a book and get a seven-figure advance for the film rights. When Ardale arrived to return Derk's credit card, driving a shiny new electric car, he suggested that Derk write his own book: *The Dummy's Guide to Prepping for Climate Change.*

"Yeah, yeah, everyone wants me to write a book. It's for people who retire," Derk said, once again dismissing the notion that he was an author. In the back of his mind, he toyed with Ardale's idea. Maybe he would write a book . . . if he ever hung up his cleats.

On his patio thoughts of relocation were in a distant recess of his mind. He was aware that living here or near any shore in Florida was akin to playing Roulette, and he didn't want to be here when the next Cat 4 came to visit. But today he was going to breathe in the salt air and allow the humidity envelop him, to lubricate his senses. It was good to be home.

The couple he had been watching on the beach kissed and embraced. That's what he would miss the most, the walks on the beach with Jenny, the star filled skies and the reflection off the moon that illuminated the shore. He inhaled as much beach air as he could and allowed it to escape along with the images of the past few weeks. Those of Susan Carlton lingered most on his mind. When he got to the Sports Page his cell phone rang. It was from an unknown caller.

"This is Doctor Bryan," he said with reservation.

"My name is Doctor Diana Wellskoff. I work with ABT. There is someone here who would like to talk with you."

"Advanced Bio-Tech?" he said and his ears rose like steel antennas.

"Yes. Susan Carlton."

He got up so fast he tipped over his orange juice. "Oh shoot!"

"Is this a bad time?"

"No, sorry." He slid back the patio door and stepped inside.

"I am aware you have been trying to contact her," said the woman from ABT.

"Unsuccessfully and at great risk," Derk said. "Where is she?"

"It's against my better judgment, but she's has been asking about you."

"Where is she?"

"I'd like to answer your all of your questions, but I need you come to Boston."

"Boston! She's in Boston?"

"I can explain everything, but there's something you need to see and ..."

Derk cut her off, "It can only be seen in Boston. I'm tired of the games. If she wants to talk with me, put her on."

"I can't do that. There is a flight waiting for you at three p.m. if you can make it," she said.

***

An unmarked electric SUV picked him up at the Logan International Airport. In less than an hour he was standing in front of an enormous, red brick building on the bank of the Charles River in Waltham, Massachusetts. According to a plaque at the entrance this historic structure had once been a successful mill. On the plaque was an address but no name. Other than the impressive restoration job done on the building the only other distinguishing characteristic was the amount of surveillance equipment present. Every movement around the building was being recorded.

The interior of the building was somewhat more appealing than the outside but still institutional with wide, antiseptic hallways and air as fresh as a grow room. As he was escorted through security, he felt two kinds of anxiety. Trepidation—every interaction with Susan Carlton involved bodily risk. The other made his stomach flutter. He felt her embrace as if he were already in her arms.

"Hello, I'm Doctor Diana Wellskoff," she said, clearly questioning his attire. He wore the same jump suit he had on when he first met Doctor Carlton. Under it were jeans and a long sleeve oxford dress shirt but no tie. "Thank you for coming," she said and offered him a seat across from her.

Diana Wellskoff's office was sparce with a desk, a phone, a computer and a window that was completely dark. A single artificial flower stayed at attention in its etched clear glass vase on her desk. Her similarity to Susan Carlton was troubling. Her handshake was firm although somewhat mechanical and she emanated the same subtle hint of perfume, something like Chanel No. 5. He knew this because it was Jennifer's favorite. Here it competed with an aroma he could only identify as cleaning fluids. His escort disappeared into a room down the hall.

Derk got right to the point. "I'd like to see Doctor Carlton before we begin."

Doctor Wellskoff swiveled her chair until she faced the dark window on Derk's right. "What I'm about to show you I'd like you to keep to yourself until we are ready to release it."

He didn't like conditions being placed upon his fundamental right to see whom he wanted when he wanted, but these folks weren't having it any other way. He pinched his face into a less than an enthusiastic form.

"What's your relationship to NASA? I gather you're on the Uncle Sam's payroll," he said.

"I am bound to secrecy when it involves national defense," she said.

Recognizing the rote response when people have something to hide, he asked, "What does Doctor Carlton have to do with national defense? She's training to be an astronaut."

His hostess hit a couple of keys on her laptop and turned the screen for Derk to see. Three women appeared. They were different in subtle ways but each one had Susan Carlton's traits. They revolved like models upon a pedestal which provided him with a three-hundred and sixty-degree view. One was Hispanic and one was Asian. The third was exactly like Susan Carlton. Their height, weight and body builds were identical. In appearance they differed only by skin color, hair-dos and wardrobes.

"Clones!" Derk said. "You've cloned these people?" The ramifications were unfathomable. "You can't keep this silent."

"No, Doctor Bryan, these are humanoids," Doctor Wellskoff said. She clicked a key and the image was gone.

Derk rolled back in his chair, his mouth agape and his eyes full of rage. What have I done? Why didn't I know? He was a professor, a scientist and an intrepid investigator, but he had been seduced by a humanoid. He was angry and he was embarrassed. He felt violated.

"No, no!" He kept shaking his head. "This did not happen. You can't be doing this."

"I can see this is a challenge for you," she sounded human but he didn't trust her. "I know you must have become close."

"Why would you assume that?" The truth was he had been pining, worrying, pursuing and risking his life for a robot, a machine that looked like a human. He got up and paced, trying to hold back a desire to tear into something or someone.

"We didn't know. You were the first person, man, she was with. This is new for us, too."

"What do you mean you didn't know?"

"It's the way she was programmed."

"Programmed?" He had been betrayed by Susan, by them, whomever they were, and by his own emotions.

She nodded repeatedly, pierced her lips and forced a smile. "Yes, programmed. Each of these NS models—"

"NS?" He jumped back up as soon he took a seat.

"New Sapiens," she said. "They are programmed for different specialties. They can perform all of the normal mechanical functions of a humanoid, but each one is fitted with a different personality."

"Fitted! You say it like you were tailoring a piece of clothing for a living, breathing person when it is really cold binary data entered one key stroke at a time."

"That's an over simplification, but that's why you're here."

He stopped fidgeting and faced her. "Wait. What do you mean by specialties? What was Susan Carlton's specialty?"

"She was programmed with extra socialization features," Doctor Wellskoff said without resignation.

"Enough with the euphemisms. What was her specialty?"

"She is a scientist, but she was also designed to be comfortable with people around her, to speak the language of emotions and even to provide pleasure to those in her presence."

"The language of emotions," he said. He had been duped by a pleasure-bot. He wrapped himself in his own arms and tried to shake the chill from his body.

"Doctor Bryan," Doctor Wellskoff applied some empathy. "She's really amazing, isn't she? Anatomically perfect in every way. And you had an effect upon her. She liked you. She developed something you and I call feelings and we didn't expect that."

He took deep breaths. He couldn't tell if the woman seated across from him was real or a bot; humanoids she called them. It was the same way when he met Susan. They were too perfect. It was difficult to find the words to express what he was feeling beyond anger and betrayal. He couldn't believe he hadn't recognized this. Later, in a more academic moment, he would ponder the possibilities for artificial humans. If they could be mass produced with programmable socialization features, they would become invaluable as home health care aids. They could perform household chores, administer medicines, play games and carry-on intelligent conversations while never forgetting appointments, names, dates or places. This would be a blessing for millions of disabled, sick, single or elderly people. Entire industries would pop up involving the manufacture, delivery, set up and service of humanoids that possessed more skills and better memories than their owners. The day would come when they could be leased like cars. Today, he was dealing with shock and disappointment, more than he wanted to abide.

He took the seat across from Doctor Wellskoff and collected himself. "Is that why she's going to Mars? To service—?" He didn't want to hear the words he was thinking.

Doctor Wellskoff's response was blunt, "She is a trained micro-biologist with an essential mission for the harsh Martian climate."

He rose again from the chair and paced. Again, he stopped to face her. "She is a woman ready and able to satisfy a male crew locked in a space capsule for nine months. That's what you really want from her, and you don't want anyone to get wind of this."

He finally said what he always feared. At the same time, he realized he had developed an attachment that had evolved into a jealousy for a machine. He slumped into the chair again. This was going to take a lot of introspection.

"Doctor Bryan, you could be of great help to us and all that follow. This is just the beginning."

His frown evolved into a scowl.

"Doctor Carlton responded to you in ways we could not have imagined. We're not good at programming human emotions, and yet she learned quickly. We want to know how that happened. What cues did she take from you? She must have learned from your reaction to her. It's clear that you developed a connection with her. There is so much we need to know. Will you please help us?"

ABT would make billions from this once it went into mass production. He sat up in his chair, searching for a revelation that may never come.

"I'm not sure I'm up to this, but if I do it will be under two conditions," he said.

"Which are?" she asked with obvious concern.

"One, I want to see her. I need some time with her."

"Okay," Doctor Wellskoff agreed.

"Two, after I see her, if I choose to, you will reprogram her for something other than a pleasure-bot. This is non-negotiable."

As his host considered his demand he got up and began to leave. "The offer is good for twenty-four hours. After that I'm calling Ardale."

"Who?"

"A dog you do not want on your trail."

Epilogue

Only two months after the completion of this book the United States Environmental Protection Agency began regulating PFAs and PFOs (forever chemicals) in the nation's drinking water supply. Cites have until 2029 to implement solutions to reduce these chemicals to safe levels.

The United Nations' Intergovernmental Panel on Climate Change (IPCC) has proposed that all countries enact a ban on single use plastics.

About The Author

G. Spencer Myers' specialty is the eco-political thriller, featuring Dr. Derk Bryan, college professor, obsessive environmentalist and intrepid EPA investigator who works only on cases involving environmental chaos and dead bodies. His blogs feature controversial issues from an ecological point of view.

His first book, <u>Pest</u>, featured a race against the clock to save his former lover from a fraudulent pesticide manufacturer and an ex-wrestler turned body guard with anger management issues. In <u>Dead Wrong</u> he exposes the link between a toxic spill, police corruption and a Johnny Cash look alike. His memoir, <u>A Letter to My Grandson</u>, inspired the 1st Palm Beach County Short Story Contest entitled, "In Search of Integrity."

WE ARE PLAYING ROULETTE WITH YOUR FUTURE is an update of A Letter to My Grandson calling upon all grandchildren to heed the challenge of global warming.

In <u>The Girl with the Red Nails</u>, the antagonist is Pendleton Danswirth III, but the real villain is plastics. Since its completion the EPA has chosen to regulate so called forever chemicals in drinking water. His recent article on sustainable cruising has appeared in newspapers throughout Florida under The Invading Seas series. A long-time environmentalist, he was the first person in the U.S. to put solar panels on a multi-family home listed on the National Register of Historic Places.

Mr. Myers is a graduate of the University of Michigan, holds an MBA from Bowling Green State University and is Certified by the American College of Sports Medicine.

He is a native of Michigan but lives in Boynton Beach, FL where he is still in pursuit of par. Contact him at <u>Author@GSpencerMyers.com</u>.